D0395598

Flaming Hot

More Erotic Romances by Lynn LaFleur

Nightshift

(with Kate Douglas and Crystal Jordan)

In a Cowboy's Bed

(with Cat Johnson and Vonna Harper)

Hot Shots

(with Anne Marsh and Stacey Kennedy)

Smokin' Hot

Published by Kensington Publishing Corp.

Flaming Hot

LYNN LaFLEUR

APHRODISIA

KENSINGTON PUBLISHING CORP.
www.kensingtonbooks.com

APHRODISIA BOOKS are published by

Kensington Publishing Corp.
119 West 40th Street
New York, NY 10018

Copyright © 2014 by Lynn LaFleur

All rights reserved. No part of this book may be reproduced in any form or by any means without the prior written consent of the Publisher, excepting brief quotes used in reviews.

All Kensington titles, imprints, and distributed lines are available at special quantity discounts for bulk purchases for sales promotion, premiums, fund-raising, educational, or institutional use.

Special book excerpts or customized printings can also be created to fit specific needs. For details, write or phone the office of the Kensington Special Sales Manager: Kensington Publishing Corp., 119 West 40th Street, New York, NY 10018. Attn. Special Sales Department. Phone: 1-800-221-2647.

Aphrodisia and the A logo Reg. U.S. Pat. & TM Off.

eISBN-13: 978-1-61773-091-7
eISBN-10: 1-61773-091-2
First Kensington Electronic Edition: November 2014

ISBN-13: 978-1-61773-090-0
ISBN-10: 1-61773-090-4
First Kensington Trade Paperback Printing: November 2014

10 9 8 7 6 5 4 3 2 1

Printed in the United States of America

CONTENTS

Fiery

1

Eve Van Den Bergh smiled as she ran her hands over the bolt of white satin. A new shipment of fabric had arrived today at Cozy Crafts Cottage. She loved unwrapping the new bolts, touching the soft cloth. The owner, Rhea Hathaway, always let Eve stock the fabric since Rhea knew Eve enjoyed it so much.

"Wouldn't this make a gorgeous wedding dress?" Eve asked her boss as Rhea cut the tape on a box of scrapbook paper.

Rhea glanced in Eve's direction and smiled. "It certainly would." Her eyebrows disappeared into her wispy bangs. "Is there something you need to tell me?"

"What?" It took a moment for Eve to realize what Rhea had asked her. "Oh, no! Marriage plans are *not* anywhere in my future."

"They could be, if you met the right guy."

"I thought I'd met the right guy. Twice. I suck at relationships."

"You don't suck." Rhea took out several stacks of plastic-wrapped paper and laid them on her worktable. "You just haven't met the right guy." She peeked at Eve over the edge of the glasses perched on her nose. "Or you won't admit you've met the right guy. I don't understand why you won't go out with Quade. That man is a walking sex object. If he looked at me the way he looks at you, I'd spread my legs in a second."

Eve chuckled at Rhea's bluntness, but she agreed with her friend. Tall, buff, copper-skinned, with long straight black hair and incredible sapphire eyes, Quade Easton had to be one of the most attractive men Eve had ever seen. She'd been tempted several times to say yes when he'd invited her out for coffee. Calling on every ounce of willpower she possessed, she managed to say no.

Going out with someone who affected her so strongly would be a huge mistake.

"No comment?" Rhea asked.

"I know it's only October twelfth, but we should think about putting some of the nicer fabric up front in a special display for the holidays."

"You're changing the subject."

"Yes, and I'll continue to do so."

Chuckling, Rhea shook her head. "Sometimes I wonder why we've been friends for so long."

Sometimes Eve wondered the same thing. She'd met Rhea in Paris their sophomore year of college twelve years ago. Rhea had gone to Paris for Christmas with two cousins. Eve had taken a few days by herself while on break from college in the Netherlands, her father's home country and where she attended school. They'd literally run into each other in a bookstore and clicked immediately.

Rhea had been there during the darkest times of Eve's life—the loss of her mother, the end of her first engagement, the end of her second engagement. She'd offered Eve a new life here in Lanville, Texas, two years ago when Eve had broken off her second engagement. Eve had gladly accepted the chance to start over.

A chime jingled through the store, indicating someone had come in the front door. Eve automatically turned her head in that direction to offer a greeting. The words died on her tongue when she saw Quade.

"Speak of the devil," Rhea muttered. "Hi, Quade," she called out to him.

"Hey, Rhea." His gaze swung to Eve, and she thought his eyes narrowed a bit. "Eve."

Eve nodded to acknowledge his greeting. She didn't think her tongue would work well enough now to speak.

"What can I do for you?" Rhea asked. "Interested in some flannel for new jammies?"

Quade chuckled. The sound tickled every one of Eve's nerve endings. "Not this time. I'm here to check your fire extinguishers."

"Oh, sure. Eve, will you show Quade where they are, please?"

They'd been friends for twelve years, yet Rhea was also her boss. Even if being around Quade left Eve tongue-tied, she wouldn't go against her boss's wishes. "I'll be happy to."

Two ladies walked into the store. Rhea hurried up front to help them, leaving Eve alone with Quade. She stopped herself before she wiped her damp palms on her thighs. "We have four."

Quade lifted the clipboard he held. "That's what's on my list." He glanced at the top piece of paper. "I also have that there's one upstairs in the residence."

"Yes, there is."

"I'll need to check it, too."

"Of course."

Eve's heart beat a bit faster. She lived upstairs in the residence, which meant she would have to take Quade into her private sanctuary. She understood the importance of the fire extinguishers being current, but the thought of having Quade so close to her bed made her palms sweat.

Dylan Westfield had checked the extinguishers last year. Having him in her apartment hadn't affected her one bit.

Quade flashed a dazzling smile, which didn't help her heartbeat at all. "I won't take up too much of your time."

Eve led the way to the fire extinguishers located throughout the store. She stood by while Quade checked the dates on the tags to verify the monthly inspections Rhea performed. He removed the extinguishers from the walls, turned them in his hands, checked the gauges and nozzles.

He wore one of the volunteer fire department's dark blue T-shirts, giving her an unobstructed view of his muscled forearms. His biceps bulged every time he lifted one of the large tanks and shook it.

She easily imagined those strong arms wrapped around her while he kissed her senseless.

He had his hair pulled back in a ponytail and secured with a leather strap. As long as she let her imagination run wild, she pictured herself untying that strap, tunneling her fingers into the soft strands, letting it fall around her face while they reclined on a soft bed of grass beneath a large tree, naked bodies pressed together. . . .

"They all look good."

His words made her fantasy disappear like a wisp of fog. "Great."

He punched the month, date, and year on the attached tag. "I don't think I've ever seen such clean fire extinguishers."

She smiled at the humor in his eyes. "Rhea's a neat nut. She hates dust."

"Her hating dust makes my job easier." He noted something on the paper on his clipboard. "One more and we're done."

Eve's smile faded. *I have to stop being such a wuss. It isn't as if Quade is going to grab me the moment we step into my apartment.*

She wouldn't acknowledge the thrill that raced through her when she realized his grabbing her might not be a bad idea.

"Let me get my keys. I'll meet you by the back door."

Eve stepped into the small employee lounge. Kathy Nantz sat in one of the cushy armchairs, eating an apple while she flipped through a fashion magazine. "I have to step out for a bit and Rhea has customers."

"No problem. My break's over anyway." Kathy tossed her apple core into the trash can. A frown drew her eyebrows together as her gaze passed over Eve's face. "You okay? You seem . . . anxious."

"I'm fine. Quade Easton is here to check the fire extinguishers. He has to look at the one in my apartment."

A dreamy look filled Kathy's eyes. "That man is so gorgeous. I love to watch him drive by on that big black motorcycle." She playfully shivered. "Makes me hot all over."

Eve knew the feeling.

Kathy playfully nudged Eve's ribs. "I'll cover for you if you want to take an . . . extended break with Quade."

She bobbed her eyebrows, which made Eve laugh. At twenty-three, Kathy still conjured up a lot of romantic fantasies. "No extended break. Strictly business."

"That's no fun."

No, but necessary for her peace of mind. She couldn't allow herself to dream of what might be when she knew it would never happen. She'd tried twice for happily ever after and both times had bombed. Her heart couldn't survive failing a third time.

Something about Eve Van Den Bergh pushed all of Quade's buttons. He couldn't help but notice her beauty—the oval face, ivory skin, shamrock-green eyes, long straight light blond hair, tall, shapely body with breasts the perfect size to fit in his palms. He loved the slight hint of a Dutch accent that colored her voice.

In the two years she'd been in Lanville, he'd barely spoken to her more than ten minutes at a time. He sensed a nervousness in her, something that kept her from completely letting go and enjoying a man's company. Nothing serious. His training as a counselor told him she'd never been attacked. But something kept her from dating, from getting close to a man. A lot of his friends had asked her out. She'd always refused.

She'd refused him, too, which frustrated him big time.

He followed her up the outside stairs to the apartment over the store, admiring the gentle swing of her hips in the dark red pants. They fit over her ass the way a man's hands would during lovemaking.

Knowing thoughts like that would only get him in trouble, Quade concentrated on his feet as he finished climbing the stairs to the small balcony outside the door. He watched her insert a key into the doorknob and deadbolt, push the door open. He followed her into a well-lit kitchen/dining room combination that he would describe as cheery with its white appliances and pale yellow walls.

"I keep the fire extinguisher in the hall closet," Eve said once he closed the door behind them. "I thought that would be the best place since it's in the center of the apartment."

She led him into a wide hall. He could see the living room to his right. Large windows gave a magnificent view of the town square. A door to his left led into the bathroom. He assumed the door at the end of the hall opened into Eve's bedroom.

She opened the closet door and stepped back to give him room. Quade slowly examined the extinguisher, taking longer than necessary so he could have more time with Eve. Whatever perfume she wore made him think of flowers during springtime.

"It looks good." He replaced it in the holding bracket on the wall, punched the tag to show when it had been inspected, and made the necessary notation on his checklist. "You're good for another year. Just keep up the monthly inspections."

"Rhea does those." Eve closed the closet door. "With all the flammable items in her store, she wants to be sure her fire extinguishers and sprinkler system are in perfect working order."

"I can understand that." He glanced into the living room again. "You have a great view."

She smiled. "Yes, I love that about this apartment. I can sit on the window seat for hours and watch people."

Quade stepped into the room, took in the furniture, bookshelves, television. "Your apartment doesn't seem as big as Rhea's store. That's about five thousand square feet, isn't it?"

"Forty-eight hundred. The apartment takes up about a fifth of the upstairs. The rest is for storage. Rhea loves to decorate for the holidays. She has all the decorations plus other seasonal stuff in plastic tubs through that door."

Quade followed her pointing finger to see a door in the wall next to the bookshelves. "There are steps up to the storage area from the store, and that door opens into the apartment. That's the way I usually come up here."

"Handy during bad weather."

She smiled again. "Very. Although it's cold in the winter and hot in the summer. Rhea doesn't turn on the heat or air conditioning in that room unless she plans to work in there for a while."

"Makes sense not to pay for the electricity when it isn't needed."

Quade had no reason to stay any longer, yet he didn't want to leave. Something about this woman drew him. He wanted to spend more time with her, get to know her better.

She'd turned him down every time he'd asked her out, yet he decided to try again.

"The new Chinese restaurant is having its grand opening

Friday night. A bunch of our friends are going. Do you want to join us?"

He thought he saw yearning in her eyes before disappointment replaced it. "I can't. I have to be here for the Friday-night workshop. But thank you for inviting me."

"Sure. Maybe another time."

He headed for the exit, but stopped halfway across the kitchen floor and turned back to face Eve. He didn't want to sound like a spoiled child not getting his way, but he had to know why she kept avoiding him. "Is there something about me you don't like? Is that why you keep turning me down when I ask you out?"

Her eyes widened in mortification. "No! I apologize if I gave you the impression that I think something is wrong with you. You're a very nice man, Quade."

"Then why won't you go out with me?"

She crossed her arms over her stomach, gave a one-shouldered shrug. "I don't go out with anyone, Quade. It has nothing to do with you. I just . . . I'm not interested in getting involved with anyone."

"Going out to eat with a bunch of friends isn't getting involved, Eve."

"I know, and I'm sure I'd enjoy it, but I do have to work Friday night. Rhea has workshops until nine every Friday night. Then there's telling everyone good-bye, and the cleanup. I don't get out of the store until around ten-thirty."

Quade understood the obligation of a job, yet he couldn't help feeling disappointed again. "If something comes up and you don't have to work, we plan to get there around seven and close the place down at midnight."

Her lips turned up in a small smile. "I'll remember."

He turned the doorknob, opened the door. "See you around."

She nodded to acknowledge his statement. Quade stepped out into the pleasant October morning. It would climb into the mid-seventies this afternoon, a bit below the normal temperature of low eighties for this time of year, but he thought it perfect. He'd be happy with mid-fifties at night and mid-seventies during the day year-round.

He wondered if the weather here corresponded with the weather in the Netherlands.

Quade knew next to nothing about the small country sandwiched between Belgium and Germany. He knew from conversations with friends that Eve had spent the majority of her life here in the States, but she visited her father often and had completed college in Amsterdam.

Perhaps he should do a little research on the country of her ancestors. It might help him understand Eve Van Den Bergh better.

2

"I don't know the sex of the baby," Grace Simpson told Eve as she perused the bins of yarn, "so I need a neutral color that would work for either a boy or girl. But I don't want yellow. That's too blah."

Eve smiled at the older woman. She'd turned eighty last week, but no one would ever believe Ms. Grace's age, even with the perfectly styled, short white hair. Slim and always impeccably dressed, Ms. Grace never looked unkempt or frumpy. Her granddaughter, Rayna Holt, possessed the same bone structure as Ms. Grace. Eve suspected Rayna would continue to be a stunning woman well into her older years.

But now, Rayna and her husband, Marcus, were expecting a baby in April and Ms. Grace told Eve she wanted to knit an afghan for her great-grandchild. "Green would work for either sex. Or lilac or lavender. You could mix ivory and brown together, or even use gray. With the right design, it would be beautiful in a baby afghan."

Ms. Grace fingered a skein the color of smoke. "I never thought of gray. That might work. Rayna loves that color."

"Or . . ." Eve moved down the row of skeins, plucked one from its bin, and returned to Ms. Grace. "What about a variegated yarn? This one has several pastel shades mixed together."

Ms. Grace patted her lips with one finger. "I like the idea of doing something a little different. Mattie," she called out to the young woman studying the different shades of cardstock. "What do you think of this for the baby afghan?"

Mattie hurried over to look at what her employer held. A bright smile curled her lips. "I like that. I never would've thought of gray, but it'll be perfect."

Ms. Grace beamed, making her smoky blue eyes sparkle. "Sold! Give me five skeins. No, make it six. I don't want to run out in the middle of my knitting."

"If you don't use that sixth skein, you can bring it back for a refund or store credit."

"In that case, give me seven. I might decide to knit a cap and booties, too."

Smiling at Ms. Grace's enthusiasm, Eve gathered up the skeins and took them to the checkout station. "Do you have the right size needles?"

"I have every size of knitting needles and crochet hooks that are available." She clapped her hands in delight. "Oh, I can't wait to get started. It'll be so nice to have a baby in the family again. I wasn't sure if Rayna and Marcus would want more children, not after they lost Derek." She leaned closer to Eve, as if about to tell her a secret. "I think the pregnancy was an accident."

"But a happy one," Mattie said.

"Definitely a happy one." Ms. Grace removed a credit card from her wallet and handed it to Eve. "Rayna is the only family I have left. I'm thrilled she decided to move back to Lanville and she and Marcus got back together."

"I'm happy for you." Eve slid the credit card receipt toward

Ms. Grace for her signature. "Keep your receipt. If you need to return some of that yarn, there won't be a problem."

"Thank you, Eve." She placed her credit card and receipt in her wallet while Mattie picked up the sack of yarn. "I appreciate your help."

"Anytime."

"Let's walk down to Mona's Place for a piece of pie," Eve heard Ms. Grace say to Mattie as they headed for the exit. "I'll bet she has pumpkin."

Eve smiled while watching the two very different ladies leave the store. Mattie worked as a full-time, live-in caretaker for Ms. Grace, although Eve believed Ms. Grace and Mattie shared more of a friendship than an employer-employee relationship. Ms. Grace had many friends in Lanville, yet no family until her granddaughter moved here.

Her smile faded. Although happy that Ms. Grace would soon have more family in her life, it emphasized the emptiness in Eve's life. She had no family other than her father, who lived thousands of miles away from her. He'd visited Eve a handful of times in the U.S., and had come for her mother's funeral. All the other times she'd seen her father had been in the Netherlands when she traveled to him.

How wonderful it would be to have her own family—a husband who adored her and children of her own. With her horrible track record with men, she didn't foresee a husband or children anywhere in her future. Eve understood that, but understanding didn't make the nights any less lonely.

She heard Rhea's firm footsteps coming toward her. "Rose Midland had to cancel tomorrow night's workshop. She has strep throat. The poor thing can barely talk."

"I'm sorry to hear that. Will you reschedule it?"

"Yes, but I don't know when. All the Friday workshops are set through the end of the year." Rhea leaned against the counter, crossed her arms over her stomach. "I've been thinking about starting some workshops on Saturday during the day. I've avoided doing that since so many mothers are busy with their kids on the weekends. But I know there's interest because I've been asked many times about Saturday workshops." She waved a hand in the air, as if to erase her statements. "I'll think about that later. I have a couple of errands to run. Could you send out an e-mail to the ladies signed up for tomorrow's workshop and tell them it's been cancelled?"

"Sure."

Rhea smiled. "Thanks, Eve. I'll be back soon."

Once Rhea left, Eve crossed the store to where Rhea's other clerk, Mary Lander, restocked ribbon. "I have to go to the office for a bit."

"No problem. I'll watch the front."

After grabbing a bottle of Coke from Rhea's mini-fridge, Eve settled at the desk and wiggled the mouse to wake up the computer. She located the mailing list in Rhea's organized files and quickly composed the e-mail to cancel the workshop. Once she clicked the button to send it, she signed out of Rhea's account and into her personal one. Nothing from her father, which didn't surprise her. He rarely corresponded by e-mail, choosing to use the telephone the few times he contacted her during the year.

Since he filled her mind so much, she decided to compose an e-mail to let him know she thought of him often, missed him, and looked forward to seeing him at Christmas. She kept it brief, knowing that was the kind of e-mails he preferred.

Once she'd completed that task, she leaned back in the chair to enjoy her cold drink. Now that she didn't have to be part of the workshop tomorrow night, she could do something else. She and Rhea could go to Fort Worth for dinner and a movie, unless her friend had a date. Rhea said all the time that she didn't care anything about getting married, yet she'd been dating Bob Rowe, a local landscaper, for several months. She claimed she only used him for sex.

Eve hadn't had sex in so long, she'd almost forgotten how it felt to have a man's lips on hers, his hands caressing her body, his cock sliding into her sheath.

Quade popped into her mind. That happened way more often than she wished it would.

She had no doubt his lips, his hands, his cock, would feel incredible.

Eve looked out the window to the wooded area behind Rhea's building. It gave a nice view of the oak and ash leaves beginning to turn colors. While parts of the country already experienced autumn in all its colorful glory, it would be another month before the trees in Lanville treated the residents to splashes of gold and red.

She wondered if Quade enjoyed the autumn colors.

Resting her head on the back of the chair, Eve sighed. Maybe he occupied her thoughts so much because he seemed to be as attracted to her as she was to him. While she knew nothing serious could ever develop between them, she considered him her friend.

She should accept his invitation to meet him and some of his friends at the new Chinese restaurant tomorrow night. She'd ask Rhea if she wanted to go, if her friend didn't already have a date.

The decision made, Eve screwed the cap on the bottle, placed it back in the mini-fridge, and returned to the retail area of the store.

"I think the new guys did very well with the ladder drills," Dylan Westfield said as he opened the restaurant's door.

Quade thought the same thing about the four new volunteer

firefighters now on the team. "Yes, they did. Clay plans to set up hose drills next week. You helping with that?"

Dylan nodded. "Talia and I are both helping." His gaze swept the area when he and Quade stepped inside the dimly lit entrance of China Palace. A smile spread over his face. "Speaking of the lady I love . . ."

Quade followed his friend while Dylan walked toward a table set up for fourteen at the back of the restaurant. He glanced over the people already seated, then did a double take when he saw Eve sitting next to Rhea. Apparently, she had decided to accept his invitation after all.

His heart beat a little faster as he slipped into the empty chair next to her. She shifted her attention from her friend to him. "Good evening."

"Good evening," she said softly.

"I'm glad you decided to come."

"The lady who was giving the workshop became ill, so we cancelled it."

"I'm sorry she's sick, but glad you're here."

"I couldn't pass up Chinese food. I love it."

A little tidbit he hadn't known about her until now. "So do I."

"I have a suggestion," Griff Coleman said from across the table. He closed his menu. "Instead of each of us ordering a plate, why don't we order a bunch of the different dishes and share? Then we'll all split the check."

"As long as I can get lemon chicken," Emma Keeton said, "I'm good."

Griff leaned closer to her and nipped her earlobe. "You're always good."

She flashed him a sexy smile. "And don't you forget it."

Quade chuckled as the lovers shared a kiss. Emma raised her left hand and touched Griff's cheek. A large diamond winked at him.

"Whoa! Emma, when did you get that rock?"

Emma wiggled her fingers, making the diamond sparkle. "Isn't it gorgeous? Griff proposed last night."

Quade reached across the table and offered Griff his hand. "Congratulations."

Griff's smile could've lit up the room. "Thanks. I figured after being together a year, it was time to make an honest woman out of her."

"I had no problem living in sin," Emma said with a playful shrug.

"Yeah, right. So that's why you called Talia at the crack of dawn to ask her to make your wedding dress."

"Hey, a woman has priorities." She looked at Eve and Rhea. "Talia and I plan to go to your store tomorrow to talk about fabric."

"Have you set a date?" Rhea asked.

"Not yet, but I want a winter wedding. Maybe in January."

"We got in some gorgeous white satin this week," Eve said. "It flows like silk. It would make a beautiful wedding gown."

Quade tuned out the three ladies' conversation while he studied the lovely woman seated next to him. Her eyes glowed, a smile curved her lips. He didn't know if her pleasure came from speaking about fabric or about wedding gowns.

He knew Eve had never been married. He didn't know why not. A woman as lovely and intelligent and charming as she should've been snatched up years ago.

Still so much to learn about Ms. Van Den Bergh.

Maysen Halliday and Clay Spencer headed toward their table. Maysen walked right up to Emma. "Let me see it."

Emma's mouth dropped open. "How did you know?"

"Rye told us when he came by Spencer's this morning."

Smiling, Emma held up her left hand so Maysen could admire the ring. "Wow." Maysen grinned at Griff. "You done good. Did Hardy make it?" she asked, referring to the jeweler in town.

Griff nodded. "I gave him an idea of what I wanted and he went with it."

"It's beautiful." Maysen leaned over to give Emma a hug. "I'm happy for both of you."

"Thank you, Maysen."

"There's Julia and Stephen," Dylan said from his place beside Griff. "Now that everyone is here, we can order."

"Lemon chicken!" Emma called out.

"Pork chow mein!" Talia said.

Dylan touched Talia's hand. "Hey, wait until we have a waiter."

"Then get one," she ordered. "I'm hungry."

Dylan looked at Quade. "Never get in the way of a hungry woman."

"I'll remember that."

The waiter arrived to take their order. Quade listened to others call out their favorite dishes, deciding there would be enough variety for fourteen people without him ordering something, too. He made a mental note when Eve ordered teriyaki wings and a glass of white wine. Something to remember for the future in case he ever decided to stop by her place with dinner.

He liked that idea. He'd always enjoyed surprising a woman with an impromptu picnic. Unfortunately, his social calendar had been far from full lately. He hadn't had a date in six months, not since he and Deborah decided their relationship would never go any further than sex.

Not that Quade had anything against sex. He loved everything about making love with a woman—the flowery scent of her hair, the silkiness of her skin, the press of firm breasts against his chest. He loved kissing soft lips, sliding his dick into a wet pussy. Yet he wanted more than sex with a woman.

He wanted a lifetime.

Quade glanced at Eve as she sipped from her water glass. He hadn't been this attracted to a woman in a long time. He didn't know if anything serious would develop between him and Eve, but he'd never know if he didn't try.

Quade didn't think he'd laughed so hard in his life. With fourteen people all telling stories, the conversation and laughter never stopped all through dinner. Time passed so quickly, it surprised him when he glanced at his watch to see the hands approached eleven o'clock.

Maysen must have noticed the time as he did for she waved to get everyone's attention. "Clay and I are leaving soon. I've divided the check by fourteen. If we all chip in twenty dollars, that will cover the bill and leave a nice tip."

Eve reached for her purse hanging on the back of her chair. Quade gently touched her hand to stop her. "I have it."

She blinked as if she didn't understand what he said. "What? No. You don't have to pay for my dinner."

"I know I don't *have* to, but I *want* to. I invited you, remember?"

Her lips curved in a small smile. "Thank you. That's very sweet."

Quade removed forty dollars from his wallet, passed it down the table to Maysen. Once she'd collected all the cash, she grinned. "Thanks. Clay's putting the dinner on his credit card. I get to keep the money."

Laughter rang out again over Maysen's joke, then everyone gathered up their items to leave. Quade waited for Eve as she spoke with Rhea. Even in a town as friendly and crime-free as Lanville, he wouldn't let a woman walk to her car alone this late at night.

She turned to him once Rhea walked away with Bob. "You didn't have to wait for me."

"A gentleman always escorts a lady to her car."

"Then I accept."

Quade placed his hand on the small of her back. He left several inches between their bodies so only his hand touched her, although he wished he could feel her entire body against his.

She led him to a newer model midsize car that happened to be parked only two spaces away from his pickup. He waved at Keely and Nick Fallon as they drove away. That left the parking lot empty except for one other vehicle besides theirs.

"Thank you again for dinner," Eve said.

"My pleasure."

The security light on the restaurant cast a golden glow over her face. He wondered what she would do if he kissed her.

"It's getting late. I'd better go."

Kissing her now wouldn't be appropriate, even though he longed to taste her. "Okay. Be careful going home."

"I will."

Quade waited until she'd withdrawn her keys from her purse and unlocked the driver's side door before he stepped back. He walked halfway to his truck, then glanced over his shoulder for one more look at her. What he saw made him hurry back to her car. "Eve, wait!"

Eve lowered her window. "What's wrong?"

"Your back tire is flat."

"What?" Turning off the ignition, she climbed out of her car. She blew out a frustrated breath when she bent over to look at the flat tire. "Well, shoot."

"Hey, it's no problem. I'll change it for you. I'll grab my flashlight while you open the trunk."

He could see the relief flash over her face. "Thank you, Quade. I really appre . . ." She stopped, closed her eyes, and blew out another breath. "Opening the trunk won't help. I don't have a spare. I mean, I have a spare, but it's flat, too. I forgot to get it fixed."

He could've reprimanded her on the danger of her getting stranded without a spare tire, but it wouldn't accomplish anything except make her feel worse than she already did. "It still isn't a problem. Your car is parked under a security light right on the main highway through town. No one will bother it. But if it'll make you feel better, I'll call our sheriff and have his deputies check it when they do their drive-throughs."

She smiled and her shoulders relaxed. "Thank you, Quade."

"Grab your stuff and I'll take you home."

Once situated in his pickup, Quade made the quick call to Brad McGuire and explained the situation with Eve's car. Since the restaurant was less than two miles from Cozy Crafts, he pulled up behind the store as he ended the conversation with the sheriff.

"All done. The deputies will check to make sure your car is okay throughout the night. I'll call Clay in the morning. One of his mechanics will take care of both tires for you."

"Thank you. Again. It seems like all I've done this evening is thank you."

"You're welcome."

He opened his door, determined to walk her to her entrance. Even though they hadn't had an official date, he still thought it the polite thing to do to see her all the way home. Taking her arm, he led her to the stairs. A security light came on when they were halfway up the steps, triggered by their movement.

When they reached her small balcony, Eve looked down at the key ring in her hand. Quade waited for her to unlock the doorknob and deadbolt and step inside. Several moments passed and she continued to stand in one place. "You okay?"

"We didn't have dessert at the restaurant."

He didn't understand why she mentioned that, but teased with her. "We had fortune cookies."

"That's not dessert," she said, still looking at her keys. "I made brownies yesterday." Now she gazed into his eyes. "Would you like to come in for dessert?"

3

Eve had no idea why she invited Quade to have dessert with her. The words had tumbled from her mouth before she could stop them. But she'd enjoyed her evening and his company so much, she didn't want it to end yet.

"With or without nuts?" Quade asked.

It took her a moment to realize he referred to the brownies. She smiled. "With, of course. In fact, the pecans came from Keely and Nick's trees."

"Does coffee come with the brownies?"

"Yes."

"Then I can't possibly say no."

Relief and trepidation battled inside Eve as she unlocked the door—relief that he'd agreed to stay, and trepidation that he'd agreed to stay. She'd told herself she and Quade could be good friends even if they couldn't have a serious relationship. What she felt in his presence had nothing to do with friendship and everything to do with a woman's desire for a man.

She couldn't allow her desire to overrule her common sense. Friends only. She had to keep telling herself that.

He leaned against the counter in her kitchen and crossed his ankles. "Anything I can do to help?"

"No, it won't take long to make coffee. I have the kind of coffeemaker that brews one cup at a time. I have several different kinds and flavors, both regular and decaf."

"Decaf works for me since it's late. You pick the flavor."

"Cream or sugar?"

"Just black."

She could feel him watching her while she prepared the first cup of coffee. Little tendrils of pleasure crawled along her skin. She imagined his touch instead of his gaze running along her arms, her back, between her legs. . . .

Eve handed him the mug of coffee. "It's French Vanilla. If you don't like it, I'll make a different flavor for you."

Quade gently took a sip of the hot brew. "It's very good. Thank you."

After starting her own mug, she took the plastic container holding the brownies out of the pantry. "They're from a mix. I've tried making brownies from scratch several times, but they always seem dry."

"Some of the best things I've eaten have come from a mix."

She thought him sweet to say that before he'd even tasted one. "You might change your mind once you eat one of these." She removed the lid, held the plastic container out to him. "Help yourself."

He chose the biggest brownie on top, took a healthy bite and chewed. "Very good."

It pleased her that he thought so. "I think the local pecans are what make them so good." Eve took her mug from the coffeemaker, added a generous splash of liquid creamer to it. "Let's take our dessert to the living room. We'll be more comfortable."

Quade finished his brownie and took the plastic container from her hands. "I'll carry that for you. Just to be helpful."

She chuckled at the mischievous gleam in his eyes. "Yeah, right."

His grin made her think of a little boy who'd gotten away with stealing cookies from beneath his mom's nose. She'd never seen this playful side of Quade. But then, she hadn't spent that much time with him over the two years she'd lived in Lanville. This evening gave her the opportunity to get to know him better. As a friend.

Eve tore a couple of paper towels from the roll and led the way to the living room. She'd left one lamp burning on the end table by the couch for she hated walking into a dark room. She turned on the other lamp as she walked past it. Once she sat at one end of the couch, Quade sat at the other and set the container between them. She handed him one of the paper towels, then chose a treat for herself. One bite and she moaned from pleasure.

"I know I made them, but I have to say they're delicious."

"Yes, they are." Quade chose a second brownie, bit off half in one bite. "I'm usually not much of a sweets eater, but chocolate is my weakness."

"Mine, too. I could gain a lot of weight easily if I gave in to my chocolate cravings more often than I do."

His gaze dipped to her breasts, her thighs. "You have nothing to worry about as far as your weight."

Her cheeks heated at his compliment. "Thank you."

He stretched his arm along the back of the couch, resting his hand mere inches from her shoulder. "You're a lovely woman, Eve." This time he looked at her face, her hair. "Your hair is an amazing color. I'll be rude and ask if it's real or if you get help from a hairdresser."

She could pretend to be offended at his question, but didn't want to play games with Quade. "It's real. Both my parents have blond hair."

Quade took a sip of his coffee. "Tell me about your parents.

I heard that your father is Dutch and your mother American. Do they live in the Netherlands?"

"My father does. My mother passed away several years ago."

A look of sympathy crossed his face. "I'm sorry."

"So am I. I still miss her." Eve drew up her knees to the couch, shifted so she could see Quade better. "My father was in Jacksonville, Florida, thirty-three years ago on business. My mother lived there and had gone out to dinner with girlfriends. She and my father had one of those moments—according to my mother—when their eyes met across the restaurant and fireworks went off. He followed her outside and asked to see her the next day. She agreed." Eve held her mug in both hands. "They spent four days together. I was the result of those four days."

"Did they marry?"

Eve shook her head. "They cared deeply for each other, I have no doubt about that, but they didn't love each other and had no desire to marry."

"Yet you have his last name."

"My father comes from a wealthy and influential family. He and my mother wanted me to be part of that family, so they gave me his last name. I was born in Amsterdam and have dual citizenship, but they decided I would stay with my mother and my father would pay for support and visit whenever possible. Or I'd go to see him. That's what usually happens. It's hard for him to get away from his job. Plus he isn't crazy about flying. So he buys my plane ticket whenever I get the chance to go to see him. It works out for us."

"But you don't get to see him very often."

"Two or three times a year. I'm going at Christmas for two weeks."

Propping his elbow on the back of the couch, Quade rested his cheek against his fist. "I'll bet it's beautiful there at Christmas."

Eve smiled in memory. "Oh, yes. There's usually snow,

which I love. Living in Florida meant it was rare for me to see snow while growing up."

"Then you should've loved last November when we got seven inches."

"I did. I loved every inch of it, even though I couldn't drive for three days."

Quade chuckled. "So what's the weather like at Christmas in the Netherlands, besides having snow?"

"The temperature varies little, only about fifteen degrees between the low and high. It usually runs from the low thirties at night to the mid-forties during the day. Although one time when I was there a few years back, it got up to sixty two days after Christmas. I saw a lot of people in short sleeves on their bicycles."

He leaned a little closer to her, as if he planned to tell her a secret. "Have you ever been to the Red Light District in Amsterdam?"

If he wanted to embarrass her or shock her, it wouldn't work. "Of course I have, many times."

A slow smile spread across his lips. "Why, you little vixen."

"I didn't say I'd *worked* there, only *been* there."

Quade laughed. "I like your honesty."

"It's much better than lying."

"True."

She watched him break another brownie in half. "What about you? Do your parents live close by?"

"In Austin. That's where I grew up. My ex-wife still lives there, and my son."

Eve stopped with her mug raised halfway to her mouth. "You have a son?"

Pride shone in his eyes as he smiled. "Adrian. He's fifteen and the best part of my life. I drive down to see him every couple of weekends. He comes up for Christmas and spring break and most of the summer. Although in another year or two, I doubt he'll want to spend spring break with his old man."

Eve smiled, sure Quade must be right. Adrian would soon be more interested in meeting girls on spring break than being with his father. "You're young to have a fifteen-year-old son."

"Natalie and I met the beginning of our sophomore year in college. Things developed quickly between us. We tried to be careful, but she got pregnant anyway. We decided to get married and did our best to make it work, but even though we cared for each other, the love needed to sustain a marriage simply wasn't there. We divorced after two years."

"That must have been hard on Adrian."

"Yeah, it was. He was daddy's boy all the way to his toenails. I stayed in Austin so I could be close to him until he got older. When the job as counselor at the high school in Lanville was offered to me, I decided to take it. I hated to leave my son, but needed a fresh start. It broke my heart to see tears in his eyes when I drove off, but I felt moving here was the right thing to do."

"Has it turned out to be a good decision?"

Quade nodded. "I love my job and love Lanville. The people here are friendly and caring. It's a great place to live. And Natalie remarried three years ago. Adrian gets along well with his stepfather. I'm thankful for that. It makes it easier for me to say good-bye when I have to leave him."

"You haven't remarried. Why not?"

"I haven't met my soul mate yet."

She gripped her mug a bit tighter. She thought she'd met her soul mate. Twice. Neither time had worked out. "Do you believe that? That there's a soul mate for everyone?"

"I don't know if I believe there's a soul mate for *everyone*, but I do believe there's one for me. I'll meet her someday, when the time is right."

"But you've dated, right?"

"Sure. I've dated several very nice women. In fact, I thought I might have met 'the one' about a year ago, but Deborah and I had little in common. We split up six months ago." Quade set his empty mug on the end table. "What about you? Why no Mr. Van Den Bergh in your life?"

"Would you like another cup of coffee?" she asked to avoid answering his question.

His eyes narrowed. She knew she hadn't fooled him. "In a minute. I told you about my past relationships. Your turn to tell me about yours."

He'd shared with her. It would only be fair for her to share with him. Eve looked down in her empty mug, wished she held a glass of wine instead. "I was engaged. It didn't work out." She lifted her gaze back to Quade's face. "Either time."

His eyebrows lifted in obvious surprise. "*Either* time?"

"I was engaged twice."

A tender look of concern passed over his face. "What happened?"

While baring her soul might be good for her, Eve couldn't talk about her failures with Quade. "I know you're a counselor and you're used to getting people to talk, but I'd rather not."

"Not a problem," he didn't hesitate to say. "If you don't want to talk about it, then we won't." He glanced at his watch. "I should be leaving anyway. It's after midnight and you have to work tomorrow."

It surprised her to realize how very much she didn't want him to go. "You don't have to leave. I don't start until noon on Saturdays. I can make you another cup of coffee."

Quade smiled. "I appreciate the offer, but I should go."

He'd mentioned he went to Austin to see his son every other weekend. Perhaps he planned to do that tomorrow and had to get home so he could leave early. "Are you going to Austin in the morning?"

"No. I went last weekend and I'll go next weekend. I'm free this Saturday and Sunday."

What a perfect opening to invite him to come back for dinner, or go to a movie, or have a picnic. Instead, she remained silent, the invitation frozen on her tongue.

Quade picked up his empty coffee mug. "Thanks for the coffee and brownies."

"Would you like to take a couple with you? I have plenty."

His eyes twinkled with humor. "I'll never turn down chocolate."

Eve led the way back to her kitchen. Quade set his mug in the sink, then moved out of her way. She placed three brownies in a plastic zippered bag and handed it to him.

"To enjoy tomorrow."

"Thanks."

This time she followed instead of led when Quade walked to her door. Not sure what to do with her hands, she slipped them in the pockets of her pants. She should be happy that he planned to leave, that she wouldn't be surrounded by his masculine, woodsy scent any longer. Truthfully, she'd enjoyed his company, his conversation, along with that amazing scent. It had been over two years since she'd been close to a man, close enough to see the flecks of silver in his sapphire eyes, feel his warmth touch her arm.

She'd missed it.

Quade placed his hand on the doorknob, then turned to look at her. "I had a good time tonight."

"I did, too."

Heat rushed through her body when she saw a flare of desire in his eyes. "Such a nice evening should end with a kiss, right?"

Say no. He won't kiss me if I say no.

Eve nodded.

She couldn't call it a kiss, but more of a whisper of his lips against hers. It lasted only moments . . . not nearly long enough for her to get enough of his taste.

"Have dinner with me tomorrow night," he said in a husky voice.

Eve nodded again.

"What time do you get off work?"

"Six."

"I'll make reservations at Café Crystal for seven-thirty."

"Okay."

She thought—hoped—he might kiss her again, but he opened the door and stepped into the night. Eve closed the door behind him, leaned her forehead against the wood. Just because she'd accepted Quade's invitation to dinner didn't mean anything would develop between them. It couldn't. She didn't have the courage to go through heartbreak a third time.

4

"You call that lean?" Quade heard Emma say in a ferocious voice. He paused inside the back door to the Café Crystal kitchen, not wanting to be in the line of fire. He'd witnessed the effect of Emma's temper and didn't want to see it again. For someone only five-three, she could slay a man to ribbons with her tongue.

"Mz. Keeton," a whiny male voice pleaded, "those are some of my best steaks—"

"Then I'll start looking for another supplier because I *will not* serve fatty steaks to my customers!"

Quade peeked around the door frame, wondering if he should step in to help her . . . or help whomever received the tongue lashing. Emma held a large knife with a thick rib eye pierced on the end of the blade while she glared at the man who outweighed her by at least one hundred pounds and towered over her by a good eight inches.

"You take these back and bring me the steaks I ordered."

"Now, Mz. Keeton, we can work this out—"

"Get out of my sight." She tossed the steak into a large

cardboard box on the counter. "And take those globs of fat with you."

The man looked like he might try to argue again, but then he sighed heavily and picked up the box. "You still want the sirloins and T-bones?"

"Yes, they're fine. But *those*"—she pointed to the box in his hand as if it were a pile of week-old garbage—"I wouldn't feed to my best friend's dog."

Quade knew his two Labs would love those steaks, fatty or not.

Emma made a shooing motion with her hand. "Get out of here. Be back Tuesday with decent rib eyes."

"Yes, ma'am."

The man sighed heavily as he walked toward the exit. When he reached Quade, he whispered, "I wouldn't go in there if I was you. She's in a mood."

"I'll take my chances," Quade whispered back.

He walked into the kitchen, but kept five feet between himself and Emma, who still held the large knife clutched in her fist. "Could you put down that weapon before I come any closer?"

Fire still shot from her eyes when she looked his way. "I hate incompetence. It really pisses me off when I don't get what I want."

"I could tell. Did Griff know what he was getting into before he proposed?"

"Oh, yeah. He's seen me mad dozens of times. He just pushes me against the wall and ravishes me, and then everything is okay." The anger disappeared from her eyes. Grinning, she laid the knife on the counter. "Was that too much information?"

"Nah. I've heard lots of things in counseling."

"Nothing like that from high school kids, I hope."

He'd made the counseling comment to tease her, but

Emma's statement had Quade thinking back on some of the conversations he'd had with abused kids. It always broke his heart when he heard about parents or relatives hurting the ones they should love the most. "Sometimes, yeah," he said softly.

Sympathy filled her eyes now. She slipped her hands into the pockets of her chef's smock. "That's so sad. I can't imagine the pleasure anyone gets from hurting a child."

"I can't either, Emma." Not wanting to go down that path, Quade decided to change the subject. "I'm here to ask a favor."

"Name it."

"I'm bringing Eve here tonight for dinner. Could you make some kind of special dessert for us, something that isn't on the menu? She loves chocolate."

Emma smiled. "I love whipping up special items. Do you want something off-menu for dinner, too?"

"I'd say yes, but I'm not sure what she prefers. I think this time it's better to let her order from the menu."

"No problem." She leaned against a counter, crossed her arms beneath her breasts. A smirk turned up the corners of her lips "So, you finally got Eve to say yes to a date, huh?"

"Perseverance pays off."

Emma's smirk faded. "To my knowledge—and you know how people in this town love to gossip—Eve hasn't dated anyone since she moved here. I hope you don't put too much hope in this date. I don't want you to get hurt."

Quade tapped the end of her cute nose. "Thank you. I appreciate what a good friend you are, but I'm fine. It's only one date. I'd like it to lead to more, but I'm okay if it doesn't."

"If I didn't love Griff so much, *I'd* push *you* up against the wall."

He grinned. "I'd let you."

"I don't understand why a woman hasn't tied you to her bed by now. You're such a great guy." Her gaze passed over his shoulders and chest. "Not to mention completely buff and gorgeous. You do know that when you ride through town on your motorcycle, every woman who sees you sighs. And I mean every one, from the teenagers to the senior citizens. Especially when your hair is free and blows in the wind." She gave a playful shiver. "Damn."

He rubbed the back of his neck while heat climbed into his cheeks. Few women could embarrass him. Emma did, time and time again. "Thank you. I think."

Her grin returned. Emma rose to her tiptoes and kissed his cheek. "I'll make something very special for your dessert tonight. What time is your reservation?"

"Seven-thirty. Or I guess I should say it'll be at seven-thirty as soon as I make it."

"I'll take care of that right now." Crossing to a small alcove that housed a desk, bookshelves, and file cabinets, Emma sat at the desk and wiggled the mouse to wake up the computer. "Wow, we're almost at capacity tonight. I love when that happens." She clicked a few keys. "Done! Got you down for seven-thirty."

"You making your prime rib tonight?"

"Of course. Every Friday and Saturday night. The chef's special tonight is a smaller cut of prime rib served with a fresh lobster tail from Maine."

Quade groaned as his mouth watered. He hadn't had lobster in months. He'd been in Austin the last time Emma served it at Café Crystal. "Thanks a lot. Now I'll be thinking about that lobster tail all day."

Emma grinned, not seeming the least bit sorry she'd tempted him. "If you think that's what you'll order, I'll save the biggest one for you."

"You're the best, do you know that?"

Her grin widened. "Of course."

"See you tonight?"

"I'll make a point to come out and say hi."

Quade headed for the exit. He'd taken one step through the doorway when Alaina Coleman plowed into him.

"Oh, Quade, I'm so sorry! I didn't see you."

Her elbow had connected with his stomach, so it took Quade a moment to straighten and be able to talk. "No problem." He studied the face of the owner of Café Crystal and The Inn on Crystal Creek. Her skin appeared flushed, her eyes shone bright with happiness. "You okay?"

"I'm great," she said with a huge smile. Cradling his cheeks in her hands, she gave him a smacking kiss on the lips. "I'm just great."

She hurried by him while Quade was still trying to recover from her elbow and the surprising kiss. He doubted if her husband, Rye, would appreciate her kissing other men.

A loud squeal from the kitchen had Quade reversing his steps and hurrying back to the room. Emma and Alaina held each other tightly and bounced up and down while they turned in a circle. "What the hell is going on?"

Emma released Alaina and beamed at Quade. "Lainy's pregnant!"

Frowning, Alaina punched Emma's arm. "Shhh! I haven't told Rye yet." She glanced at Quade. "No offense."

"None taken." Smiling broadly, he stepped closer to the two women. "May I hug the mother-to-be?"

Alaina's smile returned, even brighter than it had been when he'd first seen her. "Might as well, since I've already kissed you."

Quade lifted Alaina from the floor in a tight hug. When he returned her feet to the floor, he gave her a tender kiss on the forehead. "Congratulations."

"Thank you, Quade. I had an appointment with Dr. Dawson Monday, but I couldn't wait any longer to know for sure. I begged her to see me in her office today and do a pregnancy test." She placed both hands on her flat stomach. "It came back positive."

"How far along are you, Lainy?" Emma asked.

"Two months, more or less." A sheepish look crept over her face. "Rye and I, uh, celebrated big time after Rayna and Marcus's wedding."

Quade threw back his head and laughed. "Well, if there's a good time to get pregnant, it has to be at a wedding."

"I think so, too." Alaina turned to Emma. "Where's Kelcey? I wanted to tell her, too, but she isn't in the office."

"She had a meeting with our CPA."

Alaina closed her eyes. "That's right. I forgot." She opened them again and shrugged. "My mind has been elsewhere today." She gave Emma another hug, then gave one to Quade. "I have to find Rye. Don't tell him I told y'all about the baby. I don't want his feelings to be hurt that he wasn't the first to know."

Emma made a motion like turning a key at her lips. "Your secret is safe with me."

"Me, too," Quade said.

Tears shimmered in her eyes when she smiled again. "Thanks. We'll announce it at the family dinner tomorrow. I know Beverly and Kenneth will be thrilled to learn they have a grandchild on the way!"

She hurried from the room, practically skipping. Chuckling, Quade looked at Emma. "That'll be you someday, when you and Griff decide to start a family."

"We've talked about having a family, but it probably won't be soon. I told Griff there's still a lot I want to do with the restaurant first. He said he's willing to wait until I'm ready."

"Did you set a wedding date?"

Emma nodded. "January twenty-first. Can you be there or is that a weekend you visit Adrian?"

"I can switch a weekend with Adrian if necessary. He'll understand. There's no way I'll miss your and Griff's wedding."

Two of Emma's workers came into the kitchen. Quade took that as his cue to leave. "Thanks again for the special dessert tonight. See you later."

Quade left by the back door again, this time not bumping into anyone. His mind whirled as he made his way to his pickup of what else he could do to make tonight special for Eve.

While Café Crystal didn't have a dress code, Quade knew the people in Lanville dressed nicer when they went there than at any of the other restaurants in town. He chose to wear his charcoal gray suit with a white button-down shirt. No tie. To him, ties were for weddings and funerals only.

He reached the door leading from his kitchen to the back porch when he stopped. Rubbing his forehead, he tried to decide if he should carry condoms with him. He hoped the evening with Eve wouldn't end after dinner, that she would ask him to spend the night with her. He couldn't assume she would, yet needed to be prepared in case she did.

Retracing his steps to his bedroom, Quade opened the nightstand, removed two condoms, and slipped them in his jacket pocket. He thought a moment, then placed a third one in his pocket.

Quade left his pickup parked in the garage and took his 1969 Corvette instead. Thanks to regular maintenance and care, the car still purred like new.

He made the short drive to the back of Cozy Crafts Cottage and parked next to Eve's car. He thought a full bouquet of flowers might be too much on a first date, so had opted for a single white rosebud instead. Picking up the flower from the passenger seat, he climbed from the car and headed for the steps.

The sight of Eve when she opened the door stole his breath. She wore a long-sleeved, dark aqua dress that made the green of her eyes pop. It flowed over her curves to stop at her knees. A square neckline gave him a peek at the top of her breasts. One silver chain lay at her throat, one draped down almost to her waist. She'd pulled her hair back into what he thought women called a French braid.

"Hi," she greeted with a smile.

"Hello." Quade held up the rose for her. "You look beautiful."

She graced him with another smile. "Thank you. You look very handsome."

He dipped his head to acknowledge her compliment.

She held the rose to her nose and sniffed. "And thank you for the rose." She opened the door wider. "Come in while I put it in water."

He watched her take a slim blue vase from a cabinet and add water to it. After sniffing the rose once again, she placed it in the vase and set it on the windowsill above the sink. "I can enjoy it while I wash dishes."

Quade noticed she'd placed a lacy shawl and small purse on the end of the kitchen counter. He lifted the shawl and held it open so he could slip it over her shoulders. He took a moment to enjoy the flowery scent of her hair before she moved away from him to pick up her purse.

"Ready?" he asked.

"Ready."

Once she locked her door, Quade slipped his arm around her waist to guide her down the steps. The heels she wore made her only about five inches shorter than he . . . a perfect height for holding her against him while they kissed.

Not wanting to get ahead of himself, he pushed thoughts of kissing Eve from his mind and opened the passenger door so she could slide onto the seat. He rounded the hood, then slid behind the wheel.

She ran her hand over the dash. "This is nice."

"Thanks. It was my dad's. He bought it on his twentieth birthday, gave it to me on my twentieth."

"Will you continue the tradition with Adrian?"

"I plan to. Although I don't know if he'll want to wait until he's twenty to get it. He'll take driver's ed in the spring and is already hinting about getting the car as soon as he receives his driver's license." Quade turned on the signal to make a right-hand turn onto County Road 311. "I might buy him an older pickup to get him where he needs to go when he turns sixteen. Or I might give him this car early. I haven't decided yet."

"Does he already know how to drive?"

"Yeah. I taught Adrian to drive the summer he turned fourteen. We stayed on my property, so never got out on the highway. He did really well right away." He glanced at her and grinned. "Made me proud."

"I can tell by your voice when you talk about him how proud you are."

"He's a good kid. And I'm not saying that because he's my son. He really is a good kid."

"Maybe I'll meet him someday."

"He'll be with me over the Christmas break."

"I won't be here. I'm going to see my father over Christmas."

"Sorry. I forgot. No problem. You'll meet him another time."

Quade pulled into a parking spot at Café Crystal. Vehicles filled almost every place, making him glad he'd made a reservation so early today. He hurried around the car, arriving in time to offer a hand to help Eve from her seat.

"I looked at the dinner menu online today," Eve said as they walked toward the entrance. "I usually have lunch here, so wasn't sure about what's available at dinner."

"Did you find something you might like?"

"Yes, at least ten somethings."

Quade chuckled. "I came by earlier today to make the reservation. Emma told me the chef's special tonight is prime rib and lobster tail. How does that sound?"

"Like nirvana."

He pulled open one of the heavy wooden doors, gestured for her to precede him. "With Emma cooking, I have no doubt it will be."

5

Looking at Quade across the table, bathed in candlelight, had to be one of the most enjoyable things Eve had ever experienced. She couldn't help but admire his incredible looks, yet she also admired him. His intelligence, charm, and wit wrapped around her, making her feel warm all through her body.

That warmth soon changed to desire.

She caught the fiery looks he gave her every now and then, when his sapphire eyes seemed to glow with heat. He never made a suggestive comment, never acted like anything but a gentleman. Yet she sensed he could quickly turn into a ravishing beast with one indication from her that she wanted him.

She'd considered all through dinner about giving him that indication.

Quade exuded sex appeal. While some handsome men turned out to be duds in bed, she didn't doubt for a second that he knew exactly what to do with a woman. He had long, thick fingers that would glide over a woman's curves, dip into hollows. She wondered if he had smooth fingertips or callused ones.

The top two open buttons on his shirt let her see a bit of his smooth chest. His skin possessed that lovely light copper coloring of Native Americans. She wondered about his ancestry, if perhaps he had some Native American blood in his veins. She didn't know where he got the blue eyes. However he got them, they mesmerized her. The deep sapphire color, the flecks of silver, the long, black eyelashes . . . they combined to make her want to stare into them for hours.

He'd removed his jacket, draped it over the back of his chair. The white shirt looked like snow against his dark skin. He'd rolled up his shirt sleeves to mid forearm, letting her admire the play of muscles in his arms when he moved. The shirt stretched over a wide chest that would feel so good pressed against her breasts.

A shiver danced up her spine at the thought of Quade holding her, kissing her, making love to her. . . .

Their waitress, Shara, came by their table to pick up their plates. "How about another glass of wine?" she asked.

"Not for me, Shara," Quade said. "I limit myself to one when I'm driving."

She looked at Eve. "More wine?"

Thankful for the interruption before she did something stupid like push Quade on top of the table and jerk off his clothes, Eve shook her head. She would love another glass of the fabulous burgundy they'd had with dinner, but she wouldn't drink more if Quade didn't. "How about coffee instead?"

"Regular or decaf?"

"Decaf for both of us," Quade told Shara. "Eve takes cream in hers."

A pleasant heat spread through her that he'd remembered how she drank her coffee. It had only been one night since they'd had coffee together at her apartment, so he should remember, yet she suspected a lot of men wouldn't.

"Be right back with your coffee and dessert."

Shara left before Eve could ask her what she meant about dessert. "We didn't order dessert."

"I did. I asked Emma to make something special for us."

"When did you do that?"

"This morning when I made the reservation."

Touched that he'd been so thoughtful, Eve didn't know what to say. She didn't think she'd ever met a man as considerate as Quade. "That was very sweet. What is it?"

"I told her to go for it, as long as it's chocolate."

Shara came back with a tray. She set a plate in the center of the table. Eve's eyes widened when she saw the trails of white, milk, and dark chocolate drizzled over the top of the round dessert and decorating the plate. "What is it?"

"Emma calls it Triple Chocolate Threat. The crust is milk chocolate, the filling swirls of dark and white chocolate. It's kind of a . . . cheesecakey, custardy mousse." She held out clean spoons to both of them. "Dig in."

Eve did exactly that while Shara poured their coffee. Once she'd taken a bite, Quade tried one. The flavors of the three types of chocolate flowed over her taste buds. She'd swear they did a happy dance.

"Oh, my God, that's sinful."

"I'll second that. Shara, tell Emma she did good."

The waitress grinned. "I'll do that. Wave at me if you need anything else."

Eve scooped up another bite of the dessert. "I can't believe I'm eating this, as full as I am."

He tapped her to-go container with the handle of his spoon. "You didn't eat all your prime rib."

"I wanted to save some of it for a snack tomorrow. I ate every bite of the lobster."

"I noticed that."

She liked the way the candlelight reflected in his eyes when he grinned. So far, she'd found very little to dislike about Quade Easton.

That scared her.

Of course, one date didn't mean anything serious. Quade might be divorced, but she'd bet he didn't spend many nights alone. He'd told her last night that he'd dated since the breakup with his last girlfriend. She didn't doubt that at all. She'd seen the hot looks the women in the restaurant gave him as he walked past their tables.

She had to admit to a feeling of smugness because she had such a handsome, desirable man for her date.

"What is that?" Quade asked.

"What is what?"

He motioned toward her mouth with his spoon. "That little grin tugging at your lips."

Eve quickly sobered, embarrassed that she'd let her thoughts show on her face. "I'm not grinning."

"You were." He scooped up another bite of dessert. "What were you thinking?"

She studied his face while he chewed, trying to decide how honest to be with him. Being completely honest meant admitting how much he attracted her, how she felt fluttery whenever he looked into her eyes. Being honest meant telling him everything inside her went all soft and liquid when she thought of his body against hers, his cock pumping into her channel.

I can't tell him any of those things, not unless I want to end up naked with him.

Which wouldn't be a bad thing. It had been a long, long time since she'd been naked with a man.

"Time to come clean, Eve."

His eyes twinkled with humor, a sure sign that he was teasing her. She decided to tease right back. "A woman has the right to some secrets, Quade."

"That's true. I just thought since this is a getting-to-know-each-other dinner that we should share something that no one else knows."

A slow grin spread over her lips. "Oh, really? Is that what this dinner is about?"

"We have to talk about something personal sometime tonight. We talked about jobs and friends during dinner. Dessert is a time for sharing."

"Who made up that rule?"

"I'm pretty sure it's in the dating handbook."

He took another bite of dessert. After placing the chocolate concoction in his mouth, he slowly licked the spoon. Eve's grin faded as images of his tongue on her body filled her mind. . . .

Quade leaned forward. "I like when you look at me that way."

"What way?" she asked, her voice coming out huskier than she'd prefer.

"Like you're thinking about all the things I could do to you with my tongue."

Heat whooshed through her body. Her toes curled in her shoes. "Quade," she croaked.

Reaching across the table, he drew a figure eight on the back of her hand. "Are you going to ask me to spend the night with you?"

"I . . . don't know."

He gave a brief nod. "Honesty. I like that." He continued to caress her hand with his finger. "I won't push you, Eve. It's completely up to you if we make love. But I want you, if that helps you decide."

"I think . . . it might be too soon."

"Okay. I accept that." He glanced at the last bite of dessert remaining on the dish. "You'd better eat that in a hurry before I do."

Eve quickly spooned up the remaining chocolate treat as Shara returned with a pot of coffee. "Refills?"

"None for me," Eve said.

"I'm good, too. Tell Emma to put this on my bill."

"Already done." She smiled at each of them. "Y'all have a nice night."

"You have a bill?"

"Emma runs a tab for me and I pay once a month. I eat here a lot and it's easier to pay one bill than several." He pulled his wallet from his inside jacket pocket, laid some bills next to his plate. "I still pay the tip based on service. Shara is always good."

Quade stood, rounded the table, and pulled back her chair as Eve stood. She gathered her shawl, purse, and container holding her leftover prime rib. With his hand on the small of her back, they headed for the exit.

I won't push you, Eve. It's completely up to you if we make love.

Quade's words repeated over and over in her mind while he drove to her apartment. She didn't speak and neither did he. She looked out her window, the purr of the car the only sound breaking the silence. The half moon hadn't risen yet. Millions of stars sprinkled across the dark sky. Eve focused on the brightest one while she debated on whether to invite Quade into her home.

"Are you okay?" he asked softly.

"Yes." She turned her head and smiled at him. "Just enjoying all the stars."

"Adrian loves looking at the sky. I bought him a high-powered telescope for Christmas last year. You'd think he won the lottery."

"Is he interested in astronomy?"

"Meteorology. Weather fascinates him. I think he'll probably take whatever college courses are necessary to be a meteorologist."

Quade pulled behind Cozy Crafts and parked next to her car. It hadn't taken her long to realize he had impeccable manners, so she waited for him to come around the car and open the door for her. He offered a hand to help her from the seat, then kept it clutched tightly in his while they walked up the steps to her balcony. With a single word, she could be wrapped in Quade's arms all night long.

Eve didn't know if she was ready for that, but she did know she didn't want the evening to end yet. "It's barely ten o'clock. Would you like coffee or a glass of wine?"

He smiled. "A glass of wine sounds nice."

She handed him her container of prime rib so she could get her keys from her purse. Once inside the kitchen, Quade walked to the refrigerator and placed her leftovers in it. Eve laid her shawl and purse on the counter. "I only have red until I go to the grocery store on Tuesday."

"That's what we had with dinner, so red will be perfect."

Eve took a bottle from the wine rack in the corner, and a corkscrew from the drawer beneath it. "I know it's best to let it breathe after opening, but it's still wonderful to drink it right after removing the cork."

Before she could open the bottle, Quade laid his hand over hers that held the corkscrew. "Let me."

She relinquished the wine to him and went for their glasses. She watched him out of the corner of her eye as he expertly opened the bottle. He'd put his jacket back on before they left the restaurant. She wished he'd taken it off so she could enjoy the play of muscles while he wielded the corkscrew.

Eve set the wineglasses on the counter next to Quade so he could pour. He handed one glass to her, took the other for himself. She led the way to the living room, sat in the same spot where she'd sat last night. Quade sat a few inches closer to her than he had last night. When he stretched his arm along the back of the couch, his fingers grazed her nape.

Quade took a sip of his wine. "Mmm, that's very good."

"Thanks. I'll admit my father is a wine snob. I've learned a lot about wine from him." She swirled the red liquid in her glass. "He has a good friend who owns a large vineyard in the Rhône Valley in France. My father arranges for a case of this Châteauneuf-du-Pape to be shipped to me every year for my birthday."

"Which is . . ."

"December twenty-third. I'm usually with him then so I don't actually get the wine until a couple of weeks after I get home, but I can always count on it arriving. If I want more during the year, I let him know and he arranges for it to be sent."

"I'll admit I'm not a wine expert, but this may be the best red wine I've ever tasted."

Eve smiled, pleased he liked it. "I'm glad you're enjoying it."

"Have you been to France?"

She nodded. "Several times. In fact, I met Rhea in Paris at a bookstore." She drew her knees up on the couch, arranged her dress over her thighs so they were covered. "I've been lucky to have had the opportunity to travel a lot in Europe while visiting my father. I haven't been to any other continents yet. Maybe someday."

"Where would you like to go?"

"Everywhere."

Quade chuckled. "Could you be a little more specific?"

Eve grinned. "You asked, I answered." She sipped her wine. "Australia and New Zealand are at the top of my wish list."

"I took Adrian to Sydney two summers ago when he turned thirteen. He had a blast. So did I. I wish we'd had time to explore more of the continent. I'd love to go back someday."

She'd love to go with him. How strange that she'd been engaged twice, yet had never fantasized about traveling to other parts of the world with either of her fiancés. One mention of Quade wanting to go to another country and Eve thought about packing her bags.

He ran the back of one knuckle down her cheek. "What

happened? You looked happy, then the light went out of your eyes."

Once again, she must have let her thoughts show on her face. She quickly smiled. "I'm sorry. I got lost in memories for a second."

"Bad ones?"

"In a way. I wish I could see my father more often. I miss him."

He continued to caress her cheek with his knuckle. "I'm not trying to get too personal, but can't you afford to see him more often than you do?"

"Oh, that isn't a problem. He pays for all my trips. But he's also very busy, and two to three times a year seems to work the best for him."

"Do you have family anywhere else?"

Eve shook her head. "Only child of two only children. No cousins, aunts, or uncles. I do have my father's parents, but they live in the Netherlands, too. My mother's parents died before I was born."

"I have one brother, Quint. He's married with three boys. My father has one brother who has two boys. We Eastons can't seem to produce any girls. There hasn't been a girl born in our family for five generations."

Quade had mentioned his son many times, but hadn't said whether or not he wanted more children. "Would you like to have more children?"

"I would." His eyes shone with humor when he smiled. "Maybe I'd break the Easton curse and finally father a daughter."

The image of a little girl with her father's skin coloring, black hair, and sapphire eyes filled Eve's mind. She would be stunning.

"But maybe it would be better if I didn't have a daughter. I know she'd completely wrap me around her little finger. I wouldn't be able to tell her no."

Eve smiled at the thought of Quade jumping to do whatever his daughter wanted. "You'd have to be strong."

"That's hard for me. I'm a pushover when it comes to kids. I'd like to protect every one of them."

His comment sobered Eve. She knew Quade worked as a counselor at the high school, plus counseled adults on the side. He'd probably heard some terrible stories of mistreatment and abuse. "Your job must be hard at times."

"It is. All I can do is try to help the kids through the bad times instead of finding whoever is hurting them and throwing their ass against a brick wall the way I want to." He blew out a breath. "I guess that makes me as bad as the abuser."

"Not at all. I'd feel the same way."

He swirled his wine before taking a healthy sip. "I don't think I could ever take a life, unless I found out that person hurt Adrian. I'd protect my son with my last breath."

Eve had no doubt about that. Knowing how much Quade loved his son raised her respect for him.

Quade drained his glass. "Now that I've depressed both of us, I'll leave."

"You haven't depressed me, Quade."

"Still, I'd better go so you can get some rest."

She followed him to the kitchen. Quade placed his wineglass in the sink. "Thanks for the wine. It was excellent."

"You're welcome."

At the door, he faced her. "I enjoyed our evening. Maybe we can do it again soon."

Eve smiled. "I'd like that."

She set her glass on the counter and waited, breath held, for his good-night kiss. He tilted up her chin with one finger, lowered his lips to hers. It started the same as last night's kiss with a bare mingling of breaths, but he soon deepened it. His mouth moved over hers, then he tilted his head the other direction and kissed her again. Eve parted her lips to allow his tongue entrance, but he didn't take advantage of her movement. Instead, he continued to kiss her slowly, tenderly, using only his lips.

It had to be the most arousing kiss Eve had ever received.

Quade lifted his head. Eve struggled to open her eyes as he swept his thumb across her chin. "Good night."

"Good night," she whispered.

She stood on the small balcony, desire curling in her stomach, and watched as he descended the steps. He'd told her it would be her decision if they made love. If she asked him to stay, to be with her, he would. They'd have an incredible night of passion and then move on with their lives.

Eve battled with herself over the right thing to do. Desire won.

He'd reached the bottom step when she called out to him. "Quade."

He stopped, looked at her over his shoulder.

"Please stay."

He turned, but didn't move toward her. She thought he clenched his jaw, but couldn't be sure in the dim lighting. "If I stay, you know what will happen."

"Yes, I do."

After hesitating a few moments longer, Quade climbed the stairs.

6

It hadn't been easy for Quade not to bend Eve over his arm
and ravish her mouth the way he longed to when he said good
night to her. He enjoyed little pecking kisses, but he craved
more from her.

He'd meant what he'd said at dinner about it being her decision
if they made love. Now that she'd invited him to stay, he didn't
have to hold back and could kiss her the way he'd longed to.

He stepped through the doorway, pushed the door shut behind him. "Are you sure?"

She nodded. "I'm sure."

Quade held out one hand. Eve placed her palm against his,
let him tug her closer. He slipped one arm around her waist,
cradled her nape with his other hand. Lowering his head, he
pressed his lips to hers.

As he'd done the other two times he'd kissed her, he started
out soft and slow, giving her time to accept him. This time,
however, he didn't stop with a tender kiss. Gripping her nape,
he held her still while he deepened their kiss. His tongue tickled

the corners of her lips until they parted. He could taste the wine on her breath, along with the distinct flavor of Eve.

So delicious.

Her soft moan encouraged him to continue. Quade parted her lips more with his tongue, darted it inside to sweep against hers. He groaned when her fingernails dug into his mid-back. He took her action to mean she needed even more from him.

Ending the kiss, Quade rested his forehead against hers. "Tell me what you want, what you need."

"I want . . . I need . . . you." Her voice came out sounding as if she'd just run ten miles.

Despite the lust raging through his body, Quade teased her. "Could you be a little more specific?"

She pulled back and looked into his eyes. The green irises glowed with heat, desire. "You and me naked. How's that for specific?"

Her comment surprised him. After her hesitation earlier this evening, Quade thought he'd have to gently coax her into getting out of her clothes. He'd bare her body a bit at a time to give her the chance to relax and get used to his touch. Apparently, once she decided they would make love, she didn't want to wait one second to get close to him.

That worked for him.

"Take me to your bedroom."

Grasping his hand, she led him down the hall to her room. Once standing by the bed with the pale lamplight shining on the bedspread, Quade took a deep breath. He refused to rush this. No matter how much his body craved her, he didn't want their first time together to be a wham-bam-thank-you-ma'am situation.

Quade lifted both her hands to his mouth, kissed each palm. "Last chance to change your mind."

"I'm not changing my mind."

As if to prove her words, she slipped her hands beneath his jacket and drew it down his arms. It fell to the floor behind him. Quade let his arms relax at his sides so Eve could do whatever she wanted to. Looking into his eyes, she unfastened the first button on his shirt. She released each button, tugged the shirt from his pants.

Only after the shirt landed on top of his jacket did she lower her gaze. She touched his chest, her fingers gliding across the width, over his shoulders, down his torso. She circled his navel with a single fingertip. "I wondered if you have a happy trail." Her eyes sparkled with humor when she looked back at his face. "I like it."

The humor disappeared, to be replaced with awe. "You have a magnificent body, Quade."

She reached for his belt buckle, but Quade laid his hands over hers. "Don't you think it's my turn to take something off you?"

Eve shook her head. "Let me finish undressing you first."

Not wanting to disappoint her, he returned his arms to his sides. He helped her by toeing off his shoes, then stood still and waited for what she would do next.

She unfastened his belt, the button, and slowly lowered the zipper. Quade's breathing hitched when she dropped to her knees before him as she dragged his pants down his legs. Her position put her mouth directly in line with his cock, still covered by his black briefs. Or barely covered. The underwear stretched over his hard dick to the point of being almost transparent.

He held her shoulder while he lifted one leg, then the other, so she could remove his pants and socks. Sitting back on her heels, her gaze slowly swept up his body and back to his groin. She licked her lips.

A man could take only so much before he had to act. He tugged Eve to her feet, turned her around so he could press his body against her back and ass. "Now it's definitely my turn."

Quade lowered the zipper on the back of her dress. He slid the garment down her arms to pool at her waist while he nipped the side of her neck. Eve whimpered. Arching her back, she wrapped her arms around his neck. That left her body completely open for his touch.

He decided her breasts needed his attention first. Quade found the front closure of her bra and released it. Cradling both full mounds in his hands, he squeezed, kneaded, caressed, loving the feel of her warm flesh. Tiny bumps rose on her areolae to surround hard nipples. He flicked the peaks with his thumbs. A long moan rewarded him.

"Do you like your nipples touched?" he whispered in her ear.

"Yes."

"Sucked?"

"*Yes.*"

"How about other parts of your body? Do you like to be touched here?" He slid his hands down to her waist, splayed his hands wide across her stomach.

She shifted her hips, rubbed her ass against his groin. "Quade, please."

"Please what? You have to tell me what feels good, Eve. I can't read your mind."

She took one of his hands, pushed it inside her panties. "*That* feels good."

It pleased him to find her pussy so wet already. Quade slipped his fingers through the slick folds and easily found her swollen clit. She hissed when he rubbed it with the tip of his finger.

"Too much?" he asked.

"No. Not enough."

"What's better for you? Back and forth . . ." Gathering the moisture from her channel, he slid his finger from left to right and back over her clit. "Or is it better in a circle?" He changed his motion, rubbed his finger over her clit in a circle.

"B-both."

He cradled a breast with his free hand while he continued to caress her pussy. He alternated his movements, sometimes moving his fingers back and forth, sometimes in a circle. She spread her legs as far as her dress allowed. That gave Quade more room to fondle her.

The extra room must have been what Eve needed. Her breathing became deeper, more erratic. One arm remained behind his neck while her other hand clutched his thigh. She moved her hips in the same rhythm as his fingers. Every movement made her ass brush his dick.

"Come for me, Eve." Quade nibbled her earlobe, pulled it with his lips. "I want to feel you come."

He'd barely said the last word when a strangled gasp came from her throat. Her fingernails dug into his thigh and she threw her head back to his shoulder. Quade pushed two fingers into her pussy when her body started to tremble. The walls clamped onto his fingers, as if to keep them inside.

"My legs are weak," she said in a raspy voice.

"Good. Weak legs are a sign of a strong orgasm."

"Strong doesn't even begin to describe it." She turned in his arms, causing his fingers to slip from her channel. Sliding her arms around his neck, she kissed him long and slow and passionately. "Thank you."

"It was my pleasure."

She kissed him again while moving her pelvis back and forth over his cock. Quade clasped her ass to hold her still. It had been a long time since he'd lost control and come way too soon, but then, it had been a long time since he'd wanted a woman as much as he wanted Eve.

Eve's hands slid inside his briefs to fondle his ass. "You have an amazing butt," she whispered against his lips. One hand crept around to the front. She wrapped it around his cock. "And other things."

* * *

Eve sighed at the feel of Quade's shaft in her hand. Hot and hard with satiny skin that slid up and down with the milking motion of her hand.

She loved touching, but she also wanted to see.

She sat on the edge of the bed, urged him closer by his hips. Once she had him positioned where she wanted him, she pulled the waistband of his briefs forward so his cock sprang free. It stood out from his body, long and thick and straight with a drop of pre-cum at the slit. Eve swallowed a whimper as her pussy clenched.

She pushed the briefs past his hips and down his legs. Once he'd stepped free of them, she caressed his length with one hand, his balls with the other. She smiled when his cock surged in her hand.

"You must like this."

"Yeah." His voice sounded guttural, strained. "I like it a little too much. You'd better stop."

Ignoring his suggestion, Eve continued to play. She added her tongue, licking the crown as she continued to caress his cock and balls.

"Eve." Holding her head, he gently pulled her mouth away from him. "Not like that. Not our first time."

"You made me come with your hands. Why can't I make you come with mine?"

"Because I want to be inside you. I'm not eighteen anymore and don't . . . bounce back as quickly as I used to."

Before she could complain any further, Quade kissed her. Anything she'd been about to say vanished from her mind as his soft, warm lips moved over hers. He slid her bra down her arms. She had no idea where it landed, nor did she care. She went willingly to her back when he held her arms and pushed her backward. She landed on a diagonal on her bed with Quade on his knees beside her.

A few tugs on the rest of her clothing and she soon lay naked with him. He rose from the bed long enough to locate his jacket on the floor, remove some condom packets from a pocket, and place them on the nightstand. Eve understood the need for protection, but she hated the thought of anything separating her from Quade.

He donned one of the condoms and lay on top of her. Slipping his hands beneath her thighs, he pulled them apart and settled between them so the base of his cock rested against her clit. A subtle shift of his hips had pleasure shooting through her body. She bit her bottom lip to hold back a loud moan, but it escaped anyway.

"I love those sounds you make in your throat." Quade kissed her lips, her chin, the side of her neck. "They're very sexy."

He kept shifting his hips in the perfect motion to caress her clit. Greedy for another climax, Eve clutched his butt and pumped her pelvis to intensify the caress.

"That's the way," Quade said in a raspy voice. "Ride my cock. Take what you need."

She stared into his eyes and did as he suggested, rubbing her clit against his shaft. Sweat broke out across her skin. Her pussy clenched, needing a hard cock to fill it. A little longer and she would come again.

He pinched a nipple, rolled it between his thumb and forefinger. The extra bit of stimulation did it. Eve's back arched and her eyes slid closed as waves of pleasure washed over her.

She was still panting, trying to force air into her starving lungs, when Quade plunged into her. Eve cried out at the sudden movement since she hadn't been prepared for it.

Quade immediately stilled. Concern filled his eyes. "Did I hurt you? You're so wet, I thought—"

"Shhh." She laid two fingers over his mouth. "You didn't hurt me. It's just . . . been a while for me."

"For me, too." He drew back until only the head of his cock

remained inside her, then pushed forward more slowly. "Is that better?"

"Mmm, yes."

Lying on top of her again, he took her in his arms and kissed her. Eve ran her hands up and down his back as he began to pump. Not seeming satisfied to lie still, Quade shifted positions often until he found the perfect spot that gave her clit the most stimulation. Eve moaned.

His thrusts increased in speed, each one brushing against all her sensitive tissues. Desire built again, which surprised Eve. She'd already come twice. That rarely happened for her. She couldn't possibly come a third time.

"God, you're beautiful." He kissed her once, twice, three times. "It feels like your body was made for mine."

His romantic words and loving kisses along with his thrusts pushed her over the top again. This time, Quade made the journey with her. She held him tightly while his body jerked and he released a growling moan.

Friends had told her sometimes they'd experienced a climax so strong, they'd swear their bones had melted. She'd never experienced that feeling until now. If a tornado swept through her apartment, it would just have to take her with it because she couldn't move.

Quade shifted. The movement made her realize his cock hadn't softened. "How—"

"I'm not through."

She couldn't move and he wasn't *through?* Eve opened her mouth to ask him how that could be possible when he pulled out of her and flipped her to her stomach.

A little curious, a little eager, she waited for what Quade would do next. She heard the sound of another condom packet tearing, then he pushed her legs apart with his knees. Holding her hips, he surged into her again.

It shouldn't feel so good to have him inside her. She'd come three times and shouldn't want more. But she did. She rose to her hands and knees so he could go deeper. His deep growl told her he approved of her action.

Eve pressed her hands against the headboard to hold herself in place when Quade's thrusts quickened. She arched her back, pushed her butt back when he pumped forward. Knowing she wouldn't come again, she did everything she could to make this round of lovemaking good for him.

He cheated by sliding one hand between her legs to caress her clit.

Pleasure shot through her limbs, snaked up and down her spine, and returned to blossom in her pussy. Not as intense as her earlier orgasms, this one still stole her breath and curled her toes.

As soon as Quade released her hips after he came, she fell face-down on the bed, arms and legs sprawled. "If that's an example of you not bouncing back quickly, I don't think I could've handled you at eighteen."

The bum had the nerve to chuckle. She'd hit him if she could lift her hand.

Quade dropped kisses all along her shoulder and between her shoulder blades. "Forget it. If you still aren't through, you'll have to take care of yourself."

The thought of watching Quade masturbate sent a zing through her pussy. She turned her head toward him. "But if you do that, I want to watch."

That slow, sexy smile she loved spread over his lips. "You little vixen."

"Is that a bad thing?"

"Not at all. Just . . . surprising."

It took her two tries, but Eve managed to roll to her side facing him. "Why surprising?"

"You seemed a little . . . shy to me. Not that shy is bad," he said quickly. "I never imagined you saying you'd want to watch a guy jerk off."

"I've never said it to another man," she said, her voice low and soft.

He smiled. "I'm glad I'm the first."

Quade rested his head on a pillow. The tie holding his long hair had come loose during lovemaking. Black strands swirled over his shoulder to brush his chest. Eve picked up a tendril, rubbed it between her fingers. Soft and silky.

"Will you stay the night?"

"I'd like that. I just need to take care of something first."

Knowing he meant the used condoms, Eve nodded. Once he walked into the bathroom, she slid between the sheets. He came back moments later, turned off the lamp, and lay beside her. Content to cuddle in his arms, her head on his shoulder, she closed her eyes.

7

Quade awoke the next morning to Eve's warm lips sliding up and down his cock.

"Fuck," he muttered.

He acted before he thought and arched his hips, driving his dick deeper into her mouth. When he realized what he'd done, he relaxed his pelvis so he wouldn't gag her. Instead of letting him go, she took him all the way to his balls.

Quade grabbed the covers and threw them aside. Eve sat on her knees between his legs. She looked at him, her mouth still gliding up and down his hard flesh. "What are you doing?"

She licked up one side of his cock and all around the rim. "If you have to ask, I must be doing something wrong."

He groaned when she darted the tip of her tongue into the slit. "Believe me, you aren't doing anything wrong."

"Then just lie still and enjoy it."

Quade thought that an excellent suggestion, except he didn't think it fair for him to accept the pleasure she offered without giving some in return. "Hey." He slipped his hand beneath her chin, lifted her mouth away from him. "Swing around here so I can lick your pussy."

Her eyes flared with heat, proving she liked his idea. She gave his cock one more long lick from base to tip, then turned and straddled his face. Quade gripped her ass as she lowered her pussy to his mouth. The feminine lips flared open, letting him see the moisture produced to welcome him into her body. The scent of her arousal drifted to his nose. Quade inhaled deeply of the intoxicating scent.

He licked her slit at the same time that she took his shaft in her mouth again. Her cream slid across his tongue and down his throat. He'd never tasted anything as good as Eve's juices. He licked the full length of her labia again before concentrating on her clit. The swollen bundle of nerves beaded beneath his tongue, growing larger and firmer with his stroking.

She moaned when he nipped her clit with his teeth. Quade felt the vibration all the way through his dick. He scraped his teeth over her clit again, licked her labia to her anus. She moaned even louder when he whisked his tongue across the puckered hole.

So his lady liked anal play. More blood surged into his cock at the thought of being buried in her gorgeous ass. Quade licked all over the rosette before driving his tongue into her ass.

She moved her mouth faster up and down his shaft. Quade jerked when her wet finger slid into his ass. The intense pleasure made him groan loud and long.

His cock slipped out of her mouth. "Do that again."

It took him a moment to realize what she wanted. Quade placed his lips directly on the rosette and moaned again. Eve arched her back and pushed her ass closer to his mouth. "That feels so good."

"The vibration or my tongue?"

"Both."

He hummed as he continued to lick her, giving her as much stimulation as he could. She took him in her mouth again, flashing her tongue all around his hard length as she moved her lips up and down. Quade's eyes crossed. An orgasm bloomed at the base of his spine. He couldn't come before Eve did. Grasping her butt, he began fucking her ass with his tongue.

She pumped her hips in time to his thrusts. Her breaths came out choppy, heavy. Predicting a climax would soon claim her body, he darted his tongue quicker into the sensitive opening.

A loud moan came from her throat before she trembled. Quade pulled apart the feminine lips and watched the entrances to her pussy and anus pulse with her orgasm.

God, that was sexy.

Once her breathing evened out, she began to move her mouth on him again. Quade's desire had faded while he concentrated on Eve's pleasure. It erupted back to life with the feel of her lips and tongue on his flesh.

She pushed a second finger into his ass. Quade lost it.

"Eve. Fuck!"

Throwing back his head, Quade closed his eyes tightly as the pleasure whooshed down his spine and through his balls. His cock jerked and throbbed, his cum filled her mouth. He saw stars behind his eyelids. He'd experienced strong orgasms in the past, but he'd never seen stars.

He didn't know how long he lay there, struggling to breathe, until he opened his eyes. Eve remained on top of him, her face resting on his thigh. Her warm breath brushed his balls every time she exhaled. He ran his hands all over her ass. "Hey."

"What?" she said, her voice raspy.

"Come here."

"What makes you think I can move?"

He knew what she meant. His legs felt like overcooked spaghetti. Lifting her leg, he slid out from beneath her, turned, and lay on his side so he could see her face. Her closed eyes and parted lips proved their lovemaking had tired her as much as it had him. Several tendrils of blond hair escaped from her braid during the night. He pushed them back from her temple.

"What a great way to start the day," she said. Those beautiful green eyes opened and she smiled.

Quade returned her smile. "I agree." He gave her a gentle kiss. "You continue to surprise me."

"I hope all the surprises are good."

"*Very* good."

Eve propped up on her elbows. "I am starving and I don't have much to prepare a big breakfast, other than leftover prime rib. How about if we have breakfast at Mona's? My treat."

"That sounds good, but I think my clothes are beyond wrinkled."

Eve glanced over her shoulder at the pile of clothes on the floor. "Oh." She looked back at him, a sheepish expression on her face. "Sorry. I guess I should've hung them up for you."

"Neither of us were worried about wrinkled clothes last night." He ran his hand up and down her back. "Let's go to my house. I have a stocked refrigerator and can make you anything you want. Besides, I need to check on my dogs."

Her eyebrows shot up. "You have dogs?"

"Two Labs. I know they have plenty of food and water available, but I need to let them out so they can run and take care of business."

"Are you a good cook?"

"I'm an *excellent* cook."

"I need to shower."

"Tell you what. I'll write down directions to my house and you come when you're ready. I'll go now so I can shower, put on clean clothes, take care of the dogs, and start breakfast."

"Sold."

She rose to her knees, which gave Quade an unhindered view of her body. It looked even more magnificent in the daylight. His cock gave an interested twitch and began to harden. He grabbed her hand before she could move off the bed. "I still have one condom left."

She leaned closer until her nose almost touched his. "Do you have more at your house?"

He nodded.

"I vote we wait and use those."

She slipped off the bed before he could tighten his grip. "Hey!"

"Breakfast before sex, Quade," she said as she went into the bathroom and closed the door.

"Easy for you to say," he muttered. "You don't have a hard-on."

He waited until he heard the shower start, then rose and slipped on his wrinkled clothes. Finding a notepad and pen next to the phone, he sat on the edge of the bed and scribbled out the directions to his house. He left the notepad propped against the phone before walking to the bathroom door. The water shut off as he knocked.

"Eve, I left the directions to my house next to your phone."

The door swung open. Eve stood before him, clutching a thick blue towel between her breasts. Water dripped from her wet hair down her chest and arms. "You can't leave without kissing me good-bye."

Quade watched a drop roll down her breast and hang on the end of her nipple. His cock twitched again. "Can I kiss you wherever I want to?"

Her growling stomach answered his question. "Okay, okay, I'll go cook. Is there anything you don't like?"

"When it comes to breakfast, I like everything." Eve stood on her tiptoes, gave him a sweet kiss. "I'll make it up to you later."

"Promise?"

She smiled. "I promise."

*　　*　　*

Eve pulled up to a sprawling ranch-style house surrounded by cedar and oak trees. A wide porch ran the full length of the house and down both sides. She assumed it surrounded the entire house. Tables and Adirondack chairs sat in groupings, giving guests plenty of places to relax. The mid-fifties this morning would warm into the low eighties by afternoon . . . perfect for sitting outside.

She climbed the steps to the front door and pressed the doorbell. Chimes echoed through the house. Only moments passed before the door opened.

Quade smiled. "Hi."

She returned his smile. "Hi."

He opened the door wider. "Come in. I'm about to start cooking."

Eve followed him through a large living room filled with oversized leather furniture. The room screamed masculine. The large windows let in a lot of light, making the room cheery and warm. Very nice and very Quade, but it could do with a few feminine touches, like throw pillows on the couch and candleholders on the mantle above the rock fireplace, maybe some plants here and there. She thought live plants always made a house feel more like a home.

Quade led her into a spacious kitchen with pale tan walls and white trim. Knowing little about different types of wood, she had no idea if the cabinets were made of oak or pine or ash. Their light color blended perfectly with the rest of the kitchen.

"Sit." He pulled back the center chair of the three at the island. "Coffee just finished brewing. I'll get a mug for you."

Eve saw a carton of eggs, a loaf of thick-sliced bread, and a package of ham on the counter. Her stomach gurgled happily at the sight. "French toast and ham?"

"Yep." He set the mug, a container of half-and-half, and a spoon in front of her. "Do you approve?"

"I do. How fast can you cook?"

He grinned. "As fast as possible. How's that?"

Quade turned and began preparing breakfast. Eve studied him while he cracked eggs into a bowl and used a whisk to make them frothy. He wore a burgundy T-shirt and jeans so faded as to appear almost white. They molded to his very fine ass and thighs.

A low heat burned in her belly. She should've agreed to using that third condom this morning.

To get her mind off sex, Eve changed the subject. "Where are your dogs?"

"Outside. They let me pet them for about six seconds before they took off to explore."

"How much land do you own?"

"Ten acres. A seasonal creek cuts through my land about three hundred yards from the house. With the rain we had last week, there might even be a little water in it." He glanced at her over his shoulder. "It's a nice walk, if you're interested."

It sounded lovely. "I'd like that."

He laid slices of ham in a skillet, then dipped the thick bread slices into the egg mixture and placed them in another skillet. Soon the scent of food filled the air. Eve's stomach gurgled again. "Can I help?"

"You can get plates and silverware for us." He motioned toward one of the cabinet doors. "Plates are in there, silverware in the drawer. I have cloth napkins in the buffet in the dining room if you'd rather use them than paper towels."

"Paper towels are fine with me."

"Syrup's in the pantry next to the refrigerator."

She set their places, topped off her coffee mug, then returned to her chair as Quade set two platters piled with ham and French toast on the island. "How does that look?"

"Delicious."

"Help yourself while I refresh my coffee."

He didn't have to tell her twice. Eve took a piece of toast and a generous slice of ham. She'd cut off the first bite of meat and placed it in her mouth by the time Quade joined her.

Eve closed her eyes in pleasure while she chewed. "Oh, my God, that's wonderful." She opened her eyes again and looked at Quade to see him smiling. "That has to be the best ham I've ever tasted. It isn't too salty like a lot of ham I've eaten."

"I bought a pig from a farmer in Walnut Springs and had it butchered. I made sure the processors went light on the salt."

She washed down her bite of ham with a sip of coffee. "You bought a whole pig just for you?"

"And a side of beef from Nick Fallon. I have two big freezers in my laundry room." He cut off a bite of toast, swirled it in the syrup on his plate. "My office is here, Eve. It's more like a den than an office, which helps people feel comfortable. They talk more freely when they're comfortable. I have a regular sterile office at the high school, but I see clients here whenever I can. I fix a snack or sometimes a full meal, depending on how long the session lasts and what time of day it is. That's why I keep the refrigerator and pantry well stocked."

"I noticed all the seating places on your porch. Do you have sessions outside?"

"If that's what my client wants to do. It's whatever makes him or her the most comfortable."

She watched him as he ate his bite of toast. Handsome, charming, attentive, caring, a fantastic lover and cook. Add all those things together and they created a man any woman would be proud to call hers.

Eve hated that she could never do that.

No thinking bad thoughts today. This is a day to enjoy being with Quade. I plan to cherish every moment with him.

She forked another piece of toast onto her plate. "I shouldn't have a second piece, but it's too good to stop with only one."

"Enjoy it. We'll walk off the calories."

Or work them off making love, if I have any say about it.

Quade placed the last piece of toast and slice of ham on his plate. "Cozy Crafts is closed on Sundays, right?"

"Yes."

"Do you work tomorrow?"

"Yes. I'm off on Tuesdays."

"I didn't schedule any clients Tuesday so I'd be free to pick up some supplies in Fort Worth for the fire department. Clay should let me know for sure sometime today if I need to go. Would you like to ride along? We can have lunch or dinner, maybe go to a movie."

Spending a day in Fort Worth with Quade sounded wonderful. "I'd love to go with you."

His warm smile proved her comment pleased him. "Good." He laid his fork across his empty plate. "Did you get enough to eat?"

"Goodness, yes. It was delicious, Quade."

"I'm glad you liked it." He picked up her empty plate along with his and stood. "I'll set these in the sink and take care of them later."

"I don't mind washing them. There aren't many."

"I'll put them in the dishwasher later." He set the plates in the sink, came back to the island. "Want the grand tour of my house before we go outside?"

"Yes, please."

8
_____

Quade closed the back door behind Eve. Taking her hand, he led her down the steps into the backyard. They hadn't gone more than a few feet when he heard a loud commotion in the trees to their left.

"Daisy and Cocoa are heading this way."

As he predicted, the two Labs burst through the shrubs and made a beeline for him. Eve took a step backward, but could go no farther for Quade still held her hand. "Are you afraid of dogs?"

"No, but they're so . . . rambunctious."

"Sit!" Quade said firmly.

Both dogs stopped two feet away and dropped to their haunches. Their tails wagged, their tongues hung out of their mouths, but they remained still.

"The golden Lab is Daisy, the brown Cocoa. They're both spayed females."

"Can I pet them?"

"Sure, but then they'll love you for life."

Eve smiled. "That wouldn't be a bad thing."

"They won't move until I tell them it's okay, but then they'll be all over you."

She dropped to her knees on the ground. "I'm ready."

Quade squatted next to Eve. "Come here."

The dogs pounced, both trying to lick Eve's face. Quade worried that it might upset her, but she laughed in delight. He smiled at her efforts to pet them when they seemed determined to bathe her with their tongues.

"Okay, that's enough. Sit!"

Once again, the dogs obeyed his command. Quade stood and offered a hand to help Eve. "Believe it or not, they're great watchdogs. No one gets on the property when I'm gone. But if you're with me, they assume you're okay and want to play."

"I don't mind. They're beautiful." She scratched each dog behind one ear. Quade recognized the blissful oh-yeah-that's-the-spot look on Daisy's and Cocoa's faces. "How old are they?"

"Daisy is almost four, Cocoa is five." He added to the scratching behind the dogs' other ears. "I'm thinking about getting one more. I have Animal Control on the lookout for a Lab puppy."

"These were rescue dogs?"

"Yeah. I got Cocoa from Animal Control right after I moved to Lanville." He straightened. "Ready to go exploring?" he asked the dogs.

Excited barking met his question. Both Labs took off toward the woods, then stopped and looked back at Quade and Eve as if to tell them to hurry. Quade entwined his fingers with Eve's again and followed the dogs for several yards, then he turned to take the path to the creek. The dogs soon fell into step, Cocoa by Quade and Daisy by Eve.

"Are they protecting us?" Eve asked.

"Yeah. They'll stay right by us as long as we're walking. When we stop and sit, they'll take off to play."

"You've trained them very well."

"They were easy to train. They're very smart." He reached down to pat Cocoa's neck. "Aren't you, girl?"

He looked back at Eve to see a tender smile on her lips. "What?"

"It's sweet how much you care for your dogs."

Quade could tell her he poured all his love into the Labs since he didn't have someone special in his life. Instead, he said, "They love unconditionally, so it's easy to love them back."

Eve squeezed his hand, but said nothing else. Quade remained silent also, content to walk with her by his side.

He heard the babbling of the creek through the trees. The sound proved the creek held little water, but enough from last week's rains to flow over the rocks. He led Eve to his favorite grassy spot beneath a huge willow tree.

Her delighted gasp made him smile. "Oh, Quade, what a beautiful place."

"I'm glad you like it." Reaching into the canvas bag he'd slung over his shoulder, Quade pulled out a blanket and spread it on the ground. Once Eve sat with her legs folded in front of her, he removed two bottles of water and a plastic container of oatmeal cookies from the bag and set them on the blanket before sitting beside her. "Ready for a treat?"

"Please."

The Labs looked at Quade and Eve for several seconds, then took off down the creek. "Told you," Quade said with a grin. He removed the lid and held the container toward Eve. "Help yourself."

She chose two of the soft cookies. After biting into one, she moaned in pleasure. "Delicious. Did you make them?"

"No, I bought them from Emma. I'm a good cook, but I'm not much of a baker."

"I'm the opposite. I'm a better baker than cook."

Quade opened both bottles of water, handed one to Eve. "What's your specialty?"

She looked over the creek while she took a sip of water. "I make a chocolate cake with chocolate icing that's to die for."

"Mmm, I like cake."

"You wouldn't by any chance be hinting that I should bake a cake for you?"

He liked the teasing light in her eyes. "Now would I do something that impolite?"

"It isn't impolite to ask for something you want."

"Well, then." Quade popped his last bite of cookie into his mouth, rubbed his hands together to get rid of any crumbs. "I'm going to ask for a kiss."

She smiled before leaning closer and touching her lips to his. Quade slid his hand beneath her ponytail to cradle her nape. He tilted his head to deepen the kiss, ran his tongue along the seam of her lips. Eve parted them to allow him entrance. He touched the tip of her tongue with his and was rewarded when she did the same.

Seconds away from pushing her down on the blanket, Eve surprised him again by pushing him down first. He went willingly to his back. Their kiss continued while she yanked up his T-shirt and unfastened the button at the waistband of his jeans.

"It's private here, right?" she asked. "You don't have any close neighbors?"

"My closest neighbor lives three miles away."

The vixen smile that always led to intense pleasure for him spread across her lips. "Good."

By the time she'd unfastened his jeans and tugged them and his briefs down to his knees, his cock lay hard and thick against his belly. Eve ran one fingertip down the heavy vein. "I'm fascinated by how this more than doubles in size when you become aroused." Still caressing him, she looked into his eyes. "I told you last night and I'll tell you again. You have a magnificent body, Quade."

"So do you. How about letting me see more of it?"

He'd barely finished the question when she stood, toed off her shoes, and shucked her jeans and panties. She straddled his thighs before removing her T-shirt and bra. The sunlight bathing her body stole his ability to think.

Actions spoke louder than words anyway.

Taking her hands, he gently pulled her forward until she reclined on top of him. Her soft belly cushioned his hard cock. He loved the feel of her breasts pressed against his chest. If he slid his hand between her thighs, he knew he'd find her pussy wet and open for him.

The realization that he didn't have a condom made Quade curse beneath his breath. "We have a problem."

"What?"

"No condom."

Her vixen's smile flashed over her lips again. Sitting up and straddling his thighs, she reached for her jeans and withdrew something from a back pocket. She held up a condom packet between two fingers.

"Number three. I brought it just in case."

Quade grinned. "I do like an intelligent woman."

She also grinned, but it quickly faded. "I'm on birth control and haven't been with a man in over two years. So if we ever didn't have one of these handy, I promise I'm safe."

"My last relationship ended six months ago. We were always careful. I promise I'm safe, too."

Eve twisted her lips from side to side. "Kinda spoils the mood to talk about something so serious and personal."

"A little." He cradled her breasts in his palms, thumbed her nipples. "But I'll bet we can get back in the mood pretty quick."

Her nipples beaded beneath his caress. Quade didn't spend

nearly enough time with Eve's beautiful breasts last night. He planned to remedy that oversight today. Pulling her forward again, he arranged her so her breasts were even with his mouth. He licked each tip, getting both nice and wet and hard.

"Quade," she whispered.

Her raspy tone encouraged him to continue. Quade circled both nipples with his tongue, giving each an equal amount of time. Only after he'd made them as hard as he decided he could did he draw one into his mouth to suck.

Eve's long moan proved she liked what he did. Quade lightly bit one nipple, pulled on it with his teeth. Eve squirmed on top of him, rubbing her mound on his stomach. She made a sound of frustration in her throat before she shifted positions. Apparently, she wasn't getting the stimulation to her clit that she needed.

He'd be happy to help her with that.

With his mouth still worshipping her breasts, Quade reached between her legs and located her swollen clit. Eve gasped, then moaned again.

"Right there. Oh, yes, Quade, right there!"

He sucked harder on her nipple while his fingertips danced over the sensitive bundle of nerves. He caught glances of Eve's face when he switched nipples. Although they'd made love only a few times, Quade already knew the signs of impending bliss for Eve. Wanting that bliss to consume her, he pushed two fingers into her pussy and rubbed her G-spot.

She shattered.

Her nipple popped from his mouth when she pushed on his shoulders and arched her back. A strangled sound came from her throat, one he would mistake as pain if he didn't know better.

She wilted on top of him, her breath hot and humid against his neck. Quade left his fingers inside her channel, gently moving them to prolong her pleasure as long as possible.

"I think I'm dead."

Quade chuckled. "You wouldn't be breathing if you were dead."

"Am I breathing?"

"Yeah. I can feel your breath on my neck. It's very sexy."

She lifted her head. Her eyelids appeared heavy, as if she could barely hold them open. "*You're* very sexy."

She kissed him long and passionately. By the time the kiss ended, Quade's dick screamed at him to fuck her.

"Eve, I really need to use that third condom. *Now.*"

"I dropped it."

"*What?*"

"Wait, here it is." Eve waved the packet in the air as if it were a prize. She scrambled down his body while she tore it open, glided the latex over his hard cock. Holding it straight up, she impaled herself.

"God, you're so tight." Quade gripped her waist, arched his hips, and drove into her. "Tight and wet. So wet for me."

Placing his feet flat on the ground, he thrust into her again. Eve braced her hands on his chest and matched his movements. She pushed down when he arched, lifted her pelvis when he retreated. Sweat soon covered his body and his breathing became more labored. He wanted Eve to come again before he did, but he didn't know if he could hold back much longer.

His balls drew up tightly to his body. Quade fucked Eve faster, chasing that point when pleasure would engulf him.

All the burgeoning feelings inside him fizzled when Eve stopped moving. The lack of blood in his brain made thinking difficult, so he didn't realize she'd lifted herself off his cock until he no longer felt the snug wetness. "What are you doing?"

"Something different."

"What's wrong with the same?"

A moment later, Quade mentally took back his complaint. Eve turned to face the creek and impaled herself again. She leaned forward and gripped his knees, which gave him an unimpeded view of her ass.

"Oh, yes," she said in a breathless voice. "Feels so good."

Quade held both buttocks while Eve fucked him. He didn't move, but let her take whatever she needed. From this angle, he could see his dick slipping in and out of her pussy. Her cream covered it, letting it slide easily.

His gaze shifted to between her cheeks. He licked his thumb, rubbed it in a circle over the rosette. When Eve didn't complain, he wet his thumb again and pushed the tip past her anus.

"More. Give me more, Quade."

He'd like to shove his cock in her ass, but knew his saliva wouldn't be enough and didn't have any lube. He thought of the bottle of gel in his nightstand and longed to have it here.

Quade pushed his thumb in her ass as far as he could. Eve cried out, dug her fingernails into his thighs. Strong pulses surrounded his shaft and his thumb as the orgasm raced through her body.

The feel of those strong contractions meant Quade couldn't hold back any longer. He had to fuck her, and fuck her hard. Gripping Eve around the waist, he quickly switched their positions so she was on her hands and knees. Quade plowed into her, his thrusts firm and fast. It took only moments before he felt those pulses around his dick again. Shoving his cock all the way into her pussy, he closed his eyes and let the orgasm overtake him.

His surroundings slowly seeped into Quade's brain. He recognized the sound of the creek flowing over rocks, birds singing in the trees, the wind whistling through the leaves over his head. And Eve's heavy breathing. Opening his eyes again, he saw that she'd braced her forehead on her forearms. Her thighs trembled against his.

Gently withdrawing from her, he helped her straighten her

legs so she could recline on the blanket, then lay beside her. "You okay?" he asked.

"My bones are going to completely dissolve if I keep having so many orgasms."

Quade grinned, pleased she found such intense satisfaction with him. "Do you want us to stop?"

"Hell, no. I'll use a walker if I have to."

She gave him a quick kiss, then rolled to her back and looked up. "It's such a beautiful day. We should have a picnic right here."

"We can do that. We could walk a little more and build up an appetite, then go back to the house, fix a picnic lunch, and come back here."

"Or . . ." She rolled toward him, placed her hand on his chest. "We could go back to your house now and work up an appetite on your big bed."

He struggled not to grin again. "I don't have a walker handy."

"I don't need one yet. In fact, I'm feeling stronger by the minute."

Only three hundred yards separated them from his bed. They could make that in minutes.

Now that the idea had been planted in his head—and his dick—Quade couldn't wait to get Eve in his bed. Scrambling to his feet, he snatched up their clothes and stepped into his shoes. "Let's go."

She shot him a wide-eyed look. "You want me to walk back to your house naked?"

"Yes."

Eve grinned. "Cool."

Quade stuffed the blanket and the rest of their items into the canvas bag. Taking Eve's hand, he took off at a fast walk. He would've jogged if he'd thought Eve could keep up with him.

They made it back to his house in half the time it took them to walk to the creek. Quade led her through the house directly to his bedroom and they fell to his bed.

His kiss started out ravenous, but Quade soon slowed it. The overwhelming need to fuck that he'd experienced by the creek disappeared. From the gentle way Eve caressed his back and ass, he didn't think she felt the urgency either. This time would truly be lovemaking.

He pulled away from her long enough to roll on a fresh condom, then returned to his place between her legs and entered her with one thrust. She wrapped her ankles around his thighs. Quade linked their fingers together, laid their clasped hands next to Eve's head. He gave her soft, sweet kisses while he moved inside her . . . on her mouth, her cheek, her jaw. Even when he felt the climax brewing in his balls, he kept everything gentle.

Eve came seconds before he did. The sexy sound in her throat signaled it before her body trembled. Staring into her luminous green eyes while the pleasure flowed through him, he knew he'd found the woman he wanted to be with for the rest of his life.

Words formed on his tongue that he longed to say to her. He held back, sensing she wouldn't want to hear them yet. Whatever happened in her past with her former fiancés had caused her a lot of pain. She needed more time to heal.

He'd give her that time. She would be worth the wait.

9

Eve didn't know how life could be any better.

She'd seen Quade every day for the last four days, ever since they spent all of Sunday together. They had supper, then either she spent the night with him or he with her. She preferred going to his house because he would cook for her while she played with his dogs.

No pressure. No expectations. Just pleasure and the joy of his company.

The volunteer fire department had a practice fire tonight with the new firefighters, meaning she wouldn't see Quade until later tonight. They wouldn't be able to have supper together, but she could prepare lunch for him.

He'd sounded pleased when she invited him to her apartment for lunch. He told her he should be finished with his morning counseling sessions in time to be at her place by twelve-fifteen.

Eve covered her round kitchen table with an ivory tablecloth, added earth-toned plaid napkins. She'd walked to Flowers on the Square during her morning break and picked up a small autumn arrangement. The vase contained the same colors as her napkins.

Taking a step back, she studied the table for anything she might have missed. Even though it would be a simple meal of chicken-salad sandwiches, chips, fruit, and iced tea, she wanted everything to be perfect.

Her stomach jumped when the doorbell rang at a few minutes past noon. She made sure her blouse remained neatly tucked into her pants and smoothed back her hair before she opened the door.

She smiled. "Hi."

Quade returned her smile. "Hi."

"Come in."

He stepped across the threshold. Eve closed the door behind him and turned. Before she could say another word, he pushed her against the door and covered her lips with his.

If anything tasted better than Quade's kisses, Eve couldn't think of it. Of course, she could barely think at all when his lips touched hers. He encircled her waist with one arm, caressed her ass with his other hand. Eve tugged the leather band from his hair so she could tunnel her fingers into the silky strands while she returned the kiss.

Quade gave her three soft, pecking kisses before he rested his forehead against hers. "That's better than anything you cooked."

Eve agreed. Wrapping her arms around his neck, she hugged him tightly. He returned her hug, held her as tightly as she held him. It always amazed her how perfectly they fit together.

"Are you hungry?" she whispered in his ear.

His hand drifted to her ass again. "Mmm, yes."

Chuckling, she pulled back enough to see his face. "I meant for lunch."

"Oh." He gave a one-shouldered shrug. "You can't blame a guy for wanting dessert first."

"Sorry, no dessert today. I have to be back to work by one-thirty. But . . ." She ran her hands over his shoulders. "You could come back tonight after your practice fire."

He flashed her a crooked smile. "I do like the way you think."

She gave him a quick kiss. "Help me get our lunch."

Eve took a large bowl of mixed fruit from the refrigerator, handed it to Quade to set on the table. She followed him with a plate of chicken-salad sandwiches that she'd cut in half. By the time she uncovered the sandwiches, Quade had poured their tea from the pitcher Eve placed on the table.

Quade took a large bite of a sandwich and moaned. "I've never eaten chicken salad as good as Emma's. Until now."

His compliment pleased her. "I'll tell Emma you said that. I made it, but got the recipe from her." She smiled again when he finished his half sandwich and took another from the plate. "You either really like chicken salad or you're hungry."

"Both." He spooned a generous amount of fruit onto his plate. "I didn't have a snack like I usually do. I keep protein bars in my desk at school, but no time to eat one."

"Busy morning?"

"Yeah, unfortunately."

When he didn't continue, she gently prompted, "Something serious?"

"I can't talk about it, Eve. It's confidential."

She knew whatever a client said to Quade had to be in the strictest confidence and he wouldn't share. "I'm sorry. I shouldn't have asked."

"It's okay." He wiped his hands on his napkin before sipping from his glass of tea. "It would be nice to share some things and take the burden off me, but I can't."

"I understand."

Eve didn't speak again for several moments to give Quade time to sort his thoughts and eat his lunch. Just as she decided to break the silence, he beat her to it.

"I'm leaving about noon tomorrow for Austin. I'd like you to go with me."

The bite of banana she chewed grew in her mouth until it felt like the size of a baseball. Meeting his son didn't fall into the no-pressure-no-expectations category. That fell in the we're-getting-serious-so-I-want-my-son-to-approve-of-you category. She finally managed to swallow so she could speak. "Excuse me?"

"One of my nephews' birthday is on the twenty-fifth. The whole family is gathering at my parents' house Saturday. It would be the perfect chance for you to meet everyone."

"Quade, I don't need to meet your family."

She must not have said what he expected her to, for confusion spread across his face. "Why not?"

"Well, because we're not . . . involved."

He slowly folded his napkin and laid it next to his empty plate. "You don't think we're involved?"

"No. I mean, we've only been seeing each other a week."

"We didn't just meet a week ago, Eve. I've known you for two years."

"I know that, but I told you right from the start that I didn't want a relationship."

Eye narrowing, Quade sat back in his chair. "So we're fuck buddies? Is that it?"

She winced at his choice of words. "You don't have to be crude, Quade."

"What am I supposed to be? You say you don't call this a relationship, so what is it?" He leaned forward in his chair. "You're everything I've ever wanted in a woman, Eve." His gaze passed all over her face. "I'm falling in love with you. Hell, there's no 'falling' about it. I'm already there."

Fear wrapped itself around Eve's heart. Quade wasn't supposed to love her. She couldn't risk her heart to love again.

"Please don't say that," she whispered in a tortured voice.

He reached across the table to take her hand. "Eve—"

"No!" She yanked her hand from beneath his. "You can't love me. We're suppose to enjoy each other's company, that's all. I'm the happiest I've been in a long time. Please don't spoil it."

"I'm the happiest I've been in a long time, too. There's no reason we can't be even happier. I want more time with you. I want a *life* with you."

Eve stood and picked up their plates. She still had some of the sandwich and fruit left on her plate, but her churning stomach and clogged throat wouldn't let her eat another bite. She set the plates in the sink, turned to find Quade right behind her.

"Talk to me. We can work it out."

"There's nothing to work out."

She tried to pass him, but he took a step to block her retreat. "Why won't you talk to me, Eve? Whatever happened in the past is exactly that—in the past. You and I go forward from here."

Tears burned behind her eyelids. "There's no going forward, Quade." She crossed her arms over her stomach, creating a wall between them. "I'd like you to go now."

Disbelief flashed through his eyes, mixed with pain. "You aren't even willing to *try?*"

"I can't, Quade." She swallowed to clear the huskiness from her voice. "Please go."

Pain remained in his eyes, but anger replaced the disbelief. "I can't believe you're throwing away something so good because of fear. Whatever happened in your past has *nothing* to do with you and me."

Unwilling to say more, she looked toward the door, then back at him.

He obeyed her silent command. Without giving her another glance, he walked out the door.

It didn't hit her at first. She stood still, her arms crossed over her stomach, while she tried to figure out what happened.

Quade had been angry and hurt when he left. She couldn't blame him for that, but she'd had no choice. She had to hurt him to protect herself.

God, how selfish that sounded.

The pain struck. She pressed a fist against her chest, directly over her heart. The pain soon spread throughout her body. Tears flooded her eyes. Her knees gave out and she dropped to the floor. Huge, racking sobs soon filled the room.

She should've known better than to ever go out with Quade, much less make love with him. She should've known things with him would end as badly as with the other men in her life.

She had to accept that she would always be alone.

"Are you sure it's leaking?" Quade asked Rhea through his cell phone. "I checked the extinguishers last week and they were fine."

"I don't know what happened, but something's wrong. There's white foamy powdery stuff all around the nozzle thingy. I'm afraid the extinguisher will burst."

He couldn't help chuckling at her description, even though a leaking fire extinguisher wasn't funny. "It won't burst, Rhea."

"Please come check it, Quade. I'd feel a lot better."

He wanted to help Rhea, but he didn't want to step inside Cozy Crafts Cottage and see Eve. She'd torn his heart out of his chest with her refusal to talk to him. He couldn't handle seeing her so soon after she'd thrown his love back in his face.

"If you're worried about running into Eve, she isn't here," Rhea said as if she'd read his mind. "She looked horrible when she came back from lunch, so I sent her home."

Despite what had happened between them an hour ago, concern surged through Quade at the thought of Eve hurting. He pushed it aside. She didn't want his concern, his love, or anything else from him. "I'll be there in about fifteen minutes."

"Perfect! Thank you *so much,* Quade. I really appreciate it."

He pressed the button to end the call. He didn't know why, but something churned in his gut regarding Rhea's call. She sounded sincere, yet he couldn't help feeling that she hadn't told him everything.

With a shrug, he ignored his gut, picked up his keys from the kitchen island, and headed for his pickup.

He made it to Cozy Crafts in twelve minutes. Rhea met him as soon as he entered the store.

"Thank you for coming so quickly, Quade. It's the fire extinguisher in my back storeroom."

He followed her through the store, nodding to Rhea's clerk, Mary Lander, as he passed her. "In here," Rhea said once they got to the storeroom. He followed her through the doorway, and froze in his steps when he saw Eve unpacking a large box.

Rhea rushed past him and pulled the door closed behind her. Before he could grab the doorknob, he heard the sound of a key turning in the deadbolt.

"Y'all are going to talk and work out whatever is wrong," Rhea said through the door. "Mary and I are going to Mona's for pie. We'll be back in an hour or two. Or three."

Eve hurried over to the door and pounded on it with the side of her fist. "Rhea, open the door! *Rhea!*"

Silence, until he heard the chime of the front door. "Would she close her store and just leave?" he asked.

"There's no telling what Rhea will do."

Quade examined the door to see a keyed deadbolt above the doorknob instead of a lever to flip the bolt. "Keyed from both sides?"

"Yes."

"Do you have a key?"

"Yes, in my purse in the employee lounge." She blew out a breath. "I can't believe she locked us in here."

He took a moment to study her, noting her red, swollen eyes. "You've been crying."

She quickly lowered her head, took a few steps away from him. She could only take a few since the storeroom didn't have a lot of empty floor space. Shelves almost touched the ceiling on three sides. The other side held a long table covered with boxes, tape, scissors, box cutters, and various other tools.

He noticed a case of bottled water on one of the shelves. Tearing back a corner of the plastic, he removed one of the bottles and held it out to Eve. "Want this?"

With a huff, she accepted the bottle from him. Quade chose one for himself, removed the cap, and took a long drink. He could feel the tension flowing off her body. "Well, what shall we talk about?"

She shot him an exasperated look. "What?"

"Rhea said we had to talk." He leaned against the shelf, crossed his ankles. "She didn't specify what we should talk about."

"You know very well what she wants us to talk about."

"Yeah, I do. But I figure if you wouldn't tell me why we can't be together while we were in your apartment, you won't do it here either." He took another drink from the bottle. "Tell me why, Eve," he said softly. "The last week with you has been great. At least tell me why we can't have more days like those."

Her eyes shimmered with unshed tears. If she started crying, he'd probably lose it and join her.

"I suck at relationships," she said in a raspy voice.

"What do you mean?"

She set her untouched water on the table behind her. "I fell in love, enough to where I became engaged twice. But the feelings just . . . fizzled." He saw her throat work as she swallowed. "I can't become involved with you, Quade. I couldn't handle a broken heart for the third time." She swallowed again. "You're a wonderful man and you deserve a woman who isn't damaged goods."

He stared at her for several moments, trying to decide what

to say. He didn't want any of his comments to sound as if they came from a counselor instead of a man who loved her.

"Eve, I love you. I believe you love me, too, but you're afraid to admit it because you've been hurt in the past. I understand that. I'm not pushing you to make a commitment with me this moment. All I want is a chance."

He moved closer until they stood a few inches apart. "I'm a patient man. I'm willing to give you all the time you need to realize we belong together." He laid his hands on her waist. "How about it, Eve? Take a chance? It might turn out to be better than you ever imagined."

Quade watched the pain and hopelessness slowly fade from her eyes. Her gaze passed over his face, to his mouth, and back to his eyes. "I'm scared."

"I know you are. Trust me to always be here for you."

A gentle smile graced her lips. She touched his chest, slid her arms around his neck. "Yes," she whispered. "I want to take a chance."

He kissed her, letting his lips slide over hers with tenderness. His kiss promised a lifetime, beginning right this moment.

He pressed his forehead to hers. "I love you."

"I love you, too," she whispered. She touched his lips with her fingertips. "I'm sorry for being so selfish and hurting you."

"You have no reason to be sorry. We go forward from here. But I'll warn you right now, I'm going to do everything in my power to make you happy."

Her smile returned, even wider and brighter. "I promise I'll do the same for you."

He gave her one more kiss. "Okay, we talked. How do we get out of here?"

Eve held out her hand, wiggled her fingers. "Give me your cell phone."

Quade did as she asked, watching while she punched in a number.

"Your plan worked," she said into the phone. "Come let us out . . . No, I'm not kidding you. We made up and everything is fine between us again . . . Okay, see you then." She ended the call, passed the phone back to Quade. "She'll be right here."

"Rhea's method may have been sneaky, but I can't complain about the outcome."

"Neither can I." She pressed a tender kiss to his lips. "Thank you."

"For?"

"Giving me a chance."

Eve kissed him again. She kept right on kissing him even when she heard the sound of a key in the deadbolt.

"I guess you weren't kidding," Rhea said, laughter evident in her voice.

Eve faced her friend and employer. "I should spank you."

"Nah. You can't be mad at me since it all turned out good."

"It *did* turn out good. So good that I want to take off this weekend. Could your mom cover for me tomorrow and Saturday?" She looked at Quade and smiled. "Quade invited me to go to Austin with him and I'd like to accept his invitation."

Rhea beamed. "Of course she can cover for you. In fact, why don't you go ahead and leave now? It's quiet. I'm sure Mary and I can handle everything."

Eve took Quade's hand. "Let's get out of here before she changes her mind."

She led him to the employee lounge so she could grab her purse, then showed him the inside stairs to her apartment. Once safely inside, she wrapped her arms around his neck and cuddled close to him. "The invitation to Austin still stands, right?"

"Absolutely." He looped his arms around her waist. "Why don't you pack whatever you'll need for the next three days and come home with me? Daisy and Cocoa miss you."

She pressed her lips together to keep from grinning. "Daisy and Cocoa told you they miss me?"

"They talk to me all the time. Didn't you know that?"

"No, I didn't."

"I guess we still have a lot to learn about each other." He ran his hands up and down her back. "Luckily, we have a lifetime to do that."

Flare

1

Paige Denslow smiled at the customer as she handed him the receipt for his purchases. "Thank you for shopping at Spencer's. Have a great day."

He gave her what she assumed to be a smile of acknowledgement that barely turned up the corners of his mouth, then turned and left the store.

Paige sighed. Just once, she wished a really hunky guy would pull up to the gas pumps—maybe wearing a black leather jacket and riding on a huge motorcycle. Yeah, someone like that would get her blood pumping.

Unfortunately, Dolores Kirkland, one of the other clerks who worked for Clay Spencer in his convenience store, usually waited on the hunks. She had to be in her late sixties, maybe even early seventies, and had no interest in any of the good-looking guys who came in during her shift.

Paige wondered why she couldn't luck out and have one of Dolores's guys walk through the entrance.

She'd dated almost all the single guys in Lanville, including the ones who worked with her on the volunteer fire department. Unlike Talia King—one of her best friends who also volunteered on the fire department—she hadn't found her soul mate like Talia had found Dylan Westfield. She'd hoped to develop something with Marcus Holt, but he'd thought their six-year age difference too much. Besides, he'd gotten back together with his ex-wife when she came to Lanville to visit her grandmother. They'd remarried in August and expected a baby in April.

While happy for Marcus and Rayna, envy wrapped around Paige and made her wish for what she didn't have.

Mentally shaking herself out of the funky mood, Paige turned back to the project she'd been working on when the last customer came in the store. New lottery scratch-off tickets had arrived this morning, along with another display case. Spencer's carried the biggest selection in Lanville for those people willing to gamble a little money in hopes of winning a lot.

A *ding* from the machine that controlled the gas pumps signaled someone pressed the button to start adding gas to their vehicle. Paige glanced out the window in curiosity to see if it might be someone she knew. She blinked, looked a second time. Hand on her suddenly churning stomach, she straightened and stared at the man wearing a black leather jacket who was pumping gas into a huge black Harley.

Wavy, dark brown hair flowed over his forehead and ears and down his neck. About six-one with the broad shoulders of a swimmer. Sunglasses protected his eyes. A couple days of scruff darkened his lower face. Olive skin. Tight, faded jeans covered his legs, black boots encased his feet.

Holy shit.

Her fantasy man had materialized, as if someone intercepted her thoughts and created him just for her.

Her hormones did a happy dance.

Since most people used a credit or debit card to pay for their gas, they didn't come into the store unless they needed something besides gas. *Please, oh, please, let him need something so he comes in! Let me have the thrill of seeing him up close.*

In case he *did* come in, she ran her fingers through her hair to fluff it and straightened her T-shirt.

Paige kept glancing at the man while she unwrapped a stack of tickets. He replaced the nozzle in the pump, screwed the cap on his gas tank. Then he headed toward the entrance.

Her hormones did another tap dance.

He nodded at her once he stepped inside the store, but looked away before she had the chance to flash him her most dazzling smile. He strolled to the refrigerated section, perused the items through the glass doors before he opened one and withdrew a bottle of Pepsi.

He continued his slow-paced stroll down the snacks aisle, picked up a bag of chips and a large Snickers. Paige tried not to stare at him, but her gaze kept wandering back to him. Such an attractive man hadn't come in the store in a long time.

Apparently finding everything he wanted, he approached the checkout counter. The closer he got to her, the heavier she breathed. He had full, pale pink lips that she easily imagined pressed against hers. She couldn't call his face square, but more of a triangle with his forehead being a little narrower than his jawline. A silver stud winked at her from his left earlobe.

She wished he'd take off his sunglasses so she could see his eyes.

As if he'd read her mind, he pushed the dark glasses to the top of his head, exposing brown, almond-shaped eyes surrounded by thick, brown eyelashes. Lust churned in her stomach when his gaze met hers.

Paige had to clear her throat before she could speak. "Will this be all for you?"

"I also need some information," he said in a voice that made her think of smooth maple syrup.

"Sure." Paige rang up the items while he drew his wallet from the pocket of his jacket. "What kind of information?"

"I have an appointment at Café Crystal in about half an hour. Can you tell me where that is?"

She blinked in surprise. She couldn't imagine what kind of appointment he could have at the restaurant. "Uh, sure. It's on County Road 311. Turn left when you leave here, then take a left at the stop light. Drive about two miles and you'll see the turnoff for 311 on your right. Café Crystal is at the end of the road, next to The Inn on Crystal Creek."

He smiled, which transformed his face from handsome to panties-creaming gorgeous. "Thanks."

Paige caught herself before she fanned her face. "No problem." She slipped his items into a plastic bag. Curiosity got the better of her. It might be rude, but she had to ask him about his appointment. "Are you seeing Emma about a job?"

"A possible job. I answered an ad for an assistant chef."

"You're a chef?"

"Yeah." Grinning, he held out his hands and looked down at himself. "Not your idea of a chef, huh?"

She returned his grin. "Not exactly."

"Looks can be deceiving. That whole don't-judge-a-book-by-its-cover thing."

"That's true." She passed the bag over the counter to him. "Good luck."

"Thanks . . ." He glanced at the name tag pinned above her left breast. "Paige."

He turned and walked toward the door. With his hand on the push bar, he looked at her over his shoulder. "If I get the job, maybe I'll see you around town."

"You probably will. It's a small town."

He nodded once in acknowledgement of her comment, then left the store.

Paige placed her hand on her stomach again. A chef, of all things. She never would've guessed that about him. Not that a chef couldn't look hot, but she didn't get that kind of vibe from him. He seemed a little bit . . . dangerous.

A shiver passed through her. What fun it would be to tame him.

The sound of his motorcycle starting drew her attention back to the gas pumps. She watched him don his helmet, then drive off with a purring roar of the Harley's powerful engine.

She wondered if it would be tacky to call Emma and beg her to hire him.

Glancing at her watch, she saw that she had another ninety minutes before her lunch break. She suddenly had a craving for one of Emma's chicken Caesar salads. Picking up the phone, she punched in Talia's number to invite her to lunch at Café Crystal.

Cort Brennaman stopped his motorcycle close to the back door of Café Crystal. He'd spoken to Emma Keeton yesterday and she'd told him to enter the restaurant from the back since she would be in the kitchen.

After removing his helmet, he opened the bottle of Pepsi and drank one-third of it in a single gulp. He glanced around the area, noting the neatly manicured grounds, plants, and flowers. He didn't know one flower from another, but many still bloomed despite it being the first week of November. He knew little about architecture either, but had to admit he thought the mansion magnificent. Whoever had restored it had done an incredible job. The outside of Café Crystal bore a similar design and color scheme, so Cort assumed the same construction company had built it.

He'd learn a lot about Lanville if Emma Keeton hired him. He had to make sure he got the job. Working at the restaurant would help him blend in with everyone else in town.

Cort stepped inside the building. The warmth hit him in the face and he quickly shed his jacket. The angry female voice had him lifting his eyebrows at her fierce tone.

"You and your brothers get someone here *right now!* It's like an oven in the entire restaurant. I'm supposed to open in twenty minutes. I can't do that and let my customers bake! . . . I don't want any excuses, Griff . . . Of course I've tried turning off the heat! Don't you think that's the first thing I did? It just keeps running. Something has to be broken."

Cort peeked around the corner to see a petite brunette, phone to her ear, pacing the kitchen. He could almost see the thundercloud swirling above her head from her anger.

"That's the best you can do? Really? I have a party of thirty people tonight, Griff . . ." She blew out a hard breath. "Fine, whatever. Just get them here ASAP. I'll have to put a sign on the door for people coming for lunch that we're closed until further notice."

She jabbed a button to end the call. Cort wasn't sure whether to say anything or remain in the background where he wouldn't be in the line of her fire. "Excuse me."

She whirled around to face him. Even with her eyes narrowed and her lips pressed tightly together, he couldn't help but notice her beauty. "What," she said flatly.

"I'm Cort Brennaman. I have a ten-forty-five appointment with Emma Keeton."

Some of the anger faded from her expression. "Yes, of course. I'm Emma Keeton."

"I couldn't help hearing some of your conversation. You told that Griff guy that you tried to turn off the heat."

"I did."

"At the thermostat or breaker?"

She blinked. "Breaker?"

He would've smiled at her deer-in-the-headlights look if she hadn't been so upset. "Where's your breaker box?"

"This way."

She led him to the back wall in a large storage room. Cort opened the door to the breaker box, quickly located the correct one that controlled the heating and air conditioning. He flipped it off, on, then off again to be sure the heat's flow stopped.

"I feel like such a dunce," Emma said behind him. "I should've thought about the breaker. I've been running the AC, but that cold front last night dropped the temperature into the low forties. I turned on the heat when I got here to take the chill out of the restaurant."

"There's definitely no more chill in here."

Emma chuckled. "That's true." She held out her hand. "It's nice to meet you, Cort."

Cort accepted her hand. "Same here."

"I should give you the job right now because you saved me."

"I'll take it. When do you want me to start?"

She laughed out loud. "I'm easy, but not that easy. Let's go to my desk."

He followed Emma from the storage room back to the kitchen. A small alcove off the kitchen held a desk with a computer, calculator, and various piles of papers on it, two chairs, a bookshelf, and a file cabinet. He waited until she took the chair behind the desk, then sat in the one to the side.

Emma took a piece of paper off the top of one of the stacks on her desk. Cort recognized it as the application he'd completed online. "I've already talked to your former boss. He had nothing but good things to say about you. He claimed your pumpkin cheesecake is the best he's ever tasted."

Cort tipped his head to acknowledge the compliment.

"I have a party of thirty for dinner tonight. How about if you make that cheesecake for their dessert? I'm sure I have all the necessary ingredients. If it's a hit, you're hired."

"Sounds good."

"Let me get through the lunch rush, then come back when

you need to start preparing your dish. The party's reservation is for seven-thirty. They'll have salad, soup, and their entrée first, of course. I expect dessert will be served between eight-thirty and eight-forty-five."

"Works for me."

"If I do hire you, you'll have some shifts in the kitchen at The Inn next door. Do you have a problem with that?"

"No, ma'am."

Emma smiled. "Good. Then I'll see you back here this afternoon."

"I look forward to working with you, Ms. Keeton."

She stood and held out her hand. "Emma. We're very informal around here."

Cort also stood, accepted her hand. "See you later, Emma."

After grabbing his jacket from the counter where he'd left it, Cort wandered out the exit and back to his cycle. If getting this job depended on his pumpkin cheesecake being a hit, there wouldn't be any problem. He'd exaggerated on his application about previous chef experience, but hadn't exaggerated about his ability to cook.

Cort thought about what Emma told him as he straddled the Harley. His "former boss" had nothing to do with any restaurant. Cort had prompted him on what to say if Emma should call, which as a prospective employer she should. He must have been convincing. Emma never would have agreed to a tryout if she'd suspected the lie.

If he didn't get the assistant chef job, Cort would apply to other places in Lanville. He had no doubt he could charm his way into a position. He'd had a lot of experience with exaggeration.

He'd do whatever he had to do to stay in this town, even if it meant lying and using people to get what he needed.

An image of the blonde at Spencer's flashed through his mind. Asking her for directions to Café Crystal—even when he knew its exact location thanks to GPS—gave him the chance to check the store's layout, see how easy it would be to avoid security cameras. He'd need more time in there to research it fully.

The blonde could help. Cort had recognized the interest in her eyes. She'd stood straighter, arched her back to put her breasts on display, when he looked at her. She could be useful in his plan. It never hurt to have someone on his side, especially if that someone happened to be a beautiful woman.

2

"Thanks for agreeing to supper instead of lunch," Talia said as she picked up her glass of iced tea. "Dylan had a session with Quade, then they're going to Stephen's to tinker on his Mustang. There's too much testosterone in the air with those three guys together. I told Dylan to go and have fun and I'd spend the evening with you."

"No problem." Paige wouldn't do anything to make her friend feel guilty about not having lunch at Café Crystal today so she could drool over the stranger if she got the chance. "Having supper here is better anyway. No rush to get back to work."

"Or to pack. I don't know how I have so much stuff in that small house."

"When are you officially moving in with Dylan?"

"I've kinda already moved in with him, but didn't take all my stuff. Now that I've given Janelle notice of my move, I have until the fifteenth to get everything out and clean up the house so she can rent it out again."

"I'll help you clean."

Talia smiled. "Thanks, Paige. I appreciate that. Dylan has already conned several of our guy friends into coming over with their pickups on the thirteenth to haul boxes and furniture, or whatever is left after the yard sale on the twelfth." She leaned forward in her chair, an anxious look on her face. "You're helping with that, right?"

"Of course. So are Lucia, Julia, and Keely. We got you covered."

Talia chose a warm breadstick from the basket in the middle of the table, tore it in half. Paige could tell by her friend's wrinkled eyebrows that something troubled Talia. "Are you having second thoughts about living with Dylan?"

"Not . . . exactly. I mean, I love him and I know he loves me. It's just that living together is such a huge step. Do you think I'm rushing it?"

"You've been in love with Dylan since the first time you saw him. No, I don't think you're rushing anything. Y'all belong together."

A gentle smile curved Talia's lips. "I think so, too. He's just so perfect."

Paige snorted. Dylan worked as a mechanic at Spencer's. She knew how unperfect he could be. "You don't see his flaws because you love him."

"He has flaws?" she asked, batting her eyes innocently. Then she grinned. "Luckily, I can live with his flaws and he can live with mine." She took a bite of her breadstick, laid the rest on her plate. "I wish you could find your Mr. Right."

"I'd settle for Mr. Okay right now. It's been a long time since I've been horizontal with anyone. The last time was five months ago with Royce. That was a mistake I will *not* repeat."

Paige shuddered to think of the one time she'd given in to Royce Underwood. He'd been on the volunteer fire department about eight months when she'd let her hormones overrule her good judgment. Incredibly good looking and charming when he wanted to be, he said all the right things to get her to go out with him and invite him into her home for a glass of wine after their date. The evening should've ended with the wine. Instead, it hadn't ended until she'd awakened shortly after two in the morning to see Royce sneaking out of her bedroom.

She'd become another notch on his bedpost. Or whatever method guys used to keep track of gals they'd fucked.

While finding a man to love would be nice, Paige would be happy to simply be involved with someone she could go out to the movies or to dinner with before making love. She liked waking up with her back to a man's chest and his arms wrapped around her. Early morning sex always gave her energy for the whole day.

Shara arrived with the meals. Talia had ordered the chef's special of seafood Alfredo. After a moment of thinking about it, Paige ordered the same thing. One look at the food on her plate made her glad she'd followed her friend. One bite had her thinking about kissing Emma's feet.

"My God, this is incredible."

"I know." Talia stabbed a thick scallop with her fork. "I'd eat here every night the restaurant is open if I could afford it just to have Emma's chef's special."

"I'm glad you're enjoying it," Emma said as she stepped up to their table.

"Hey, Emma." Paige wiped her mouth with her napkin. "This Alfredo is to die for."

"I tried some different spices this time. I like the way it turned out."

"I should get a to-go order for Dylan," Talia said. "Then I can convince him to share it with me."

Emma smiled. "Be sure and save room for dessert. My new assistant chef made two pumpkin cheesecakes for a dinner party. There are four pieces left. I'll save two for you and Paige. My treat."

Paige stopped with her fork raised halfway to her mouth. "New assistant chef?"

"Yes, I hired him today. Cort Brennaman. I told him he was hired if the party liked his cheesecake. Everyone raved about it."

Cort Brennaman. Paige liked that name. It fit him. "He, uh, came into Spencer's this morning and asked for directions to get here."

"So you saw how gorgeous he is."

Talia straightened in her chair. "How gorgeous?"

"He rates right up there with Dylan and Griff. Tall, dark hair, brown eyes, killer body. *Very* nice ass."

"And you met him this morning?" Talia asked Paige. "Why didn't you tell me?"

"There was nothing to tell. He was in Spencer's for ten minutes, tops."

Talia turned back to Emma. "Is he moving to Lanville?"

"We haven't discussed that. He's from Garland, so I doubt if he'll want to commute that far."

"I'm moving out of Janelle's house next week. I don't think she plans on putting an ad in the paper until I'm gone, but I'll check with her to be sure. If he's looking for a place to rent, it'll be available after the fifteenth."

"I'll let him know." She glanced toward the entrance to the kitchen. "Cindy is waving at me, so I'd better get back to the kitchen. I'll tell Shara to bring out the cheesecake after you finish your meal."

Paige thought about what Talia said regarding the house she rented from Janelle while she and Talia ate their meal. Talia's boss may be kind and generous, but she also knew how to pinch a penny until it screamed. Paige wouldn't be surprised if an ad for Talia's house already appeared in the newspaper. "Are you sure Janelle didn't put an ad in the paper for your house?"

"No, I'm not sure. She told me she would, but I assumed she'd wait until I was gone."

"The paper comes out on Wednesday. I'll bet there's an ad in there for your house even though you paid rent through the fifteenth."

Talia sipped her tea. "Maybe, but Janelle won't pressure me to leave early so she can rent it to someone else. Like you said, I'm paid through the fifteenth."

"But rentals are in short supply in Lanville, especially cute little houses like yours where the rent is reasonable. If Cort needs a place to live, that house would be perfect. Emma may have gotten busy in the kitchen and didn't mention it to him. That means we should."

"Janelle will probably raise the rent on the next tenant."

Paige waved a hand, as if to erase Talia's statement. "It'll still be a great deal. We should talk to him before he leaves."

"We haven't had our dessert."

"We'll tell Shara we'll take it with us." Paige laid her napkin by her empty plate. "C'mon, let's find Cort."

Cort signed his name on the W-9 form and dated it. He now officially worked for Café Crystal as an assistant chef. He never would have imagined his pumpkin cheesecake would get him exactly where he wanted to be.

From his position at the desk, he could see the bustle in the kitchen. Although petite, Emma Keeton ruled her domain. Yet she didn't yell or admonish someone roughly, even when one of the busboys dropped two plates that shattered on the floor. She calmly told him accidents happened and to clean up the mess.

It would be interesting to work here while he took care of his other plans.

He thought he heard a female voice mention his name, but decided he had to be mistaken. No one other than the people in the kitchen knew him. The next moment, the blonde from the gas station appeared in the doorway, along with another blonde who appeared as petite as Emma.

"Remember me?" the Spencer's clerk asked with a smile.

"Of course. You're Paige." He stood. "It's nice to see you again."

"Forgive us for bothering you, but Emma told us she hired you. Congratulations."

"Thanks. I think I'll really enjoy working here."

Paige looked at the other woman, as if urging her to say something. The other blonde stepped forward. "I'm Talia King, Paige's friend. Emma mentioned you're from Garland. If you plan to move here and need a place to live, I'm renting a small, two-bedroom house in the city limits that I'll be vacating on the fifteenth. If you're interested, I can tell the owner, who's also my boss. It would save her the hassle of putting an ad in the paper and interviewing prospective renters."

It surprised Cort that these two women would be so willing to help a complete stranger. "That's very kind of you, but you don't know me. How do you know I'd be a good renter?"

"Emma is a great judge of character," Paige said. "If she hired you, that's enough for us to trust you."

The trusting souls in this small town would make his task much easier.

"We can show you the house now," Talia said, "if you think you might be interested in renting it."

"Why are you giving it up?"

"I'm moving in with my boyfriend. I can call him and tell him and his two friends to meet us there."

Smart girl. Taking a strange man to your home wouldn't be a good idea. "If it isn't too much trouble, I'd appreciate it."

Talia stepped to the side to make her call. Cort studied Paige, admiring the way she looked in a blouse the color of oyster shells with a denim jacket that matched her jeans. She stood about five-five or five-six with a slim build. The ends of her curly hair teased her breasts. Very nice breasts.

Lust curled in his belly. With him being on the move most of the time, he rarely had the chance to indulge in sex. The last time had been a one-night stand several weeks ago that he'd regretted as soon as it ended.

Approaching thirty had him examining his life and what he wanted to do with it. Staying constantly on the move no longer appealed to him. He had this final task to complete, then he might consider a different way to make a living, one that would give him time to get involved with someone.

She turned her head and looked at him. Heat flared in her eyes as her gaze passed over his shoulders, down his chest, to his fly. It lingered there for several seconds before she looked back at her friend as Talia approached.

"They'll be there in five minutes, so they should get to my house about the time we do."

"I'll follow you and Paige after I ask Emma when she needs me to be back."

After finding out Emma wanted him at The Inn Monday morning to meet the manager, Kelcey Ewing, Cort followed the two ladies out the back door. He walked them to their cars, then went back for his motorcycle. They led him to a small brick house a couple of blocks from the downtown square and parked on the street in front of the house.

Two pickups and a classic Mustang Fastback pulled up behind his motorcycle before he had the chance to turn off the key. A tall man emerged from each vehicle. One of them had him beat by a couple of inches in height and a good thirty pounds. His long black hair practically screamed "badass."

The men approached him the same time the women did. Cort offered his hand to the buff man first. "Cort Brennaman."

He accepted Cort's hand. "Quade Easton. This is Stephen McGettis and Dylan Westfield."

Each man offered Cort his hand to shake. Cort had become an expert at picking up vibes from people. He didn't sense any distrust or suspicion from any of the men. Either they hid their true feelings, or Cort's cover of an assistant chef looking for a place to live held.

"Come in, everybody," Talia said.

She slipped her hand into Dylan's. He must be the boyfriend. Cort noticed Paige didn't touch the other two guys, so must not be involved with either of them. That didn't mean she wasn't involved with someone else. Although the way she'd devoured him with her eyes in Spencer's and Café Crystal, he didn't think so.

Talia unlocked the front door, flipped a switch to turn on a lamp on either side of the couch. "Excuse the mess, Cort. I'm still packing."

"There's no bigger job than moving." His gaze swept the living room, neat despite the boxes stacked in the corner. "This is nice."

"Thanks. Dylan and I are still trying to decide which furniture to keep and which to sell since we have duplicates of everything."

"I like my bed better, but her couch is nicer," Dylan said.

She continued to speak as she led the group to the small kitchen. "The appliances come with the house, so at least we don't have to try and sell a stove or refrigerator. The laundry room is through that door. We both have washers and dryers that are within a year of each other, so we'll probably keep his and sell mine. I'm having a yard sale next Saturday. Hopefully, I'll sell everything I no longer need."

Cort wandered through the kitchen, checked in cabinets that contained no food. Talia had apparently already moved most of the kitchen supplies to Dylan's home. "How about if you sell whatever furniture you don't want to me?"

"You don't have any furniture?" Talia asked.

"Not of my own. I live in a furnished studio apartment

now." He shrugged. "It's just me and I've never been one to collect stuff. I have dishes and sheets and blankets. That's about it."

He thought he saw pity in Paige's eyes. Her sympathy to what she must consider his sad loneliness could work to his advantage.

Talia turned to Paige. "If Cort buys the extra furniture, I won't need to have the yard sale."

"What about all your knickknacky stuff you said you'd sell?" Dylan asked. "I don't have room for all of it."

Talia's cute little chin lifted an inch. "Then you'd better make room, because I changed my mind and want to keep all my knickknacky stuff."

Stephen chuckled. "It's called compromise, my friend. Get used to it."

"I have stuff to get rid of, too," Dylan said. "Since I have to make room for the things Talia has decided to keep, I think we'd better stick with having the yard sale. Whatever doesn't sell, we'll donate to The Thrift Store, like we planned."

She smiled at him. "Okay."

Stephen elbowed Dylan in the ribs. "See? Compromise can be easy."

"I don't know how easy it is, but she's worth it."

A lovely blush colored Talia's cheeks. She stood on tiptoe and gave Dylan a gentle kiss.

Cort shifted his gaze to Paige to find her watching the couple. Then, as if she felt him looking at her, she turned her head toward him. Cort would swear something flared between them, something hot and impossible to ignore. His heart slowed to a heavy thud while blood rushed to his dick. He'd have a full-blown hard-on in moments if he didn't break the connection.

"So you're sure you want to rent the house?" Talia asked.

Grateful for the excuse to look away from Paige and get his

hormones back under control, Cort faced Talia. "Yeah, if the owner agrees to rent it to me."

"I'll introduce you to her Monday. The fact that Emma hired you to work in her restaurant is the best reference you could give Janelle."

"Why don't you come over to my house tomorrow, Cort?" Dylan asked. "You can look at the couch and other items I'll probably sell to make room for Talia's nicer things." He wrapped one arm around Talia's shoulders. "With your help, maybe we can finally decide what to keep and what to sell."

"I'll write down the address and directions for you," Talia said. "Do you want to look through the rest of the house now?"

"Sure."

He followed Talia and Dylan to the two bedrooms and one bathroom with Stephen trailing them. He noticed neither Paige nor Quade went with them. Maybe he'd been mistaken about Paige not being involved with anyone. Perhaps she had a thing with the big guy.

The tour didn't take long since the house couldn't be over eleven hundred square feet. Cort stepped back into the living room to see Paige and Quade talking with each other, their heads close together. Their conversation stopped when they saw him.

Little shivers danced up and down his spine. Maybe his vibes had been wrong and Quade Easton didn't buy Cort's assistant-chef cover.

Damn it.

"Here." Talia held out a piece of paper to Cort. "The directions to Dylan's house."

"Thanks." He slipped it into his jeans pocket. "I see no reason to go home tonight and come back tomorrow. Is there a reasonable motel in town? I assume The Inn on Crystal Creek is over my budget."

Paige opened her mouth as if to speak. Quade shot her a

sharp look. She frowned, but closed her mouth before saying anything.

"I have an extra room," Quade said. "You're welcome to stay with me."

Cort had learned to mask his feelings and emotions a long time ago, so didn't let the surprise at Quade's offer show on his face. "I don't want to be any trouble."

"It's an empty guest room. Won't be any trouble at all for you to sleep there."

So you can pump me for information? Cort had been in much worse situations than having an overprotective lover grill him. "Thanks, Quade. I appreciate the offer."

Cort followed everyone outside. He wished he had the chance to speak to Paige alone, but it didn't appear that would happen tonight. He said good-bye to the group, nodded to Paige, then straddled his Harley. A moment later, he pulled away from the curb to follow Quade.

3

The sprawling ranch-style house made of cedar blended in perfectly among the trees. Cort couldn't see much of it due to darkness, but sconces on either side of the front door illuminated a wide porch with five steps leading up to it.

He grabbed the canvas bag he'd used to pack a few clothing and personal items from the storage compartment behind his seat. After hooking his helmet over the handlebars, he turned to find Quade waiting at the bottom of the steps.

There had been a moment on the way here that Cort thought about motioning Quade to stop so Cort could tell him he'd go to a motel after all. He decided not to. As quickly as Quade had offered a stranger the guest room in his home, Cort figured he'd be subjected to a lot of questions . . . ones he could easily dance around. Cort knew how to avoid offering too much information about himself.

He walked up the steps next to Quade. His host opened the front door and led the way into a spacious living room. Cort's gaze immediately latched onto the lovely blonde sitting in a corner of the couch, holding an e-reader.

Damn, what's with all the gorgeous blondes in this town?

She looked at him with eyes the color of spring clover. A smile curved her lips, the kind she would give a stranger she passed on the street.

"Eve, this is Cort Brennaman. He'll be staying in the guest room a few days. Cort, Eve Van Den Bergh."

Cort tipped his head. "Eve, a pleasure."

"For me, too."

"We're going to have a beer in my study."

"Okay. There are fresh banana nut muffins on the island if you want a snack later."

Quade smiled. "Thank you, sweetheart."

So Quade wasn't involved with Paige after all. The tender kiss he gave Eve proved that.

Cort followed Quade down a wide hallway lined with book-shelves and through an open doorway into a masculine room that gave Cort chills.

Quade crossed to the built-in shelves and cabinets on the back wall and opened a mini-fridge. "Beer? Or would you prefer a Coke or coffee?"

"Beer sounds good." After dropping his bag to the floor, Cort removed his jacket and draped it over the back of one of the leather armchairs and sat. A large, L-shaped desk occupied a lot of floor space, but the armchairs didn't sit before the desk. Instead, they faced each other at a forty-five-degree angle in the center of the room, each with a small table beside them.

Interesting.

Quade removed the caps from both bottles, tossed them in the trash. He handed one bottle to Cort before sitting in the other chair. "I guess you're wondering why I invited you here."

"The question crossed my mind." Cort took a drink of the cold brew. "I'm not much for Q-and-A sessions, so why don't you just tell me?"

"You're the undercover cop who's tracking the thieves that have hit all around North Texas."

Cort almost choked on his swallow of beer. Quade hadn't asked the question, but made a statement. "How did you know?"

"Several things. I'm a counselor. It's my job to read people. Brad McGuire, the sheriff, and I are good friends. He trusted me not to tell anyone about your assignment. He didn't tell me when you'd be here, but I had this feeling in my gut the longer I was with you." A smirk lifted one corner of his mouth. "And you don't look like a chef."

"Looks can be deceiving. I told Paige that when I met her."

Quade's smirk disappeared. "Speaking of Paige, I saw the way y'all looked at each other at Talia's house. You're a good-looking guy and I understand her being attracted to you. But don't hurt her, Cort."

"I have no intention of hurting anyone, except the thieves. I'll gladly hurt them if I get the chance."

"I'm with you on that. But Paige is vulnerable now. She cared for someone and he didn't return the feelings. She wants to be in love. Don't let her fall for you when you know you won't be in Lanville for long."

Cort scratched loose a corner of the bottle's label. He knew Quade was right. No matter how much he desired Paige, he had to avoid getting too close to her.

"Are you really a chef?" Quade asked.

Cort nodded. "I've always enjoyed cooking. I never went to any kind of cooking school, just picked up stuff on my own." He let a small smile touch his lips. "I make a pork roast so tender, you'll get tears in your eyes while eating it."

Quade chuckled. "I may take you up on that."

"I wouldn't want to step on Eve's toes in her kitchen."

"Actually, it's *my* kitchen. Eve has a small apartment on the

square above the crafts shop where she works. We've been together less than a month and we're still learning about each
other. She visits me and I visit her, but no plans to move in together anytime soon." Quade scratched his cheek. "And I have
no idea why I told you all that."

Cort laughed, more at ease in Quade's presence. He believed
they could be good friends if he would be in Lanville more than
however long it took to catch the thieves. "Maybe you couldn't
resist my charm."

"Yeah, I'm sure that's it." He rested one ankle on the opposite
knee. "I'll help you any way I can, Cort. You only have to ask."

"Thanks, Quade. I appreciate that." He took the last drink
from his bottle. "Actually, there is something you can do. I
need to meet your sheriff. We've spoken on the phone and ex-
changed e-mails and texts, but haven't met face-to-face yet.
Could we meet here? I don't want anyone to see me go into his
office."

"Sure. That isn't a problem at all. Like I said, Brad and I are
good friends, so no one would think twice about him coming
to my house. When do you want to meet?"

"Whenever it's convenient for him. I'm supposed to be at
The Inn on Crystal Creek Monday morning at nine to meet the
manager and find out my schedule. Emma told me I wouldn't
work Monday or Tuesday, but she wants me to work in The
Inn's kitchen Wednesday morning."

"I'll call Brad in the morning and see if he can come over
Tuesday."

"That'd be great."

Quade nodded toward the empty bottle in Cort's hand.
"Want another?"

"No, thanks. If you don't mind, I'd like to take a shower
and hit the sack."

"I'll show you to your room."

Cort followed Quade from the study and down a short hallway to another part of the house. Quade pushed open a door to expose a furnished guest room with a queen-sized bed. "Bathroom's across the hall. Remote for the TV is in the nightstand closest to the wall. Let me know if you need anything."

"I'll be fine." Cort offered his hand to Quade. "Thanks, man."

Quade smiled as he shook Cort's hand. "See you in the morning."

Cort shut the door, dropped his jacket and bag on the bed, and sat beside them. He'd never expected to be invited to stay in someone's home, but had to admit he liked the comfort of this room more than any motel room he would've gotten in town. They always seemed so sterile, while this room seemed . . . homey.

As for renting Talia's house, he had to pretend he planned to be in Lanville longer than a few days or weeks. If he had to sign a lease, he would. He'd done so in the past and had help from his captain getting out of it. Sometimes an extra month's rent had done the trick, sometimes the owner let him out of the lease without complaint because he'd caught "the bad guy."

Fatigue hit him so hard, he could barely keep his eyes open. He'd started the day early and it had been like riding a roller coaster. A hot shower would do him in for the night. Before he did that, he had to call his sister.

Despite being older than his sister or brother, his sister demanded he contact her as soon as he got settled in his new assignment. Daphne had a husband and two children to take care of, yet couldn't help worrying about her brothers.

Cort adored her.

Removing his boots, Cort stuffed a pillow behind his back and leaned against the headboard. He located his sister's phone number at the top of his favorites list on his cell phone and pressed it to place the call.

She answered after two rings. "Hey, bro."

Cort smiled. Daphne always sounded so cheerful. "Hey, sis. What's shakin'?"

"Donnie's weewee. He's running around naked after his bath."

Cort laughed at the mental picture of his naked two-year-old nephew being chased by his mother. "Do you need to catch him?"

"Nope, that's Don's job."

"Why is Donnie awake so late? It's after ten-thirty."

"Long story that has to do with chocolate pudding. So, you're in Lanville?"

"I am. In fact, I'm staying with one of the residents, a good friend of the sheriff's."

"Nice guy?"

"Very nice. He already knew about me from the sheriff and wants to help if he can."

"Having an in with a local is always good for the undercover work, right?"

"You've learned well, sis."

"I was taught by the best cop in the Metroplex."

Her comment brought a tightness to his throat. Daphne always said the right thing to make him feel good. "Thanks, Daph."

He heard his nephew laughing in the background. "Did Don catch him?"

"Yes, but I don't think he was trying all that hard. We love to listen to Donnie giggle."

So did Cort. At only three months old, Daphne's daughter still slept a lot, but Cort had no doubt he'd soon have fun spoiling her the way he did Donnie.

"I'm gonna hit the shower and then the bed, sis. It's been a long day."

"Okay. I know you can't keep in close touch while you're undercover, but call when you can, okay?"

"I will. Kiss my beautiful niece for me."

"Okay. Love you."

"Love you, too."

Smiling, Cort disconnected the call. Talking with his sister always made him smile. His brother, not so much. He and Neal loved each other, but fought over stupid things thanks to Neal's fast temper. Still young at twenty-four, Neal had a lot of growing up to do.

Which Cort couldn't worry about now. Shower and bed. Those were the only things on his to-do list.

Fifteen minutes later, Cort crawled naked between jersey sheets that smelled like the outdoors. Blowing out a soft sigh, he closed his eyes and let sleep take him.

Paige never had trouble falling asleep. She considered that a gift since she knew so many people suffered from insomnia or difficulty sleeping. She dropped off within a couple of minutes of her head hitting the pillow and slept straight through the night until her alarm buzzed at six-thirty.

Tonight, sleep eluded her.

She flipped her pillow, punched out all the lumps. It didn't help. She still couldn't sleep.

Maybe a midnight snack would help. Or in this case, a two-o'clock snack.

Throwing back the covers, Paige rose and donned her robe and slippers. She never ate her pumpkin cheesecake from dinner. That and a glass of milk might settle the gnawing in her stomach.

She sat at her small kitchen table with her treat. One bite of the cheesecake had her moaning. Sinful. She imagined spreading the creamy concoction all over Cort's body and licking it off.

Hence why she couldn't sleep. Her mind churned with thoughts of the handsome chef.

Paige had experienced physical love many times. She knew

how it felt to desire a man, to kiss him, to touch him. She especially loved when they'd both reached the highest peak of lust possible before he slipped his hard cock into her pussy. The pounding thrusts, the scratching and biting, the ultimate act of surrender . . . Paige loved it all.

And wanted it with Cort.

Finding a lover wouldn't be difficult. Despite Royce sneaking out of her bedroom the one time they'd been together, he flirted with her every time they ended up at the fire hall together. If she wiggled her finger at him, he'd probably follow her to the nearest bed.

No. Paige didn't want anything to do with Royce. She saw nothing wrong with two people being friends with benefits, but she didn't want that with Royce or any of the other single guys on the fire department.

She wouldn't mind being friends with benefits with Cort.

Paige scooped up another forkful of cheesecake. She'd felt a flare of awareness between them today, first at Spencer's and then again at Talia's house. She had no doubt it wouldn't take much for that flare to become a conflagration that would engulf both of them.

She shivered at the delicious thought of Cort's naked body brushing against hers. She'd never fucked a guy on a motorcycle. It would be fun. And seriously hot.

Paige drummed her fingers on the table while she tried to decide what to do. She'd never felt such a strong pull for a man and knew she had to examine it further.

So what's the best way to seduce him? I could invite him over for dinner. It would be a friendly gesture since he's new in town. We can eat and talk and then I'll tear off his clothes.

Paige sighed. She liked the tearing off his clothes idea, but not the cooking dinner part for a chef. She could cook, but nothing worthy enough to be served at Café Crystal.

He didn't seem like a froufrou kind of guy. He'd probably be as happy with a juicy hamburger as he would a gourmet steak. Sunday would be a great day to invite him over for a hearty meal of hamburgers, baked beans, and potato salad.

Inviting him could be a problem since she didn't know his phone number. She could call Quade and ask him to give Cort a message to call her. Or she could ask Emma for Cort's phone number. Ethically, Emma shouldn't do that, but she probably would if Paige begged enough.

Paige swallowed the last of her milk. Now that she'd satisfied her hunger and figured out a way to be with Cort, she should fall asleep in seconds.

4

The buzzer announcing someone had come into Spencer's made Paige look up from her position on the floor where she unpacked a box of potato chips. Her boss and the owner, Clay Spencer, walked in. Paige hadn't expected him to be back from his trip until Tuesday. "Hey, boss."

Clay smiled. "Hey, Paige. How's it going?"

"Great. It's been super busy thanks to that motorcycle rally by the river."

"Super busy is good." He offered his hand to help her from the floor. "Got a minute to talk?"

He seemed so serious, unlike the usual friendly way he spoke to her. Apprehension crawled up her spine. She believed she'd done a good job since she started working here almost a year ago. Surely he wouldn't fire her.

"Of course."

Clay looked over his shoulder at his other clerk, Lesa, who waited on a customer. "Lesa, I'm stealing Paige for a couple minutes."

"Okay."

"Let's go to my office."

Paige's palms broke out in a sweat. Jobs in Lanville didn't fall in someone's lap. She knew that from past experience. She'd had no choice but to live with her parents while she went to college. Once on her own, she took whatever part-time jobs she could find to make ends meet until she went to work here. People in Lanville tended to keep their jobs. She knew people who had worked at the newspaper for over thirty years.

She had no idea what she'd do if Clay fired her.

Clay sat behind his desk and Paige took one of the chairs in front of it. She told herself not to fidget and clasped her hands together in her lap to keep from doing that.

"You know I've been in Tempe for business meetings this week."

Paige nodded, even though he'd uttered a comment and not a question.

"The board has decided to expand farther north, from coast to coast. We especially want to be in the Pacific Northwest and New England. I have a fantastic team who does the research for future stations, but I'll still be needed for the final decision on anything we purchase. Maysen and I will be out of town a lot. I need to know this store will be taken care of in my absence." He leaned forward, propped his forearms on his desk. "I'd like you to be my manager."

She'd been prepared to hear the I-have-to-let-you-go speech, so it took Paige a moment to realize Clay had said something entirely different. "What?"

He smiled. "Caught you by surprise, huh?"

"Well . . . yeah. I thought you were going to fire me."

His smile faded and his eyebrows drew together. "Why would I fire you? You're one of the best employees Spencer's has. I'd clone you for every one of our stores if I could."

Warmth spread through her cheeks at his compliment. "Thanks. That's nice of you to say."

"It's the truth." He leaned back in his chair. "Want details before you say yes or no?"

"You don't honestly think I'm going to say no, do you?"

The corner of his mouth quirked. "Let me lay out what I expect of you before you make your decision. Your hours will increase. You're working thirty-two to forty now. Expect that to jump to closer to fifty. You'll be put on a set salary instead of paid by the hour, so no overtime for those extra hours. But I'm going to double what you're making now to compensate for the extra time you'll work."

Paige's mouth dropped open before she could stop it. *"Double?"*

Clay smiled. "Double. Beginning today if you accept the position. You'll also receive medical insurance, a pension plan, one personal day to take whenever you want to, two weeks paid vacation, and twelve paid sick days per year. But you'll also have a lot more work here in the office, like inputting sales and creating spreadsheets for the home office. There's a lot of paperwork in being a manager."

More work didn't bother her at all. The extra benefits would be wonderful, but doubling her salary meant she could save to buy her own house instead of renting the little one where she lived now. That's what she wanted more than anything. She laid a hand on her stomach, which tumbled with excitement.

"You okay?" Clay asked, glancing at her hand.

"Yeah. I'm . . . You just . . . Wow."

A grin spread over Clay's lips. "I'll take that as a yes."

"Of course it's a yes! I'd be crazy to turn down such a wonderful opportunity."

His grin widened. "Great. I have some errands to take care of this morning, then I promised Maysen I'd take her to Fort Worth this afternoon to look for furniture for the guest room. Once it's furnished, the house will be completely finished. Thank God."

Paige knew Clay and Maysen had been working on the remodel of their house for several months, doing a lot of the work themselves before hiring Coleman Construction to finish it and build a new garage. "I'm sure you're glad it's done and you don't have to smell sawdust anymore."

"You got that right." He reached into the jacket he'd hung over the back of his chair. "I had something made for you, in case you said yes."

Paige accepted the tissue-wrapped item from Clay. She unwrapped the tissue to see a new silver name tag that said "Paige Denslow" and "Manager" beneath her name in bold black letters. Tears sprang to her eyes as she ran her fingers over the letters. "Thank you, Clay."

He winked at her. "Okay, I know you work Tuesday through Saturday now, but your hours will vary from now on. We'll start your training first thing Monday morning. You'll still get Sundays off, but you'll probably work six days a week at first. After you get familiar with everything, you'll drop back to five days a week, probably after the first of the year."

"Any chance of hiring another clerk or two to work on the weekends when special events are in town? It gets pretty crazy in here, especially on Saturdays."

"We'll go over the budget for this store Monday. I have to look at the bottom line, but don't want to overwork the employees I have."

Paige nodded. That made sense to her. She understood the store had to make a profit.

"For now, do whatever you normally do on Saturdays and we'll figure out your duties Monday."

"Okay." Paige stood, the new name tag clutched in her hand. "Thank you, Clay."

"Don't thank me yet. You don't know how hard I'll work you."

Paige laughed, then left his office. Eight customers stood in line at Lesa's register. Paige jammed the name tag in her pants pocket and hurried to the second register to help. As quickly as she rang up two customers, three more walked in the front door. A glance out the window showed her ten of the twelve gas pumps were in use. Clay wouldn't be able to complain about today's receipts.

She finished sacking up a couple's purchase, bid them a good day, then turned her smile to the next customer in line. Her heart sped up when she saw Cort.

"Hi."

"Hi." He smiled. "Busy, I see."

"It's been crazy, that's for sure." A quick glance out the window showed her three vehicles remained at the pumps. "Lesa, why don't you take your break before it gets busy again?"

"I can help this gentleman if you want to take a break."

Paige pressed her lips together to keep from laughing. At twenty-two, Lesa didn't know how to be subtle. If she could eat Cort with her eyes, she'd be doing it right now. "That's okay. I rested while I talked to Clay."

"Oh." Her bright smile abruptly faded. "Are you sure?"

"I'm sure."

After giving Cort one more long look, Lesa stepped from behind the counter and headed toward the empty office they used as a break room.

Paige shook her head. "Sorry about that."

"I'm flattered she wanted to flirt with me." He set a twelve-pack of longnecks on the counter. "How about you? Are you going to flirt with me?"

"Nah. I don't want to give you a big head."

"Too late. I'm already hopeless."

She laughed when he flashed a devilish grin. "I believe you." She tapped the top of the beer. "Is this all for you?"

"Yeah. This is the brand Quade gave me last night, so I thought I'd restock his supply."

"We do have the best beer prices in town."

"I know." He leaned closer to her, as if to tell her a secret. "I checked."

She rang up his purchase on the cash register. "Everything okay at Quade's house?"

"It's great. He has a beautiful home."

"Quade's the best. He's like a big brother. A *protective* big brother."

She accepted his credit card, ran it through the scanner, and returned it to him. Now would be the perfect time to invite him to her house tomorrow for lunch.

Before she had the chance to do that, Cort gestured toward her pocket. "You're about to lose your name tag."

Paige pulled it from her pocket, ran her thumb over her name. She wanted to tell someone about her promotion. Cort could be the first. She turned the tag so he could read it. "I got a promotion."

Cort's eyes twinkled when he smiled. "Hey, that's great! Congratulations."

"Thanks. It was a complete shock."

"Your employer must think you can handle the job or he wouldn't have given it to you." He propped his forearms on top of the twelve-pack. "Do you plan to celebrate tonight?"

"I was thinking about tomorrow. How do you feel about an old-fashioned, tummy-filling meal of hamburgers, baked beans, and potato salad?"

His smile turned into a lazy grin. "I feel very good about that."

"Come to my house tomorrow. I'll fix it for lunch."

Cort shook his head. "You shouldn't have to cook for your own celebration. Quade and Eve left early this morning for Austin. He told me to make myself at home. How about if you come over tonight and I'll fix dinner for you?"

She liked that idea a lot. "Okay."

"How do you feel about pork loin?"

Her mouth watered at the sound of the word. "I love it."

"Great." He straightened, picked up the beer. "What time do you get off?"

"Five."

"How about six-thirty?"

"I'll be there."

She watched him walk out of the store and climb into what looked like Quade's pickup. Paige frowned. Even though Quade believed he could find good in everyone, she'd thought it strange for him to invite a stranger to stay at his home. It seemed even stranger to her that he would lend his pickup to Cort.

What's going on? Who are you really, Cort Brennaman?

Tonight would be a good chance for her to find out.

You let your dick rule you, Brennaman. That should've stopped in high school.

The mental admonishment that ran through Cort's brain when he'd left Spencer's didn't stop him from going to the grocery store and picking out the perfect pork loin roast to prepare for Paige tonight. Quade had shown him the well-stocked freezers and told him to help himself, but Cort didn't feel right taking any of Quade's food. He'd decided to buy what he would use for tonight's dinner.

He had borrowed Quade's nicest dishes, glassware, and linen napkins to set the table. A small vase of various flowers sat on the table between two tall white tapers in glass candleholders. He'd light the candles and dim the overhead lights as soon as he heard the doorbell ring.

A quick glance at his watch showed him Paige should be here any minute. He'd already opened the bottle of Chardonnay and put it back in the refrigerator to keep it cold. The pork roast, seasoned mashed potatoes, green beans, and yeast rolls sat in the oven to stay warm. A quick toss of the salad and he'd be ready to serve.

He wanted to do this for Paige, to give her a little celebration for her promotion.

Cort shook the small carafe of vinaigrette dressing he'd made and started to pour it on the salad when the doorbell rang. Setting it back on the island, he wiped his hands on a dish towel, jogged into the dining room to light the candles, and headed for the front door.

To say Paige looked amazing would be a vast understatement. Her blond hair fell in a riot of curls to her breasts. She wore a blouse of various shades of green and brown all mixed together that made her hazel eyes appear huge. Several gold chains in different lengths and designs hung down over the blouse's buttons. Brown slacks covered her legs, brown flats her feet.

"Wow."

She smiled. "Thank you."

Cort stood to the side so she could enter. "Come in."

She stepped over the threshold, giving him a close-up view of her ass as she walked past him. Round and tight with the right amount of fullness to fill a man's hands.

"Something smells wonderful."

Her comment snapped Cort out of his trance. He closed the front door, took her arm to lead her to the kitchen. "Roast pork loin with apple rosemary glaze. I hope you like it."

"If it tastes as good as it smells, I *know* I'll like it."

Cort placed his hands on Paige's waist and lifted her to one of the island's tall chairs. She gripped his shoulders before he had the chance to step back. This close to her, he could see the streaks of green and brown and gold in her eyes. She wore green-and-brown eye shadow; dark brown mascara thickened her lashes. She didn't wear lipstick, but some kind of gloss made her lips shiny. Kissable.

He involuntarily squeezed her waist before he released it. "Do you like Chardonnay?" he asked as he rounded the island, putting it between them. He ordered his cock to behave instead of trying to jump out of his briefs.

"Yes," she said, her voice a bit husky.

He glanced at her to see that flare of desire in her eyes again. Cort never took anything for granted when it came to a woman, but he strongly suspected his and Paige's evening would end up in his bed if he didn't stop it.

Dinner first. Then he'd see where the evening went.

"I set the wineglasses on the table. I'll get them and pour a glass for you before I toss the salad."

"Go ahead. I'll get the glasses."

Cort gave the salad a final toss as Paige came back into the kitchen. He'd already taken the wine from the refrigerator, so removed the loose cork and filled the glasses half full. He lifted his glass toward her. "To your new promotion."

"To my new promotion." Paige clinked her goblet against his, took a small sip. "Ooh, that's good."

"You can thank Quade. I pilfered this from his selection of wines. I'm not much of a wine expert, so didn't know what to buy."

"I'm no expert either, but I know what I like." She lifted her glass an inch. "I like this very much."

Cort grinned. "Then it's a good thing there are two bottles chilled."

"You don't really expect us to drink two bottles of wine, do you?"

He liked the teasing light in her eyes as she took another sip from her glass. "I never try to predict the future. How about if I serve dinner and we'll see where the evening goes?"

"I say that sounds perfect."

5

Cort prepared a plate for her, giving her about half the amount he put on his plate. She ate every bite and asked for seconds. His eyes shone with pleasure when she complimented him on how good everything tasted.

She suspected other things would taste just as good. Perhaps even better.

So many little things built up her desire over the evening. A brush of his hand, the way his gaze heated when it slipped to her breasts, the way he looked into her eyes when she spoke to him. She switched her attention from his eyes to his mouth and back to his eyes when he spoke. She imagined those well-shaped lips worshipping her body, those deep brown eyes staring into hers while he fucked her.

A sharp clutch in her pussy reminded her how long it had been since she'd had a hard cock filling it.

She had no doubt she and Cort would make love before the evening ended.

Cort tilted the wine bottle toward her glass. "More?"

"I'll split it with you."

He emptied the bottle into both their glasses. "I made a light vanilla custard for dessert, whenever you're ready for it."

"I'd like to wait a while, if you don't mind."

"I don't mind at all. This is *your* celebration, so you make the rules."

She sipped her wine to hide her smile. If she made the rules tonight, they would definitely end up in Cort's bed.

"It's cool enough this evening for a fire," Cort said. "Would you like me to build one in the fireplace?"

"That would be nice."

"Okay. I'll clear off the table, then we'll relax in the living room."

"I'll help you."

Working side by side, Paige helped Cort clear the table, put away the rest of the food, and load the dishes into the dishwasher. She carried their wineglasses into the living room and relaxed on the couch while he knelt before the large rock fireplace. His jeans pulled across his ass. She had plans for that amazing ass later . . . plans that included her fingernails digging into it.

For now, she would enjoy the wine and the fire and talking with Cort. If she could get him to talk about himself. Every time she'd steered the conversation in his direction so she could find out more about him, he'd steered it right back to her. She'd ended up telling him practically her entire life story, which would have bored him to sleep if he hadn't been so polite.

She'd never known a guy who didn't like to talk about himself.

Unless he had something to hide.

She studied his back while he arranged the wood and kindling. Emma had to have thoroughly researched Cort before she hired him. Quade wouldn't have let Cort drive his pickup, much less left him alone in the house, if he didn't think Cort could be trusted. Quade had all those patient files in his office.

He had them in a locked file cabinet, but a lock could be broken if someone wanted in the cabinet badly enough.

The fire caught, throwing a pale yellow light into the room. Paige turned off the one burning lamp so it wouldn't interfere with the fire's glow.

Cort stood, looked at the darkened lamp, then back at her. With the fire at his back, she couldn't read his expression, so didn't know if it pleased or angered him that she'd turned off the lamp.

He joined her on the couch, picked up his wineglass from the end table. "This is nice."

Paige relaxed. His comment had to mean he liked that the only light in the room came from the fire. "Yes, it is."

After taking a sip of his wine, he stretched his arm along the back of the couch behind her. Paige drew up her knees and shifted so she faced him. "I told you all about myself over dinner. Now it's your turn."

Cort stared into the fire while he took another sip of Chardonnay. "There's not much to tell. I'm the oldest of three kids. My sister and I get along great, my brother and I tolerate each other most of the time."

When he didn't say anything else, Paige prompted, "Are your parents still living?"

"Divorced and remarried to other people. My dad and stepmom live in Abilene, my mom and stepdad in Phoenix."

Another lapse in the conversation. Deciding she'd have to prompt him for every morsel, Paige opened her mouth to ask the next question. She closed it again when she heard the patter of running feet on the hardwood floors. She quickly set down her wineglass before Daisy jumped on the couch beside her.

"Hey, Daisy." Paige buried her hands in the Lab's scruff. She laughed as she tried to avoid the dog's kisses. "Where's your shadow?"

As if on cue, Cocoa ran into the room and plopped her front

paws on Cort's lap. He winced and shifted one paw from his groin to his thigh. "Easy on the family jewels, Cocoa."

Paige snickered. "Maybe she's curious."

"She can be curious with someone else."

Paige continued to pet Daisy, who now lay with her head on Paige's lap. "Quade usually boards his girls when he goes to Austin."

"He told me that, but I told him I don't mind taking care of them." He scratched behind Cocoa's ears, causing her eyes to close to half-mast. "You'd rather be here than in some dumb kennel, wouldn't you, Cocoa?"

The way he obviously liked the dog sent warmth all through Paige's body. Any man who loved animals had to have a good heart.

"I'm surprised they didn't beg for scraps while we were eating."

"They're well trained." He gave Cocoa one more scratch behind each ear. "Daisy, Cocoa, go lie down."

Both dogs immediately moved to the rug in front of the fireplace and flopped down on it. It surprised Paige how quickly they'd done as Cort ordered. "They really are well trained."

He stretched his arm behind her again. Paige picked up her wineglass, took a sip. "You were telling me about your parents before the dogs came in."

Cort shrugged one shoulder. "Not much to tell. I think we three kids turned out okay despite coming from a broken family."

"How did you end up in Garland if your folks live in Abilene and Phoenix? And why did you come to Lanville?"

Paige could sense the walls going up around Cort. "Paige, I don't like to talk about myself. I'm not that interesting."

"You are to me. I want to get to know you better."

"You know me now. My past doesn't matter."

Disappointment wrapped around her heart and squeezed. She understood someone wanting privacy. She understood someone having secrets he'd rather not share. But not telling her anything about his past didn't make sense to Paige unless he really did have something to hide.

She drained her wineglass, set it on the end table. "Dinner was wonderful, Cort. Thank you so much for inviting me over."

"That sounds like a good-bye."

"It is."

"But it's early. We haven't had dessert yet."

She looked directly into his eyes. "Cort, we met yesterday. I'm not asking you for any kind of long-term thing. I won't be sad if a relationship develops between us, but right now I just want to spend time with you. I have no problem telling you anything about me. I proved that at dinner. You obviously don't feel the same way."

Paige stood and headed for the kitchen to pick up her purse from the island. She reached for it when Cort grabbed her hand.

"Wait." Holding her hand, he turned her body toward him. "I don't want you to go."

"Then talk to me, Cort."

Releasing her hand, he cradled her face in his palms. "How about if we communicate another way?"

He slowly lowered his head, perhaps giving her time to say "no" or "stop." That's exactly what Paige should do. Curiosity about his kiss kept her silent.

His lips felt soft and warm against hers. A hint of wine on his breath made his taste more intoxicating. She laid her hands on his waist, needing more contact with him than simply their mouths.

He must have wanted the same as she for he soon wrapped his arms around her, pulled her against his body. Paige moaned at the sensation of his hardening cock against her mound. She slid her hands up his back to his shoulder blades. Rising on her tiptoes, she tilted her head and parted her lips for his tongue.

Cort didn't deepen the kiss, but kept it gentle, tender. He ran his tongue across her lips, yet didn't venture past the seam to the inside of her mouth. Paige finally took the lead, stroking her tongue over his lips before darting it into his mouth.

That must have been the signal Cort needed. He inhaled sharply through his nose, a growl came from deep in his throat. He slid one arm beneath her ass and lifted her. Paige automatically wrapped her legs around his hips.

"Tell me now if you don't want me," Cort whispered against her lips.

Instead of speaking, Paige tunneled her hands into his hair and kissed him again. She didn't stop kissing him, even when he started walking. He carried her down a hallway and through an open doorway. Darkness filled the room, but Paige didn't need to see. She only needed to feel.

He lowered them to the bed. Paige loosened her legs from around his hips, letting them fall apart to give him more room between them. She caught her breath when he pressed his hard cock against her clit.

Cort lifted his head, stared into her eyes. "I want to kiss you everywhere."

Paige's pussy clenched at the thought of Cort's lips, his tongue, on every part of her body . . . especially between her thighs. "Only if I can return the favor."

Cort had already wanted Paige more than he could remember ever wanting a woman. Her words sent that desire through the roof. He imagined her pink tongue circling the crown of his dick, darting into the slit to gather the pre-cum. She'd dig her fingernails into his ass and hold him so he couldn't get away from her.

Not that he'd be stupid enough to try and get away.

Cort kissed Paige once, twice, before he rose from the bed.

After turning on the lamp, he whipped his T-shirt over his head and dropped it on the floor.

Paige curled on her side, a pleased smile curling her lips. "Do you plan to take off everything?"

"Is that what you want?"

"Yes."

If she wanted to watch him strip, he'd let her. He looked into her eyes while he pulled off his boots and socks. He unfastened his belt and jeans, pushed them and his briefs down his legs, and stepped out of them. When he straightened, her gaze snapped to his hard cock. She moaned softly.

"See something you want?" he asked.

"Very much." She crooked her finger at him. "Come here."

As soon as Cort placed one knee on the bed, Paige leaned toward him and took his shaft in her mouth. He hissed at the intense pleasure. "No fair. I'm naked and you're still dressed."

She ran her tongue from the head to his balls and back again. "I think it's kinky for me to be dressed while you're naked."

She drew his cock back into her mouth. Cort slipped his hand beneath her hair to cup her nape. If she wanted to suck his dick, he certainly wouldn't argue with her. At least, not yet. While he loved oral sex and loved coming in a woman's mouth, he didn't want his first time with Paige to end that way.

He remembered she'd mentioned it being kinky for her to be dressed and him naked. He wondered exactly how "kinky" she liked sex to be. Glancing at the nightstand by the wall, he thought of his handcuffs in the top drawer. Not that he was into bondage and submission, but playing around could be fun.

First, he had to get her naked.

Holding her nape, he stepped back until his shaft slipped free of her mouth. "I want you naked, too. Get up on your knees."

She obeyed him after giving the head of his cock one more lick. She touched the top button on her blouse. Cort stopped her before she could unfasten it.

"Let me."

Paige lowered her arms to her sides. Cort reached for the top button, but stopped when he noticed all the chains hanging down her torso. "Uh, you'd better take off your jewelry. I don't want to break anything."

"They're all hooked together." She slid her hands beneath her hair, pulled them back out holding the single hook for the chains. "See?"

Cort took the piece of jewelry from her, carefully laid it on the nightstand before returning to her blouse. He unfastened it, one slow button at a time, and drew the cotton down her arms. Letting it fall to the bed behind her, he pushed aside her hair so he could kiss her neck. One finger gently tugged her bra strap off her shoulder while he nibbled on the soft skin beneath her ear.

"The hook is in the front."

He smiled at her raspy tone. "In a hurry?"

"Well, you're already naked . . ."

"That I am." He pulled back far enough to see her face. "I like naked."

"I like it, too."

He located her bra's hook, opened it, and palmed her breasts. The size of apples, they fit perfectly in his hands. Dark coral nipples jutted forward, as if searching for his mouth.

He couldn't resist tasting them.

Lifting her breasts, Cort latched on to one nipple, drew it into his mouth. He caressed the other tip with his thumb, keeping it as hard as the one he nibbled with his teeth. Paige arched her back and gripped his shoulders. Her warm breath flowed over his face as her breathing grew heavier. He pressed his fingertips against her chest to feel her heart pounding.

Wanting to give her even more pleasure, Cort released her breasts long enough to remove her bra and unfasten her pants. He took a nipple back in his mouth as he slid his hand inside her panties. His fingers passed over a bare mound and to the soft folds of her pussy.

So silky.

So creamy.

"You're wet for me."

"Mmmmm."

Cort kissed his way up her chest, her neck, to her mouth. "And your clit is swollen."

"Mmmmm."

Lust galloped through his body, but he couldn't resist teasing her. "Can't you talk?"

"No."

"Well, I guess sometimes talking isn't necessary." He slid his fingers farther into her panties until he reached the entrance to her channel. "Like now."

With one motion, he pushed two fingers inside her. Paige cried out and threw back her head. Contractions milked his fingers, proof of her climax.

He waited until she straightened her neck and looked into his eyes before he spoke. "That was fast."

Worry filled her eyes. She bit her bottom lip. "Too fast?"

"Hell, no. I loved it." He pumped his fingers a couple of times, and smiled when her eyes crossed. "Feel good?"

"Yes."

"Want more?"

"Yesssss."

"Lie back."

She did as he said, lifting her hips when he tugged on her pants. He slid them down her legs, stopping long enough to remove her shoes before he pushed her pants over her feet to land on his T-shirt. She lay diagonally on the bed, wearing nothing but a tiny pair of green panties the same color as her bra.

"You are so beautiful, Paige."

"Inside me, Cort. Now."

Cort shook his head. "Not yet." Gripping the waistband of her panties, he slowly pulled on it. "How about if I make you come again first?"

6

Paige couldn't think of one reason why she should say no to Cort's offer.

She enjoyed sex a lot, but rarely came more than twice. That didn't mean she couldn't still enjoy the touch of a man's hand, his kisses, his body pressed to hers. The closeness of lovemaking mattered more to her than orgasms, although she'd never complain about having those.

Cort climbed onto the bed. He hooked her legs behind her knees, drew them farther apart. Paige helped him by placing her feet on the bed and letting her knees fall open. His nostrils flared. Using his thumbs, he spread her cream all over her labia, paying extra attention to her clit. Each pass of his thumb over the nub sent a pleasant zing through her body.

"I like the way your eyes turn a different color when you're aroused." He rubbed her clit with one thumb, caressed the swollen folds with the other. "They look more green than hazel now."

A man had never commented on her eyes during sex. She

didn't know for sure if a man had ever *looked* at her eyes during sex. He usually focused on her body between her shoulders and her thighs.

Two fingers pressed inside her again. Paige's breath caught when Cort found and massaged her G-spot. He continued to caress her clit, giving her twice the sensation.

Good, but not good enough.

Paige cradled her breasts in her hands. Cort's gaze snapped to them and his nostrils flared again. She kneaded the firm mounds, dusted her fingertips over her nipples.

"Oh, yeah," he said hoarsely. "Touch yourself for me."

Paige twisted and tugged her nipples. She'd like to tell Cort to suck them again, but the things he did with his hands felt too good for her to ask him to stop.

She lifted her hips, silently asking Cort to give her more. He did, moving his fingers faster against her, inside her. Paige pinched her nipples harder, pulled on them with her thumbs and forefingers. Warmth flowed through her, a prelude to the pleasure she knew would soon follow.

She couldn't hold back her orgasm if she tried.

"Yes! Oh, *yessssss!*"

Paige bucked in time to the contractions deep inside her pussy. She began to wonder if they'd go on forever when the last one finally faded. She collapsed on the bed, struggling to remember how to breathe.

Movement of the mattress had Paige prying her eyes open. Cort leaned over her, propped on his hands and knees. "God, you're even more beautiful when you come."

His long, passionate kiss caused desire to flare once more. Paige wrapped her arms around his waist, tried to tug him down on her. He drew her arms away from him, positioned them next to her head and held her wrists.

Paige had never been into any kind of submission, but she had to admit a thrill shot through her at the feeling of helplessness from Cort holding her in place. She wondered what it would feel like to be handcuffed to the bed and completely at his mercy. Thinking about it made her moan.

Cort ended their kiss. "What are you thinking?"

Heat rushed to her cheeks. She couldn't tell him she'd been fantasizing about being handcuffed to the bed. "Who could think after such a strong climax?"

He flashed a wicked grin. "Liked it, huh?"

"Very much."

He nipped the tip of her chin. "Want another one?"

Paige burst out laughing. "Yeah, right."

A determined look crossed his face. "Is that a challenge?"

"Cort, I've had two orgasms. You haven't had any. It isn't right for you to think only of me. You need to come, too."

"Don't worry. I will definitely come. But right now . . ." He rose to his knees between her legs. "I want to please you."

Paige looked at his cock, so hard the skin appeared shiny. She couldn't help wondering if it hurt to be so hard. "Are you sure you're okay?"

Cort palmed his shaft, ran his hand from crown to base and back again. "I'm good. I'm enjoying the anticipation of being inside you."

Seeing him touch himself made her mouth water and her womb clench. Paige licked her lips. "You could be inside me right now."

"Soon."

Taking her hands, he pulled her to a sitting position. With his help, Paige moved until she lay in the middle of the bed with a pillow beneath her head. He took her hands, pushed them over her head, and wrapped her fingers around two of the thick posts that ran along the headboard.

"Hold on."

She didn't think her pussy could get any wetter. The soft command from Cort made cream dribble from her channel and flow between her buttocks. "I'm making a wet spot on the bed-spread."

The wicked grin turned up his lips again. "We're going to make a lot of wet spots before the night is over."

Paige almost cheered when Cort reached into one of the nightstand drawers and withdrew a condom packet. Finally, *finally*, he'd fuck her the way she longed for him to.

She clutched the posts when Cort lifted her legs. He held her calves, drew them apart, and stared at her cunt. He glanced at her face, then returned his gaze to her mound. Bracing her calves on one arm, he ran his other thumb from her clit through her slit, all the way to her anus. He circled the rosette with his thumb, causing Paige to moan again.

"You like me touching you here?" he asked, his voice sounding rough and rusty.

"Yes."

"You have an incredible ass." He squeezed one cheek, then the other. "So firm. I'll bet your asshole is really tight."

Paige jerked as her womb clenched again. She'd tried anal sex a couple of times and hadn't been impressed. She imagined it would be so hot with Cort.

"Do you want to fuck my ass, Cort?"

"Yeah." His voice came out even rougher than a few moments ago. "But I need inside your pussy first."

He held his cock against her slit, slowly moved it back and forth so it caressed her clit and feminine folds. After two strong orgasms, Paige thought her clit would be too sensitive to touch. Cort gently caressed her, as if he knew anything rough would be uncomfortable.

She'd had four lovers before Cort. None of them had tried so hard to make sex this good for her.

"Cort, please," she whispered. "Don't make me wait any longer."

After dragging the head of his cock over her labia once more, he positioned it at the entrance to her channel. One shift of his hips and he entered her.

He released her legs, wrapped his arms around her. Paige let go of the posts so she could hold him instead. She dragged her fingernails up and down his spine . . . not enough to hurt him, but enough to satisfy her craving to touch him.

She shifted her hips a bit to the side to get a more direct contact with her clit. Cort must have felt her movement for he slipped one hand beneath her ass and lifted to help her. The new position brushed her clit every time he pumped.

So very, very good.

That glorious warmth shot out to her fingers and toes and the top of her head before rushing back to her pussy. She dug her fingernails into Cort's ass as she felt his body lurch. He squeezed her tightly, pumped twice, then lay still on top of her.

Three orgasms. Wow.

She had no idea how much time passed—nor did she care—when Cort lifted his head from her shoulder. His damp hair stuck to his temples and forehead. She gently pushed it back from his face. "Are you okay?" she asked.

"Sure. Just don't expect me to walk anytime soon."

Paige giggled. "And here I thought you'd offer to get our dessert for us."

"You mean that wasn't dessert?"

"It was a . . . pre-dessert."

Cort grinned. "I wonder if Emma would put it on the menu at Café Crystal."

"You'd better not mention it to her. She might consider it."

He chuckled, then gave her a soft kiss. "That was amazing."

"Yes, it was."

"Do you want dessert in here, or do you want to eat it at the island?"

"The island is good."

"Okay." He kissed her again. "I think my legs might work well enough now for me to stand."

He groaned as he lifted to his elbows, which made Paige giggle again. Her giggle abruptly turned into a moan when Cort pulled out of her. His softening cock passed over sensitive tissue that hadn't been used in a long time. Well, except for an occasional vibrator.

She watched him pull on his jeans without bothering with underwear. "Do you want a T-shirt to wear?" he asked.

"Please."

He reached into the second drawer of the chest of drawers and drew out a navy T-shirt. "Last clean one. I'm going home tomorrow to pick up more clothes and stuff. Hey, do you want to go with me?"

Paige pulled the shirt over her head. "You have to buy me lunch."

"Works for me."

She picked up her panties from the floor. She could only imagine how she must look with her wild hair and smudged makeup. If nothing else, she had to pull a brush through her hair. "I'll meet you in the kitchen."

Cort whistled as he added the pieces of crispy shortbread to the sides of the two custard dishes. A dollop of whipped cream on top and they would be ready to eat.

He set them in front of two of the chairs at the island. He hadn't thought to ask Paige if she wanted something to drink, but prepared two small glasses of iced water anyway. When he turned to set the glasses next to the custard dishes, he saw her walk into the room. Lust hit him square in the chest, even though he'd come hard enough to see stars only moments ago.

She'd brushed her hair. It still hung to her breasts in curls, but the curls were tame now. She wore less makeup, so must have washed off some of it. Her nipples clearly showed through the soft cotton of his T-shirt. Her tanned, shapely legs seemed to go on forever.

He knew how good they felt wrapped around him and could hardly wait to feel them around him again.

She climbed onto the tall chair at the end. "This looks wonderful."

"Thanks. I hope you like it."

She waited until he sat next to her before picking up her spoon and digging into the custard. Cort watched her place the fluffy treat in her mouth. Her eyes slid closed and she moaned softly.

"Delicious." She opened her eyes and smiled at him. "Is there anything you don't know how to make?"

"Yeah, lots of things. But I like experimenting and trying new dishes. I got this recipe online today. I didn't think you'd want a heavy dessert after the big meal we had."

"This is perfect." She picked up one of the shortbread pieces and took a bite. "Did you make these, too?"

"No, I bought those. Although I have a great recipe for shortbread cookies. I make them every year at Christmas and give them to my family. My sister likes them so much, she almost hoards them. I give her an extra small box just for her that she doesn't have to share with her husband or son."

Her eyes turned soft and she gave him a tender smile. "Thank you."

Cort paused with his spoon halfway to his mouth. "For what?"

"For volunteering a tidbit about yourself."

It surprised Cort to realize he'd done that. It surprised him even more not to be upset about it. He rarely talked about himself, too afraid of letting something slip to damage his undercover work.

He gave a one-shouldered shrug in response to her comment and decided to change the subject. "So when do I get the old-fashioned, tummy-filling meal of hamburgers, baked beans, and potato salad?"

He could tell by the pleasure in her eyes that she liked his question, since it meant he wanted to see her again. "My new position at Spencer's means more hours. The only day I get off is Sunday, at least until I've finished my training. How about next Sunday?"

"Sounds good to me, but I won't know my work schedule until tomorrow."

Paige reached into her purse, withdrew a small notepad and pen. "Here's my cell number. Call me when you know your schedule."

He looked at her number, memorized it, then stuck the paper in his jeans pocket. "I can request next Sunday off. Being the new guy, I might not get it, but I can ask."

He watched her replace the notepad and pen in her purse. For the first time, he noticed the pager clipped to her purse's handle. "What's that for?" he asked, pointing to the pager.

"I'm on the volunteer fire department. The number of beeps that sound indicates what type of fire is burning. Two is a grass fire, three is a house fire, and so on."

"I think you're the first female firefighter I've ever met."

Paige grinned. "Impressed?"

"Very."

"Don't be. Luckily, there aren't many fires in Lanville, or serious accidents or illnesses where an ambulance is needed. The department has regular drills and practice fires to keep up our skills, but we rarely have to fight an actual fire." She plucked the last cookie from her custard. "Do you want to join?"

Cort almost automatically said no since he wouldn't be in Lanville that long, but stopped before he gave away his plans. "I'll think about it."

Paige scooped up the last bite of her custard. "This was delicious, Cort. Thank you."

"There's more in the fridge. Do you want another one?"

She laughed and laid one hand on her stomach. "I'd love it, but I don't have room."

Her hand on her stomach drew the T-shirt tighter across her breasts. As if they felt him watching, her nipples beaded. His cock responded, growing longer and thicker.

"I think I want a little more."

He moved the dishes to the other end of the island. Rising from his chair, he walked around Paige and swiveled her chair toward him. He lifted her and set her on the edge of the island.

She gave a squeal of surprise and grabbed his shoulders. "What are you doing?"

"I told you I want more. I didn't say anything about the 'more' being custard."

Slipping his hands beneath the shirt, he palmed her breasts as he covered her lips with his.

7

Cort loved nothing more than watching a woman's ass in a tight pair of jeans. That little side-to-side movement of her hips when she walked always made him hard. He loved squeezing firm cheeks, pulling them apart to caress and lick the tight rosette. He loved burying his dick deep inside a woman's ass, fucking her there until she cried out with her orgasm.

Other parts of a woman's body were also very nice . . . like the pair of breasts he now held. Round and full, they fit perfectly in his hands. Her nipples responded immediately, becoming bigger and harder with each pass of his thumbs.

He enjoyed touching them. He'd enjoy sucking them even more.

Clasping her upper arms, Cort gently guided Paige backward until she lay on the island with her legs dangling over the edge. He kissed the spot between her navel and the top of her panties. Moving up her body, he pushed up the shirt as he dropped kisses along the way. When he reached her breasts, he licked each tip, then blew on them.

"Cort." A soft sigh escaped her lips. "That feels good."

It felt good to him, too, but he wanted to do more. He'd touched her pussy when they'd made love, but hadn't tasted it. He planned to change that oversight right now.

Cort gave each nipple one more sharp suck, then he moved back down her body until he reached the waistband of her panties. He continued to drop kisses on her belly while he drew the piece of lingerie over her hips and down her legs. Tossing it in the general direction of her chair, he kissed his way to the inside of one thigh, switched to the other one. He stopped long enough to move Paige farther up the island until only her legs from the knees down hung over the side.

Looking into her eyes, he ran his hands all the way down to her ankles. He placed her feet on the island, pushed on her knees until she let them fall open. Only then did he lower his gaze to the sleek flesh between her thighs.

Her cream glistened on the puffy folds. He watched a single drop drift toward her anus. He caught it on his thumb before it reached its mark. Lifting his thumb to his mouth, he licked off the drop.

Paige whimpered.

One taste not nearly enough, Cort slid his hands beneath her ass, leaned over, and feasted.

The scent of her musk made his dick throb. He alternated between breathing in her scent and laving every part of her pussy. Wrapping his hands around her upper thighs, he reached in with his thumbs and pulled her labia apart. He sucked on her clit, circled it with his tongue. He licked down one side and up the other, circled her clit again, darted his tongue into her channel. Over and over, he repeated his actions, unable to get enough of her taste.

Paige played with her breasts the entire time he ate her cunt. He watched her knead them, push them together and up, tug on her nipples . . . completely lost in her pleasure.

Exactly what he wanted.

"God, Cort, I'm close."

He shoved two fingers in her pussy while he sucked her clit. Gathering the wetness that flowed between her cheeks, Cort thoroughly wet his thumb before pushing it into her ass. Paige moaned loudly and bucked her hips. Taking that as a sign she liked what he did, he fucked her pussy with his fingers, her ass with his thumb.

"Cort! Yes, just like that. Oh, *yessssssss!*"

The walls of her cunt and her anus clamped around his fingers and thumb. He pushed them as far inside her as he could reach to draw out her pleasure as long as possible. Paige arched her back so high, only her shoulders and ass touched the island.

Smaller contractions kept milking his fingers as she relaxed. He could see the pulse pounding in her throat. Her chest rose and fell rapidly with her heavy breathing. Although his dick cried out to fuck her *now*, he wanted to let her enjoy the sensations galloping through her body as long as possible.

Slowly, he pulled his fingers and thumb from her body. She whimpered again. "Did I hurt you?"

She released a bark of laughter. "Hardly."

"Good. Because I'm not anywhere near through with you."

Cort lifted her into his arms and headed for his bedroom. After placing her on the bed, he quickly shed his jeans, donned a condom, and joined her. Rolling her to her stomach, he placed his cock in the cleft between her buttocks and began rocking his hips.

He pushed her hair aside, nipped the back of her neck. "God, I want to fuck your ass."

She lifted her hips, which settled his shaft more firmly in the cleft. "Do it, Cort. Please."

"I don't have any lube."

"There's some in my purse."

Her comment stilled him. "What?"

"There's a small bottle in my purse."

"Why do you carry lube with you?"

She huffed out a breath. "Will you just go get it? I'm dying here."

Cort knew the feeling. He scrambled off the bed and hurried to the kitchen. Not daring to dig into a woman's purse, he grabbed it off the island and jogged back to his room.

The sight when he walked through the doorway made him freeze and his dick jerk.

Paige had removed her T-shirt. She'd positioned her knees right at the edge of the bed, spread wide. She rested her forehead on her folded arms. Her pose left her pussy completely exposed.

With a groan, Cort tossed the purse in the vicinity of Paige's hands before he speared her asshole with his tongue. Using his thumbs, he pulled her anus open so he could go deeper. He fucked her with his tongue for several seconds before he felt a bump on his hand. Reluctantly lifting his mouth away from her, he saw Paige holding a two-inch-tall bottle of lube.

Cort didn't waste any time in coating his cock with the clear gel, then squeezing a generous amount into Paige's ass. No matter how much he wanted to fuck her, he had to be sure she could take him. He eased two fingers into her ass to see if she had any reservations.

The way she pushed her hips toward him proved she wanted this as much as he did.

Cort replaced his fingers with his cock. He slowly pushed the head past the tight ring of muscle. Paige didn't utter any complaint, didn't flinch, so he withdrew and pushed in again. After each time he withdrew, he pushed in another inch until his balls rested against her pussy.

"God," he muttered.

So tight.

So hot.

Cort remained still, absorbing the pleasure of having his

dick inside Paige's ass, before he began to thrust. Careful not to hurt her, he pulled back until only the head remained inside her, then thrust forward again.

"You okay?" he asked.

"Mmmmm."

He chuckled at the same sound she'd made when he'd first slipped his hand into her panties. Taking it as the sign of enjoyment he knew it to be, he gently increased the speed of his movement until he steadily pumped into her.

"More," Paige breathed.

Gripping her hips, he plunged faster and deeper. Paige reached back with one hand and gripped his wrist, as if she needed an extra anchor. Worried her legs would start hurting, he nudged her forward, following her until she lay on her stomach with him on top of her. He grabbed a pillow, shoved it beneath her stomach, and started pumping again.

"Better?" he asked in her ear.

"Mmmmm."

Cort suspected that moan would quickly become his favorite sound since it signaled Paige's satisfaction. Sliding his hand between the pillow and her tummy, he lifted her a few inches to give him a better angle. She must have liked his new position for she groaned loud and long.

Her obvious enjoyment urged him to move even faster. Cort pounded his cock into her ass, climbing a little closer to the heavens with each thrust. He didn't want to reach the stars without Paige getting there before him.

When she dug her fingernails into his thigh, he couldn't stop the climax. Pleasure started at the base of his spine and surged through his body. It grabbed his balls before barreling up his dick to explode out the end.

Cort had enough brain cells left to remember to prop himself on his elbows so he wouldn't smash Paige. His arms shook with weakness, as did every part of his body. If he didn't know he needed to pull out of Paige, he would've been happy to close his eyes and sleep right there on top of her.

"Cort, could you move, please?"

"Yes. Absolutely. Give me a second."

The second turned into several moments, but he finally gathered enough strength to move away from her. The sight of her anus grabbing his softening cock as he pulled it out of her looked so sexy, he had no doubt he'd be ready for a round three soon.

He fell to his back on the bed, one arm over his eyes. Then again, he might not be ready until next week.

The mattress shifted, so he assumed Paige rose. He heard the bathroom door close. As soon as she finished, he'd go in there and get rid of the condom.

The toilet flushed, water ran in the sink, the bathroom door opened. The mattress shifted again, then warm lips touched his. Cort uncovered his eyes so he could tunnel his hand into Paige's mane of hair while he returned her kiss. He slipped his other arm around her waist, slid his hand down to clasp one firm butt cheek.

She gave him two more pecking kisses before she lifted her head and smiled. "Hi."

A wide smile spread across his lips. "Hi. How do you feel?"

"A little sore, a lot weak, and very good."

He swept his hand up and down her spine. "I'm sorry I came before you did."

"Cort, I've had four orgasms tonight. I *never* do that. You have no reason to be sorry."

"You sure you were satisfied?"

"Completely, positively satisfied."

"Good." He kissed her quickly. "My turn in the bathroom. You're staying the night, right?"

"I'd like that."

Cort found her beneath the covers when he returned to his

room. He shut the door in case Daisy or Cocoa explored through the night, turned off the lamp, and crawled beneath the covers with her. She cuddled next to him, her arm over his waist, her leg between both of his.

More comfortable than he ever remembered being after sex, he wrapped his arms around Paige, kissed the top of her head, and closed his eyes.

The puppy kept pinwheeling his little legs, trying to climb higher up Paige's chest to lick her face. She laughed in delight. The little black Lab had been the perfect gift from Cort. He'd told her he couldn't resist picking up the puppy from the animal shelter as soon as he looked into those big brown eyes.

Paige laughed again when the puppy barked. But instead of a normal yip, two beeps came from its mouth. Her laughter faded and she lifted the puppy to her face. The young animal beeped twice again before it began to fade away as consciousness seeped into her brain. She blinked to bring the room into focus. She lay half on her side, half on her stomach, with Cort's head resting on her shoulder blade and his hand on her ass.

Two beeps sounded again. Immediately awake, Paige pushed Cort away from her, threw back the covers, and scrambled from the bed.

"Whazup?" he asked, rubbing one eye.

"Two beeps. That's a grass fire. I have to go." She picked up her blouse from the floor, shoved her arms into the sleeves.

He sat up in bed, pushed his hair back from his face. "Can I fix you something to eat or drink to take with you?"

"Thanks, but I don't have time." She stuffed her bra into her purse, searched the floor for her panties. Not finding them, she decided she could go commando. She drew on her pants, slipped her feet into her shoes, and leaned over to give Cort a quick kiss. "Last night was great. Can't go to Garland with you. Bye."

"Hey, will I see you later?" he called as she ran out the room and down the hall.

"Don't know. Depends on the fire."

Once in her car, Paige called her captain to find out the location of the fire. Depending on the address, sometimes going straight to the fire instead of to the fire hall saved time. The locale ended up being only a few blocks outside the city limits. Paige disconnected the call, laid her cell phone on the passenger seat, and headed for the fire hall.

Paige accepted the cold bottle of water from Talia and gulped down half of it. While the firefighters had gotten the brush fire under control before it turned toward any homes, the heat and smoke quickly caused an almost unquenchable thirst. She'd drink a lot for the rest of the day, both to replenish her body's moisture that she'd sweated away, and to try and get the taste of smoke out of her mouth.

She took another gulp as her gaze traveled to Edward Riley, who spoke with one of her captains. A simple act of burning brush on the Rileys' property had gotten out of hand when the wind suddenly shifted. When Mr. Riley couldn't control the fire on his own, he'd called the fire department. If he'd delayed a few minutes longer, his home could've been destroyed.

Talia took a bottle of water for herself from the ice chest. "I feel sorry for Mr. Riley. You can see the guilt on his face from here."

"He has no reason to feel guilty. It isn't his fault the wind whipped up the way it did."

"I heard him telling Tate that his wife told him not to burn today, but he did it anyway."

"If we don't get some decent rain soon, a fire ban will probably be enforced."

"I wish it would. People shouldn't even think about burning

brush when it's so dry." Talia unscrewed the cap from her bottle, took a long drink. "Hey, did you hear about the robbery?"

Paige paused in the act of picking up her shovel. "What robbery?"

"One of the convenience stores in Glen Rose got hit Thursday night. The thieves broke into the safe and stole close to three thousand dollars."

"Who told you?"

"Lonnie."

If anyone would know the truth, it would be one of Lanville's deputies who also volunteered for the fire department. Paige picked up her shovel and headed for the brush truck. "That's close."

"Yeah. Lonnie said the robbery appeared to be just like all the ones in the Metroplex, so there's a good chance it's the same thieves."

"Thieves? More than one?"

Talia shrugged. "Maybe. Lonnie said it's impossible to tell, but he and Brad believe there have to be at least two committing the robberies."

Paige laid her shovel in the bed of the truck. "Surveillance cameras?"

"All disabled. These guys are pros."

Goose bumps broke out on Paige's skin at the thought of the robbers being so close to Lanville. Spencer's closed at ten at night and had an excellent security system, but it sounded as if a security system didn't matter to the thieves. From what she'd read about the Metroplex robberies, they seemed to be able to bypass anything.

She made a mental note to call Clay later today and make sure he'd heard about the robbery so close to Lanville. As the new manager of Spencer's, she wanted to be sure to do everything she could to protect her employer.

8

Paige collapsed in her recliner, leaned her head back, and closed her eyes. Today had been her third day as the manager of Spencer's and it had been insane. Clay had crammed so much information into her brain since Monday, it surprised her that she could form one coherent thought. He and Maysen left this afternoon for the Pacific Northwest and Paige had no idea how long they'd be gone. She'd be able to reach him via phone or text or e-mail, but it wouldn't be the same as having him right there at Spencer's to answer the questions that would arise.

She could do the job, she knew she could. She just wished she had a little more time with Clay for training.

Managing to pry open one eyelid, she peeked at the clock on the wall above the TV. Seven-thirty. Her stomach had been rumbling for the last forty-five minutes, yet she doubted if she could find any strength in her legs to carry her to the kitchen for something to eat.

The ringing of the doorbell made her groan. It couldn't be Talia or Lucia. They would simply come in without bothering to ring the doorbell or knock. That meant she had to get out of her chair and attempt to walk.

With another groan, Paige pushed herself out of the chair and shuffled to the door. She opened it to see Cort standing on her porch. He smiled. "Hi."

"Hi. What—"

"Take this." He held out a plastic grocery bag. "I have to get the Crock-Pot."

Frowning, she watched him jog the few steps to his motorcycle, reach inside the storage area, and lift out a silver slow cooker. She peeked inside the bag he'd handed her to see a package of spaghetti, one of garlic bread, and two covered plastic containers. "What is all this?" she asked once he joined her on the porch again.

"Supper." Without waiting for an invitation, he gave her a quick kiss as he walked past her. "Where's your kitchen?"

"That way," she said, pointing in the general direction.

Paige followed Cort to her small kitchen. He set the slow cooker on the cabinet next to a plug. From the items in the sack she still held, she assumed there must be some kind of pasta sauce in the appliance. "What's in that?"

"Spaghetti sauce. It's been cooking all day, so should be just about perfect by now." Taking the sack from her, he began removing the items. "Spaghetti, obviously. I'll need a pot to cook it. The garlic bread needs ten minutes in the oven. I brought a salad, too, because I didn't know if you had salad stuff here. I didn't bring any dressing since I wasn't sure what kind you like."

"I have a couple of different kinds in the refrigerator."

He smiled. "Perfect." He removed the last plastic container from the sack. "Peanut butter cake, still warm."

Her stomach rumbled again, even louder this time. Cort chuckled. "Good. You're hungry."

"Starving. I had snacks at work, but that's not the same as a real meal."

"That's for sure." He clapped his hands together once. "So, where's that pot? I'll start the spaghetti so we can eat."

She hadn't seen him since she left his bed Sunday morning. She'd assumed he would call her, but he hadn't. Perhaps he'd been busy getting settled in his new job, the same as she. Neither of them had mentioned seeing each other again when they made love.

"How did you know I'd be home?" she asked, reaching into a cabinet for the pot he requested.

"I called Spencer's to find out when you got off. Lesa told me when you left. I allowed you enough time to get home before I came."

"And how did you know where I live?"

"Emma told me." He placed the pot of water on the stove, turned on the burner. "You don't mind that she gave me your address, do you?"

"No, not at all." She smiled. "You brought food. How could I be mad?"

He ran one finger over her cheek in a sweet caress. "Good." He leaned toward her and she met him halfway for a soft kiss. "I brought more than food, if you're interested." He bobbed his eyebrows and gave her a wicked leer.

Paige laughed. "Now you have me curious."

"Supper first. Then I'll satisfy your curiosity."

Twenty minutes later, Paige sat across from Cort at the kitchen table. She'd snitched a piece of garlic bread as soon as it came out of the oven to stop her stomach from making noise. And because she loved garlic bread. She selected her second piece from the napkin-lined basket in the center of the table. "This is so good."

"That's a talent I don't have." He also selected a piece. "Making bread. I've tried all different kinds of recipes, but it never turns out as good as I'd like it to."

"My grandmother makes the most amazing yeast rolls." Paige rolled her eyes in pleasure at the thought of biting into the soft, buttery bread. "They are so delicious."

"Would she share her recipe?"

"I doubt it. She won't even give it to me. She said she'll leave it to me in her will. Which, as healthy as she is, means I won't get it for a long time. And that's fine with me. I'm not in any hurry to lose her."

Paige ate a bite of her spaghetti and rolled her eyes again. "Who cares if you can't make bread when you can create food like this? Cort, this is amazing."

He smiled. "Thanks. I'm glad you like it."

"Like it? I *love* it." She took another bite and moaned. "I want to hire you for my personal chef."

Laughter flashed through his eyes. "Think you can afford me?"

"I just got a raise. I'll match whatever Emma is paying you."

"You don't know what she's paying me."

"Doesn't matter. I'll match it. And . . ." She leaned closer to him. "I can give you benefits she can't."

Now she bobbed her eyebrows, which made Cort laugh. He speared a grape tomato in his salad. "Your offer is very tempting. How about if I keep my job and cook for you whenever you want me to? That way you won't have to pay me, but can tip me with those special benefits."

Paige grinned. She really liked the playful side of Cort. "Deal."

She'd taken a bite of her salad and another of the spaghetti before Cort spoke again. "I want one of those special benefits now."

Paige looked at him to see a devilish gleam in his eyes. "While we're eating?"

"Yeah." He motioned toward her polo shirt with his fork. "Take off your top."

She couldn't believe he'd ask her to do that. "You want me to sit here and eat without my shirt?"

"Yeah."

Paige didn't want to take off her top. She'd worn a plain bra today that supported her breasts nicely in the polo shirts she had to wear at Spencer's, but didn't qualify as pretty by anyone's definition. Vain, perhaps, but she and Cort had only been together once and she'd worn her nicest set of lingerie then. She wanted to be wearing something pretty beneath her clothes when she took them off.

His eyes narrowed. "Is there a problem?"

That tone—a little rough, a little edgy—sent a zing straight to her clit. And a little chill through her body. She didn't believe Cort would do anything she didn't want him to, yet she barely knew him. The anal sex on Sunday proved he liked things in the bedroom on the kinky side. She'd never been with a guy who wanted to fuck her ass the first time they had sex.

He openly stared at her breasts. Paige's nipples puckered. Deciding that he couldn't care less about which bra she wore, she pulled the shirt over her head and tossed it on one of the extra chairs.

"Nice," he said, still staring at her breasts. "The bra you wore on Sunday was hot, but there's something about a plain white one that makes me wonder what it's covering." He raised his gaze to her face. "Show me."

Not a question, but a command. Looking into his eyes, she reached behind her, unhooked the bra, and drew the straps down her arms. She tossed the piece of lingerie on top of her shirt.

Cort laid his napkin by his plate and rose. Paige glanced at his fly as he circled the table, noting the large bulge. She swallowed with the desire to slide his cock into her mouth, take his essence down her throat.

He dropped to his knees before her, took one nipple between his teeth, and bit gently. Paige gasped at the combination of pleasure and pain. He palmed her other breast, flicked the nipple with his thumb while he licked the one he'd bitten. Each swipe of his tongue sent another zing to her clit.

Taking gentle nips along the way, he moved up her neck until his lips covered hers. Her hunger for food disappeared, to be replaced by a stronger hunger for Cort. She grasped handfuls of his hair and returned his kiss.

"Bedroom?" he asked against her lips. "Or somewhere else?"

Her little house didn't have a lot of options like Quade's house. Draping herself over the table would be hot, if their supper didn't still cover it. "Bedroom."

Standing, she took his hand and led him to her room. She cringed at the basket of unfolded clothes on top of her dresser, then realized Cort probably wouldn't even notice it. She suspected he thought of nothing but getting her naked.

Which is exactly what she thought, too.

She stopped by the side of her bed and switched on a lamp. Before she could face him, he slipped his arms around her waist. "I've been anticipating this ever since you left my bed Sunday." He nuzzled behind her ear as he unfastened her pants. He slid his hands inside the opening, splayed them over her tummy. "I've thought about how free you were with me, how good you felt in my arms." One hand dipped into her panties. "I've thought about this shaved pussy and how wet it got for me."

Paige whimpered when he pushed two fingers into her channel while he tugged her pants and panties down to her thighs. He withdrew his fingers to spread her cream over her clit, then pushed them in again. He repeated his action over and over, massaging her clit longer each time.

"You gonna come for me, Paige?" he whispered in her ear. "I love it when you come."

The combination of his caressing and sexy voice drove her to an orgasm. Closing her eyes, she rested her head against his shoulder and bit her bottom lip to keep from crying out as pleasure flowed through her body. Little pulses continued to shoot through her, each one a bit weaker until they faded away.

"My God, you're an amazing woman." Cort turned her around, gently pushed on her shoulders until she sat on the bed. "I don't think I've ever known a woman as sexy as you."

His compliment sent warmth through her, almost as delicious as the orgasm she'd experienced.

Almost.

He knelt before her, removed her shoes, socks, pants, and panties. She didn't wait for his instruction, but moved to the middle of the bed. She sighed softly when he began to undress. He tugged off his T-shirt, exposing his smooth chest and the sexy trail of hair that ran down from his navel. He removed two condom packets from his back jeans pocket and placed them on the nightstand before he pushed the denim over his hips.

No underwear.

Paige propped up on one elbow so she had a good view of his body while he finished undressing. She waited until he climbed on the bed before she pushed on his chest to urge him to lie on his back. Once he did, she straddled his hips and settled over his cock.

Cort hissed. "Damn, your pussy is hot." Gripping her waist, he surged upward, which brushed his shaft over all the sensitive nerve endings. "Climb up here and sit on my face."

"Tempting, but I have another idea." She opened one of the packets, slid back on his thighs to give her room to roll on the condom. After she sheathed him, she impaled herself on his cock.

"Oh, yeah, you have good ideas." Once more holding her waist, he arched his hips to drive himself farther inside her. "*Really* good ideas."

She soon established a rhythm with him, lowering her hips as he raised his. Since she'd already experienced a toe-curling orgasm, she was content to do whatever she could so Cort could have one now.

He must have wanted more. He thumbed her clit while they fucked, apparently not satisfied to be the only one to come.

Her second climax hit only moments before Cort moaned loud and long. She could feel his cock jerking inside her as his cum filled the condom's reservoir. She waited until the sensation stopped, then lay on top of him.

He wrapped his arms around her, kissed the top of her head. "Yep, really good ideas."

Paige smiled against his chest. "You started this with telling me to take off my shirt."

"Yeah, I did."

The smug tone in his voice made her lift her head so she could see his face. "You could've let me finish my supper first."

"You could've left your shirt on."

"How could I have done that when you sounded all . . . alpha?"

Cort frowned. "What the hell is alpha?"

"Bossy. Confident. Used to getting whatever you want."

His eyebrows shot up. "Is that how I sounded?"

"Yeah."

"Did you like it?"

"Kinda."

His eyebrows lowered again and his eyes took on that slumberous, I-want-to-fuck-you look. "You into the whole Dom/sub thing?"

She drew a circle on his chest with one forefinger. "No."

"I hear a 'but' after that no."

"I'll admit I've thought about maybe, *possibly*, being tied to a bed."

His cock jerked inside her. "Yeah?"

He sounded entirely too eager at her confession. "I said I've *thought* about it, not that I want to do it."

"Well, if you decide you want to play . . ." He slid his hands down to grasp her ass. "I'll be happy to assist."

"What would make me happy now is more of your spaghetti."

"Do you have a microwave?"

"I'm a single woman and you have to ask that?"

He grinned. "Sorry. Lost my head for a minute."

Although very comfortable lying on top of him, Paige reluctantly moved. "Bathroom is to the right."

"Thanks." He gave her a quick kiss before he walked out of the room.

Paige donned a large T-shirt and faded jeans and headed back to the kitchen. Cort had finished everything on his plate, so she warmed hers first. The microwave dinged with her hot supper as he came into the room, once again dressed. He'd even put on his shoes, which Paige thought strange. He'd just have to take everything off again when they went to bed.

He picked up his empty plate from the table, carried it to the stove, and refilled it with spaghetti and sauce. Out of politeness, Paige knew she should've waited until his plate had warmed before she started eating again. Her growling stomach won over politeness. She leaned against the cabinet next to him and took a large bite of the pasta.

Cort smiled. "I'm glad you like my cooking."

"It's incredible. But I'm going to have to either taper back or add more time to my exercise routine. If I keep eating your wonderful food, I'll be the size of a barn in no time."

"I have lots of low-cal recipes, too. I'll prepare one of those next time. I'll bet you won't be able to tell the difference."

He threw out "next time" like it was a done deal they'd continue to have meals together. Paige didn't want to rush anything or make Cort think she expected more than he wanted to give now, but she couldn't help the thrill that ran through her at the thought of spending more time with him.

She suspected she could easily fall in love with him.

He warmed a couple more pieces of garlic bread before they sat at the table. Paige assumed he'd been busy with his new job and that's why she hadn't heard from him. "Is Emma keeping you hopping?"

"And then some. But I love it. I've already learned some shortcuts from her that I can incorporate into my cooking."

"What have you been doing after work for the last two days?"

He shot her a sharp look, one that froze her in the act of chewing her bite of bread. "Why do you ask that?"

Paige swallowed the bread that felt three times as big as the bite she'd taken. "This meal is wonderful and I'm glad you're here, but we had a very nice Sunday. I thought you might call me before now."

He looked down at his plate as he wrapped spaghetti around his fork. She didn't understand why a simple question would make him react the way he had.

A tingle niggled at the base of her neck, a warning that Cort wasn't being completely honest with her. "I would've called you, but you didn't give me your phone number."

"No, I guess I didn't." He looked at her and smiled. "Sorry about that."

His smile didn't reach his eyes. Nor did he offer his phone number. Paige opened her mouth, ready to ask him another question, when she heard her cell phone ringing from inside her purse in the living room. She couldn't ignore it since it might be Clay. "Excuse me."

Locating her purse where she'd dropped it on the couch, she

dug out her cell phone to see a local number she didn't recognize. "Hello?"

"Paige, it's Talia."

"Where are you? This isn't your number."

"I'm with Dylan at China Palace. I let my cell phone battery die again, so I'm using the restaurant's main phone line. I didn't want to wait to get home to call you. Lonnie and Brad and a couple more deputies are here, too. Lonnie told me there have been two more convenience store robberies—one in Walnut Springs and one in Tolar. The owner of the Tolar store surprised the burglars and was shot!"

Paige gasped. "Oh, no!"

"He's okay. The bullet went through his shoulder. He's in the hospital in Granbury."

"So how many thieves are there?"

"There were two. The owner didn't see their faces because they wore ski masks. I wanted to tell you so you can let Clay know, and to be careful at work."

"I'll call him right now. Thanks, Talia."

Paige got Clay's voice mail. Preferring to tell him what happened herself, she left a message for him to call her as soon as he could.

She returned to the kitchen to find Cort spooning the rest of the sauce into one of her plastic bowls. "Everything okay?" he asked.

"That was Talia. There have been two more convenience store robberies in nearby towns. The owner of the one in Tolar was shot."

She sensed a tenseness in Cort that she didn't understand. The churning in her stomach told her it was more than just concern for the man who had been shot.

He snapped the lid on the sauce, picked up the empty slow cooker. "Dishes are in the dishwasher. The cake's in the fridge.

I bought some of those throwaway containers, so you don't have to worry about returning anything to Quade."

Those comments sounded like ones someone would make who planned to leave. "Are you going?"

"Yeah. I have to be at Café Crystal at six tomorrow morning. Emma's giving me a lesson in making her giant cinnamon rolls. I don't want to wake you when I get up."

"I don't mind."

He smiled, and this time it looked genuine. "And I'd like nothing better than to wake up next to you, but not tonight. Maybe this weekend, okay?"

It appeared she didn't have a choice but to agree. She couldn't force him to stay. "Okay."

Paige followed him to the front door, where he gave her a soft kiss. "Bye."

She watched him walk to his motorcycle. He stashed the cooker in the storage bin, donned his jacket and helmet. After starting the bike, he waved before he took off.

Leaving her alone and confused and full of suspicion.

And still without his phone number.

9

Cort refilled Brad McGuire's and Lonnie Atwater's mugs with hot coffee. "I think Lanville is next." He topped off his own mug before setting the carafe on a hot pad at the side of the breakfast-nook table. "It fits their pattern of hitting the smaller stores first before they hit a major one." He tapped the map of Lanville spread on the table, directly over the spot of Spencer's location. "There are six other gas stations in Lanville, but they'll hit Spencer's. It's the biggest and busiest, so logically will have the most money in the safe. Plus there's a music festival in town this weekend, which means a lot more people spending money."

"I have my deputies making more drive-throughs, ever since I heard about the robbery in Glen Rose," Brad said before taking a sip of his coffee. "I don't have the manpower to post a deputy at every station. Besides, we don't know for sure they'll strike here. They may decide to move on and not hit anyone in our town."

"True, but I don't think so. I've been following them for months. They started in Missouri and have been moving southwest. Lanville is southwest of Tolar." Cort tapped the map again. "They'll hit here in the next few days. I'd bet my badge on it."

It terrified him to think of the robbers hitting Spencer's while Paige was there. They hit at night after the stores closed and Spencer's closed at ten, but a churning in his gut told him Paige could be in danger.

He cared too much about her to let anyone hurt her.

"I have a meeting scheduled with all my deputies this afternoon." Brad set his empty mug on the table. "I'll assign some extra patrols at night."

"I'll continue to keep watch, too," Cort said. "A new guy still trying to get the layout of the town shouldn't raise any suspicion."

"You think that big black Harley doesn't draw attention?" Lonnie asked. "Especially if you take the same route all the time?"

Lonnie had a good point. "Quade told me I could use his pickup any time. I'll alternate between the two."

With a plan finalized, Brad and Lonnie left Quade's house. Cort straightened up the kitchen, not wanting anything amiss when Quade brought Eve here tonight. He'd told Cort this morning Eve planned to spend the weekend with him. Cort offered to get a room at the motel or one of the B-and-Bs in town, but Quade told him not to be silly. It wasn't as if he and Eve planned to run around the house naked. Then he'd grinned and said at least not while he had a guest.

Still, Cort decided to be absent for a good part of the weekend. He would help Talia and Dylan with their yard sale tomorrow, and visit Spencer's two or three times to check on Paige. He planned to ask her to spend Sunday with him, doing whatever she wanted to do.

Cort wandered through the house, making sure he didn't leave a mess anywhere, while thinking about Paige. He'd met her one week ago today, yet it seemed as if he'd known her most of his life. He felt so comfortable with her, so at ease. That had never happened with a woman.

He hated that he hadn't been honest with her about his reason for being in Lanville, and the fact that he'd be leaving soon, but he had no choice. The fewer people who knew his true profession, the better.

"That one is two dollars," Talia said when Paige held up the small bowl. Paige nodded before marking the price on a piece of masking tape and applying the tape to the bottom of the bowl. She couldn't be here tomorrow to help her friend at the yard sale since she had to work at Spencer's, but she could price items until midnight if necessary.

Pricing items that Talia and Dylan hoped to sell didn't require Paige to concentrate, which left her mind free to think about Cort. She couldn't get over the way he'd tensed when she'd told him about the local robberies, or when he'd snapped at her when she'd asked him what he'd done on the two days prior to Wednesday. She knew he hadn't been working. Some subtle questions to Emma when she came into Spencer's let Paige know he'd gotten his schedule Monday morning and Emma hadn't seen him again until Thursday morning. She'd originally assigned him to work in the kitchen at The Inn Wednesday morning, but changed his schedule to Thursday to give him the cinnamon roll lesson.

Paige supposed he could've gone to Garland to get more of his personal items.

Or he could've been in other towns, committing robberies.

Paige rubbed her forehead. She had no reason to think Cort could be behind anything illegal, except for the knot in her stomach and the cold chill that kept racing up and down her spine.

He still hadn't told her about his past. Granted, they hadn't spent much time together, and most of the time they *had* spent together had been in bed. They'd communicated with their bodies, not their mouths.

He'd come into Spencer's both yesterday and today, but hadn't stayed long for he said he didn't want to interrupt her work. He'd called her last night from Café Crystal before she went to bed to say good night to her. Yet he still hadn't given her his phone number or made any plans to get together.

"Here," Talia said right before something cold bumped Paige's arm. She looked at her friend to see her holding two bottles of Dr Pepper. "Break time."

"We still have a ton of stuff to price."

"Stuff can wait. We need to talk."

Assuming Talia needed to confide in a friend, Paige set down her Sharpie and tape and followed Talia to the side of the garage, where she'd set up two folding chairs. "What's up?" Paige asked, unscrewing the cap on her drink.

"You tell me. I don't know where you've been tonight, but it hasn't been here."

Paige didn't realize she'd been that transparent. "I have a lot on my mind."

"Like?" Talia gently prompted.

"Like my new job. There's a ton of work that goes with being manager. Clay told me there would be, but I didn't know *how* much until I started doing it. The hot dog machine isn't working. The company promised they'd send a repairman out by nine tomorrow morning. I hope so. There's a music festival in town and we can't serve hot dogs. That's a lot of money to lose."

Talia's eyes narrowed. "That's not what you were thinking about. A new job wouldn't put that sad look in your eyes."

Her friend had always been much too observant. Perhaps confiding in Talia would make Paige feel better. "I was thinking about Cort."

"Now, why doesn't that surprise me?" Talia asked, then grinned. Her grin faded when Paige didn't return it. "What's wrong?"

"He won't talk to me. I know he has two siblings and used to live in Garland, but that's it. We've made love twice, but I still know next to nothing about him."

"Paige, you only met him a week ago. You gotta give the guy more time to open up. Men are horrible about sharing their feelings. I've had lots of experience with that problem with Dylan."

"Yeah, but don't guys love to talk about themselves? Shouldn't he have told me *something* about his life before he moved here? For all I know, he could be the one robbing the convenience stores."

Talia's eyebrows shot up. "You're kidding, right?"

"I don't know if I am or not."

"You don't honestly think Cort could be one of the robbers."

"The timeline fits. He shows up in Lanville the day after the Glen Rose store is hit. Then he goes missing on Monday and Tuesday, which was when the stores in Walnut Springs and Tolar were hit. Maybe he's using Lanville as a base to hit the stores in all the surrounding towns. Maybe he's planning a bigger hit." Paige's eyes widened and her breath hitched. "Like Spencer's."

"Okay, stop it right now, Paige Denslow. Just because Cort hasn't told you the name of his childhood pet doesn't mean he's hiding a life of crime from you. You can't accuse him of something so horrible without proof." She reached over and squeezed Paige's arm. "Talk to him. Don't give up until he talks back to you. I had to almost pry the information out of Dylan about his past, but I was determined not to give up until he realized he's nothing like his abusive father and would never hurt me." She squeezed Paige's arm again. "Do you love him?"

"I care about him a lot. I think that caring could turn into love if we had more time together. He's charming and witty and amazing in bed."

Talia grinned again. "That's always a plus."

"He hasn't even given me his phone number. Doesn't that prove he has something to hide?"

"No, it proves he forgot. The next time you see him, shove your phone in his hand and demand he enter his number in your contacts list."

"And if he won't?"

"Then he isn't worth your time," Talia said, her voice softening. "Don't give your heart to a man who doesn't want it."

It worried Paige to realize she may have already done exactly that.

Cort casually strolled to the back of Spencer's to check the security cameras and lights on the outside of the building. The lights didn't burn during the daytime, but he'd driven along the narrow dirt road behind Spencer's at night and they lit up the entire area brighter than the sun at noon.

A good deterrent to thieves. Except some of the other stores they'd hit also had security cameras and lights, which were somehow disabled long enough for the robbers to get in and out of the stores without any detection.

His stomach churned and tumbled with anxiety. He knew the robbers would hit Spencer's, if not tonight then tomorrow night. The three-day music festival in town provided plenty of cover for strangers to blend in and meant lots of extra cash for all the businesses. Cort assumed the owner deposited the day's earnings every day, but since the two banks in town closed at noon on Saturdays, he would have to keep any income in Spencer's—presumably in a safe—until Monday morning.

He wanted to tell Paige his identity and why he'd come to Lanville. Yet if he did that and made her suspicious of every stranger who entered Spencer's, she could accidentally tip off the robbers should they decide to enter during the day to check the layout. Even though they'd previously hit stores at night, they might decide to go ahead and hit Spencer's then. And at gunpoint. He couldn't take the chance of anyone getting hurt.

A vacant house sat on a tree-covered lot right across the street from Spencer's. He could hide there tonight and watch the store after his shift ended at Café Crystal.

For now, he needed to see Paige.

At least a dozen people wandered the aisles of Spencer's, selecting chips and drinks and sandwiches or hot dogs. Paige stood behind one of the cash registers, Lesa behind another, and an older woman he hadn't met stood behind the third. They all had at least three people in line to pay.

Cort stood to the side, out of the way, and watched Paige handle her customers. She smiled and greeted each one warmly. One good-looking guy openly flirted with her, which raised the hair on the back of Cort's neck and had him clenching his fists. No other man had the right to flirt with Paige.

He heard the guy say something about seeing her later at the music festival, to which Paige replied that she had to close the store tonight, so wouldn't make it to the festival. The guy gave her a you-don't-know-what-you're-missing look before he sauntered away.

Cort wanted to punch him, the conceited ass.

He grabbed a bottle of Pepsi from one of the refrigerated sections and got in line at Paige's register. She glanced at him while waiting on her customer. A pleased smile spread over her lips, a much bigger one than she'd given the ass. Then it quickly faded and doubt filled her eyes, leaving him to wonder what happened.

"Hey," he said once he reached the front of the line.

"Hey," she returned, not nearly as friendly as he expected.

"Is something wrong?"

She didn't speak for several seconds, then shook her head. "Just tired. It's been really busy."

"I noticed. Can you take a short break?"

She looked around the store—he assumed to check how many customers remained—then nodded. "Lesa, Dolores, I'll be back in a couple of minutes."

"Okay, boss," Lesa said.

She led him away from the checkout counter and toward the back, where he assumed the offices were located. She stopped in front of a door marked PRIVATE, crossed her arms over her stomach. "What's up?"

"I just wanted to say hi and ask when you get off tonight."

"I have to close, so I won't get out of here until close to midnight."

He didn't like the sound of that at all. "You'll be here alone?"

Her eyes narrowed. "Why are you asking?"

"I don't like the idea of you being here all alone that late at night."

"I've closed lots of times. I have Lonnie's number programmed into my phone. He's one of the deputies and on the fire department with me. If I have any trouble at all, he'll be here in a flash."

Naturally she would describe Lonnie's position for she had no idea Cort already knew him. It relieved Cort to know Lonnie would respond quickly, yet he also wanted Paige to call him. He hadn't purposely neglected to give her his phone number, but kept forgetting to do so. He would rectify that right now. "Do you have your cell with you?"

"Yes."

He held out his hand, palm up. Paige tugged it from her front pocket and laid it on his palm. Cort quickly located her contacts, added his name and number to them. "Call me if you feel uncomfortable about anything, okay?"

She replaced her phone in her pocket, crossed her arms over her stomach again. Cort recognized the action as putting distance between them. "Are you sure something isn't wrong?"

She looked at the floor for a moment before looking back at his face. "Why did it take you a week to give me your phone number?"

"It wasn't on purpose, Paige. I just forgot."

When she looked away again, he placed his finger beneath her chin and turned her face toward him so she'd meet his gaze. He needed to tell her the truth and trust that she wouldn't panic if someone suspicious entered the store. Her safety meant everything to him. "Paige, there's something I—"

Lesa stuck her head around the corner. "Paige, it's getting really busy again."

"Be right there." Once Lesa left, Paige took Cort's hand from beneath her chin and squeezed it. "I have to go."

"I can come by after my shift and keep you company. I get off at ten-thirty."

Her pleased smile made warmth spread through him. "I'd like that."

"Then I'll see you later."

The churning and tumbling in his stomach came back with a vengeance, even though he'd made arrangements to be with her after Spencer's closed. Something would happen tonight. He had no doubt about it.

10

Cort glanced at his cell phone on the raised ledge above his work station. 9:46. Only fourteen more minutes until Café Crystal officially closed. Diners still lingered in the restaurant, but they would soon finish their meals and leave. He'd already started his cleanup routine, so should be finished and out of here in an hour.

"How're you doing?" Emma asked from behind him.

He smiled at her over his shoulder. "Great. Almost finished."

"Not quite. Shara wasn't feeling well and I sent her home. She usually helps me with the Sunday brunch advance preparation. I need you to stay a while longer and take her place. Okay?"

The words "I can't" formed in his mouth, but Cort didn't utter them. As far as Emma knew, this was his only job and he couldn't do anything to blow it. "Sure. No problem."

Once Emma walked away, Cort blew out a heavy breath. Damn it. He should be on his way to Spencer's in fourteen minutes, not in the middle of making cinnamon rolls or chopping vegetables for omelets.

He picked up his cell to call Paige.

Paige rolled her neck to relieve some of the tightness. She'd been inputting on the computer for almost two hours, and her neck and shoulders screamed at her. Normally, she could've done a lot of the weekly paperwork today, but she'd had to work in the store since they had so many customers. She could either tough it out and finish everything in another hour or so, or come back tomorrow on her only day off and work.

She opted for toughing it out.

She picked up her cup of Dr Pepper, only to discover nothing left in it but a few ice cubes. Another shot of caffeine would help her get to the end. She started to rise from the desk when her cell phone rang. A quick glance at the display showed her Cort's name.

Her heartbeat sped up at the sight of his name. She'd been thrilled when he'd entered his phone number in her contacts list. She took that to mean he had nothing to hide from her.

She pressed the button to accept the call. "Are you on your way here?"

"I wish. I'm helping Emma with tomorrow's brunch preparations, so I'll be later than I thought. Everything okay there?"

"Everything's fine. I'm trying to get all the paperwork done so I don't have to come in tomorrow."

"Do you have plans for tomorrow?"

"Nothing specific. I just don't want to see the inside of Spencer's."

Cort chuckled. "I can understand that. So, since you aren't busy, how about if we go to a movie and out to dinner in Fort Worth?"

That sounded wonderful. "I'd like that."

"Is there a movie playing you want to see?"

"There are a couple I wouldn't mind—"

Paige stopped when the lights went out. Her contentment at talking to Cort disappeared in a flash, to be replaced by fear. "Cort," she whispered, "the lights just went out."

"Get out of there, Paige," he ordered in a stern tone. "Right now."

It could simply be a power outage, but she didn't think so. Cort's demand to leave the store sounded like a good idea.

"Stay on the phone with me," he said.

"No problem there." She reached for the handle of the bottom desk drawer where she kept her purse, but froze when she heard the warning tone that signaled someone opened the back door. "Someone's coming in the back door."

"Shit," Cort muttered. "Okay, Paige, listen to me. Are you listening?"

"Yes," she said in a small voice. She'd never been so frightened in her life.

"Where are you?"

"In the office."

"Is that where the safe is?"

"Yes."

"Then that's where they're heading. Is there a place you can hide?"

"I can go in the restroom and lock the door."

"Good. Do that. Keep your phone with you. I'm on my way."

"Shouldn't I call the sheriff?"

"I'll take care of that. You hide. Now!"

Voices outside the office door prompted her to follow Cort's advice. Making as little noise as possible, she rose from her chair and hurried into the bathroom, locking the door behind her.

She heard two distinct male voices in the office, but that didn't mean there couldn't be more than two out there.

Paige slowly turned the lock on the doorknob until she could push down on the lever and open the door a crack. She saw a man dressed in dark clothes with a ski mask over his face. He held a penlight while he looked behind pictures on the walls and behind bookcases.

"Hey." Another guy, also dressed in dark clothes and wearing a mask, stepped out of the supply closet. "It's in here."

He'd found the safe.

These guys would crack that safe and be out of here with the money before the sheriff or Cort could get here. Paige couldn't let that happen.

Once the second robber stepped into the closet, Paige hurried from the restroom, slammed the supply closet door closed, and jammed one of the metal armchairs beneath the doorknob to keep them from getting out. Grabbing her keys from the top of the desk, she hurried from the office while the robbers kicked at the door and yelled some inventive curse words. After locking the office deadbolt, she ran to the front of the store. Three police cars pulled up as she pushed open the entrance door and ran outside.

Cort's motorcycle screeched to a halt no more than three yards from her. He barely had time to throw one leg over the seat to stand when she jumped into his arms. Now that Cort held her, the adrenaline rushing through her body made her tremble.

"I've got you." He stroked one hand down her hair. "You're safe. I've got you."

Lonnie walked over to them, looking official in his uniform and Kevlar vest. "Are they still in the store?"

Paige nodded. "I locked them in the supply closet in the office." She held up a key on her ring. "That's the office key."

Lonnie looked at the deputies behind him. "Let's go."

"Wait a minute." Cort held her upper arms. "You locked them in a *closet?*"

"That's where the safe is. When I saw them go inside, I—"

"What do you mean, you saw them go inside?"

"I peeked out from the restroom. I know there are at least two. There might be more. They made a lot of noise kicking at the door to get out."

A thundercloud passed over Cort's face before he shook his head and chuckled. "I don't know whether to be proud or furious."

"I vote for proud."

He pulled her back into his arms and Paige went willingly. She heard the door open behind her and turned her head to see two deputies leading each handcuffed man from the store. Now that the robbers no longer wore ski masks, Paige immediately recognized one of them.

"He's the hot dog machine repairman! He was in the store this morning."

"That's a great cover," Lonnie said. "He could come in and basically be ignored while he checks out the store before they hit it."

"He may have been in the store before today," Cort added, "and disabled the machine so he'd have to come back and 'fix' it."

"That's possible," Paige said. "I don't wait on every customer and don't remember most of the ones I help since they're in and out as they drive through town."

Lonnie handed Paige her ring of keys, then looked at Cort. "Guess this wraps up your case, Cort."

"I guess so."

"Thanks for your help." Lonnie touched the bill of his hat. "Both of you."

Paige looked back at Cort as the deputy returned to his car, confused by what Lonnie had said. "Your *case?* What does that mean?"

He inhaled deeply and blew it out slowly. "We need to talk. May I follow you home?"

Whatever he had to say to her, Paige knew she wouldn't like it. Not liking it didn't mean she wouldn't listen. She nodded.

Cort looked around the parking area. "Where's your car?"

"In the garage. Dylan changed the oil for me today, so I left it there." She wrapped her arms around herself. "If I'd moved it out to the parking lot, maybe the robbers would've realized someone was still in the store and not hit it."

"Then we wouldn't have caught them and they wouldn't be on their way to jail, where they belong."

"I guess that's true." She hitched her thumb over her shoulder at the store. "I'll get my purse and meet you at my house."

Cort dreaded the conversation with Paige. He didn't want to leave her. They'd known each other only eight days, but he knew in his heart he'd never in his life feel as close to another woman as he did her.

She pulled beneath her carport barely a minute after he'd arrived at her house. He silently followed her into her living room. She stopped in the middle of the room, crossed her arms beneath her breasts. The blank expression on her face didn't give him any hint as to her thoughts. "You're a cop, aren't you."

She didn't ask a question, but stated a fact. Cort took off his jacket, laid it over the back of the recliner. "Yeah. I'm an undercover detective for the Dallas Police Department."

"And you didn't tell me this . . . why?"

"I couldn't. Going undercover means exactly that. No one but Brad and a couple of his deputies knew my real reason for being in Lanville."

"Quade knew, didn't he?"

"Quade *suspected* because Brad told him an undercover cop would be coming to Lanville on the trail of the robbers. When we got to his house and he asked me if I was the cop reporting to Brad, I couldn't lie to him."

"But you could lie to *me,* the woman you were fucking."

Cort winced at her bluntness. He took a step closer to her. "We *made love,* Paige. There's a huge difference."

She waved a hand in the air, as if to erase his words. "Whatever you call it, it means the same thing. It was okay to get me naked, but not okay to tell me the truth." Her eyes narrowed and anger darkened her expression. "Well, you know what, Cort? It's *not* okay, not by a long shot."

He reached out to touch her face. She jerked her head to the side so he couldn't. He let his arm fall back to his side.

She blinked rapidly several times. It broke Cort's heart to know she might be fighting back tears. "I'm sorry if I hurt you. I never meant to do that."

"Yeah, well, shit happens. That's life."

Cort shifted from foot to foot, unsure what to say. He couldn't leave without telling her of his feelings. "I care about you, Paige."

She released a humorless laugh. "You're slipping, Cort. You were supposed to say that to get me into bed. But you didn't need to use any lines, did you? I started falling for you the moment I saw you putting gas into your motorcycle at Spencer's."

He had to touch her, to hold her. He reached for her again, but she batted away his hands. "No! Don't touch me. I want you to leave. Now."

Cort didn't want to leave, but Paige obviously wanted nothing to do with him. He couldn't blame her for that, not after he'd hurt her. He picked up his jacket and headed for the front door. After grasping the knob, he looked at her over his shoulder.

"I do care about you, Paige. Please remember that."

Cort walked out of her house. He'd helped capture the thieves, but that didn't cure the empty feeling inside him.

11

Eleven Days Later

Paige removed the two pumpkin pies from the oven and set them on hot pads on the counter. Ever since her grandmother had shared her pie-crust recipe, Paige's pies had turned out perfect. She'd become the official pie maker for all the family functions. She had to be at her parents' house early tomorrow morning to help with the Thanksgiving preparations, so she'd taken off from Spencer's this afternoon to bake pies.

They looked and smelled wonderful. Paige would wait until one of the pies cooled a bit before she cut a sliver from it. She couldn't possibly take anything to the meal that didn't taste good, so had to test the pie first. She grinned, already anticipating the way her brothers would tease her about the same mouse getting into her pies every time.

Her doorbell rang. Expecting the books she'd ordered to be delivered today, she hurried to the door and threw it open. Her automatic greeting for the man in brown died on her lips when she saw Cort.

He gave her an uncertain smile, as if she might not welcome him. "Hi."

Surprise stole her ability to speak. She hadn't expected to ever see him again. Although her heart felt as if it had broken into a million little pieces, she'd accepted the fact that she had to go on with her life without Cort. And now he stood on her porch, looking so handsome and making her long for him all over again.

"What are you doing here?"

"I need to talk to you. May I come in?"

Paige hesitated, not wanting to invite more heartache. Curious at what he wanted to talk to her about, she opened the door wider so he could enter. Small snowflakes dusted the shoulders of his leather jacket. The meteorologists had predicted snow flurries today. It appeared they'd gotten the forecast right.

"Something smells good," Cort said after removing his jacket. He draped it over the back of the recliner, the same thing he'd done on the few times he'd been in her house.

"Pumpkin pies for Thanksgiving dinner tomorrow."

Paige stared at him while desire curled low in her stomach. He'd hurt her, but that didn't destroy the feelings she still carried in her heart. She'd longed for him during the dark nights . . . longed to feel his arms around her, his lips on hers, his cock pumping into her pussy.

She'd missed everything about him.

He wore a long-sleeved gray henley, black jeans, and black boots. His hair dipped over his forehead and ears. She didn't think he'd ever looked so edible.

Don't get too excited about his visit. You don't know why he's here.

"Why are you here, Cort?"

"I would've been here sooner, but I had some details to take care of before I could officially move to Lanville."

Paige blinked, certain she hadn't heard him correctly. "What?"

He smiled. "I got my job back at Café Crystal."

That didn't make any sense. "But you're a cop. Will you be happy working as a chef?"

"Yeah, I'll be very happy working as a chef. I love to cook. But I'll also be a cop. Brad agreed to take me on as a part-time deputy. I'll fill in when other deputies are out sick, or on vacation, or in court."

She didn't want to get too excited, but she couldn't help the pleasure that whooshed through her body. "You're really moving here? For good?"

"I'm really moving here, if a certain beautiful blonde will have me."

Happier than she could ever remember feeling, Paige threw her arms around his neck and kissed him. Cort wrapped his arms around her, held her tightly to his body, as he returned her kiss.

Paige had one question when the kiss ended. "When?"

"Now. Quade told me I could stay in his guest room again until I find a place to live. Talia's house was rented, so I have to house hunt."

Oh, no. Him living with Quade wouldn't do at all. "You're kidding, right? You honestly don't think you're going to stay anywhere else but with me, do you?"

"I didn't want to assume anything, Paige. I know I hurt you by not being honest with you. I figure we need time to get to know each other before we do something as serious as live together."

"There's no better way to get to know each other than by living together. If you hog the covers or leave the toilet seat up, I'll throw you out."

He chuckled. "That's fair."

He kissed her, sweetly. He hadn't said the words, but Paige could feel his love in his kiss. She didn't feel right sharing her blossoming feelings for him yet. She agreed that they needed time to get to know each other. Confessions of love could come later.

"You'll go with me to my family's Thanksgiving meal tomorrow," she said firmly. "Unless you already have plans with your family."

"I celebrate the Friday after Thanksgiving with my brother, sister, dad, and stepmom. That way, my sister can spend the holiday with her husband's family. But, Paige, I don't want to interfere with your family's dinner."

"I want everyone to meet you. That's not interfering."

"Then you have to come with me on Friday and meet some of *my* family."

"Deal."

He ran his hands up and down her upper arms. "Any chance of getting a taste of your pumpkin pie before tomorrow?"

She loved the humor shining in his eyes. "Maybe. I might be willing to let you taste it after we make love."

A slow smile turned up his lips. "Is that a proposition?"

"Most definitely."

"In that case . . ." Cort reached into his jacket pocket, brought out a pair of handcuffs. "I thought we might play a little."

A thrill coursed through Paige's body at the sight of the shiny cuffs. "Then let's not waste any time." She took off for her bedroom with Cort right behind her.

Flash

1

Kirk Wilcox tugged his heavy work gloves back in place to get a better grip for another stack of two-by-fours. His twin, Kory, worked beside him, as did two of Coleman Construction's laborers. He and the other men worked as quickly as possible, hoping to finish the outside work before the cold front blew in later this afternoon.

Even though the calendar said December 5, Kirk knew the cold wouldn't last but a few days. Texas weather in the winter often resembled a roller coaster with below-freezing temperatures for a day or two and then highs in the seventies with lots of sunshine.

He preferred the cold over the hot nineties and one hundreds of summer. Kirk liked nothing better than to take off a few days from working at his father's lumberyard–hardware store and head for the ski slopes in New Mexico. He usually went alone because Kory hated cold weather. Kory would always head for the beach while Kirk headed for the snow.

Going alone didn't bother Kirk. It gave him the chance to get away from small-town life and meet other people.

Preferably other men.

"Stack that next batch here," Marcus Holt said, pointing to a spot next to the new house foundation.

The foreman turned as Kirk approached, giving Kirk a nice view of Marcus's ass below the denim jacket he wore. He knew Marcus dearly loved his wife, Rayna, and they expected a baby in a few months. That didn't stop Kirk from admiring the very handsome man.

Not that admiring *any* man in Lanville did him any good.

Kirk hadn't worked up the courage to "come out of the closet" in his hometown, which meant he traveled to the Dallas–Fort Worth Metroplex to find lovers. He hadn't even told his twin, and he and Kory shared everything. But it worried Kirk about how his friends and family would react to the news that he was gay.

His mom would understand. Mothers usually accepted and loved their kids no matter what. His father, not so much. A big, barrel-chested man, Henry "Hank" Wilcox had always pounded into his sons about playing "man" sports like football or baseball. None of that froufrou gymnastics or skating stuff. Those sports weren't for "real" men.

Kirk figured he'd lose his father and his job if he admitted the truth about his sexual preference. And maybe his brother.

God, it would kill him to lose Kory.

Griff Coleman walked up to Marcus, clipboard in hand. "How's it going?"

"Good," Marcus said. "This is the last delivery of two-by-fours today." He smiled toward Kirk. "We can always depend on Wilcox Lumber to be on time."

"My dad won't do anything to screw up his best customer," Kirk said, flashing a grin toward Griff.

"And Coleman Construction appreciates that." He flipped a page on his clipboard. "Kirk, do you know if the kitchen sinks we ordered have come in?"

"They're due today. I can check on them as soon as I get back to the store."

"I'd appreciate it." He glanced toward the house across the street. "As soon as we install the kitchen sink in the Andersons' house, we can finish the kitchen and they can move back in."

Kirk also glanced at the Andersons' house. It had almost been destroyed by fire in July, but no one would be able to tell that now. Fourteen houses in Parker Place had been touched by the grass fire and needed to be repaired or rebuilt. Now Coleman Construction would start building the brand-new homes in the housing development, which meant a lot more business for Wilcox Lumber.

More business always made his dad happy.

"That's it for the wood," Kory said after he'd placed three more boards on top of the stack. "What do you want next, Griff?"

Griff checked his clipboard again. "I need another load of cement blocks and the shingles for the Moores' house."

"You got it." Kory punched Kirk's upper arm. "You ready, bro?"

Kirk nodded and turned toward the passenger side of the truck. They should be able to load and make the next delivery before the cold front hit.

"I need a vacation," Kory said once he sat behind the wheel. "Whatcha think, bro? Want to run away to somewhere warm for a couple of weeks?"

"If you try to leave this close to Christmas, Mom will whup you."

"It'd be worth the whupping to be warm. I hate cold weather."

"Kory, it's in the mid-fifties."

"Now, sure, but it'll be in the low thirties tonight and tomorrow and barely thirty on Wednesday with a chance of snow and ice."

"A twenty percent chance of snow and ice."

"If it's over zero percent, I don't want to be around here." He shivered. "I hate cold weather."

"You said that already."

"It needed to be repeated." He punched Kirk's arm again. "C'mon, bro, let's go find some babes in Florida who need suntan lotion spread over their bodies."

Finding babes in Florida didn't appeal to Kirk at all, yet he wouldn't admit that to his brother. He and Kory had double dated lots of times. Kirk knew how it felt to hold a woman, have her skin next to his, sink his cock into her. None of that appealed to him. He'd rather have a strong, muscled body lightly covered with hair and a big hard cock to suck or sink into his ass.

He shifted on the seat as his mental image made his dick react. Of course, if Kory noticed anything, he'd think Kirk reacted to the thought of those Florida babes.

"Not until after Christmas."

"Shit," Kory muttered. "Am I gonna have to go without you?"

"If you're determined to go before Christmas, yes. I won't disappoint Mom."

"Hell, Kirk, I would never do anything to disappoint Mom either. I just want some warmth. I hate cold weather."

Kirk chuckled at his twin saying the same thing a third time. "I'll try to remember that."

Kory sighed heavily. "Okay, if you won't go to Florida with me, how about hitting a club this weekend in Fort Worth? Maybe we'll get lucky and find some babes with big tits to keep us warm for a night."

That idea didn't appeal to Kirk either. But he could go with his brother, have a drink or two and enjoy some music, and not make any attempt to hook up with a gal. "Sure."

Kory smiled. "Great. We'll make plans later in the week."

He pulled the big delivery truck into Wilcox Lumber and headed toward the storage area for the cement blocks. Kirk jumped down from the seat and rounded the hood. "I'll go get Gus to help us load the blocks and shingles and check with Dad to see if there are any more deliveries to make today."

" 'K."

Kirk made his way to the back door of the business. He passed the employee break room, where he found Gus Lindell pouring a mug of coffee. "Hey, Gus, Kory and I need some help loading the next delivery."

"Be right there."

Not seeing his father in the office, Kirk continued to the main part of the store. He nodded at customers as he walked by them. A quick count produced a dozen people—mostly men— wandering through the aisles. Perhaps the onset of the freezing weather had people winterizing their homes to keep their water pipes from freezing.

Kalinda Meyers stood at one register, his father at the other, while they checked out customers. Kirk waited until his dad had finished ringing up Red Wilkerson's purchase before he stepped behind the checkout counter.

"Kory and I are making another delivery to Parker Place. Anything else need to go?"

"Nothing yet. Check back again after you finish there."

"Will do."

He started to turn to walk back outside when his father's next words stopped him.

"Kirk, there's a guy in the plumbing section who's looking for a job. I told him I couldn't talk to him until I finish checking out some of these customers. Would you talk to him?"

"Sure. I'll tell Kory I'll be a few minutes. He can come in and have some coffee. Maybe that'll warm him up."

Hank grinned. "Is he bitchin' about the cold again?"

"Always." Kirk glanced toward the plumbing section, although he couldn't see down the aisle from there. "What's the guy look like?"

"Tall, about your age, black hair. Said his name's Joshua Stafford."

Customers stepped up to be checked out, so Kirk moved out of the way so his dad could wait on them. He called his brother's cell while he headed toward the part of the store where Joshua Stafford should be.

"Yo," Kory answered.

"Dad asked me to interview a guy looking for a job. Why don't you come in and have some coffee? I'll only be a few minutes."

"You don't have to tell me twice to go inside. I'll be in the break room when you're ready."

Kirk disconnected the call, turned the corner, and headed down the plumbing aisle. He saw the back of a man with black hair, broad shoulders, and a gorgeous ass in tight jeans perusing the array of plastic pipes. "Joshua?"

The man turned . . . and Kirk instantly fell in lust.

Joshua's black hair fell over his forehead and ears in gentle waves. A square jaw carried a day's worth of stubble. The first two buttons of his blue Oxford shirt were open, revealing a sprinkling of dark chest hair. Those broad shoulders tapered to a trim waist, followed by long legs. He topped Kirk's five-eleven by a couple of inches.

Kirk didn't dare look at Joshua's fly.

The man stepped closer and offered his hand. "My friends call me Josh."

Having lots of practice at hiding his true feelings, Kirk smiled and accepted the other man's hand. A flash of sensation shot up his arm and through his body at the contact. He caught himself before he groaned. "I'm Kirk Wilcox. My dad asked me to speak to you. You're looking for a job?"

"Yes, but I kind of have a unique situation. Could we go somewhere more private to talk?"

"Sure. We can go to the office. This way."

Kirk kept his gaze trained straight ahead of him, instead of straying to the side to look at Josh. The high cheekbones and olive skin, combined with that black mane of hair and brown eyes, made Josh one of the most handsome men Kirk had ever seen.

Kirk waited until Josh stepped into the office before closing the door. "Sit down. Would you like a cup of coffee or something else to drink?"

"No, thanks. I'm fine."

Kirk sat behind the desk while the other man took the steel armchair in front of the desk. Josh crossed one ankle over the opposite knee, hooked his hands together across his stomach. Kirk didn't see a wedding band on Josh's finger, but that didn't mean he wasn't involved with a woman. A man as good looking as he probably had dozens of women chasing him.

Damn it.

"What kind of job are you looking for?" Kirk asked.

"Something physical. I've spent the last several years in school . . . first college, then law school."

"You're a lawyer?"

Josh wiggled his hand back and forth. "Technically, yeah. I passed the bar, but I'm not ready to practice law yet. I've had enough of using my brain for a while. I want to use my body instead."

Kirk could think of several ways the handsome man could use his body.

Josh patted his stomach. "After all that classwork, I feel like I've turned into a mass of putty."

Kirk couldn't see that at all. Josh's stomach wouldn't be that flat without some work. "You don't look out of shape."

"Good metabolism. All the men in my family are lean. That doesn't mean strong or healthy. Hitting a gym isn't me. I'd rather do something that builds muscles other than working out on a hunk of metal."

He admired Josh's determination and goal. Unfortunately, business dropped off in the winter and he couldn't offer Josh a full-time position now. "We're busier in the spring and summer, so I don't have anything now but a part-time position."

Josh smiled. "Part-time would be perfect. It'll give me the chance to explore the area in between the days I would work."

Hiring Josh would be strictly personal for Kirk. While his father owned the business, he depended on Kirk more and more for the management of Wilcox Lumber. They didn't need any more part-time help now, but he hated to turn away anyone looking for work. Especially a man he'd be happy to look at every day.

Josh leaned forward in his chair. "I have no job experience, Kirk, so I can't give you any references. Like I said, I've been in school. All I can do is promise I'll do the best job I can. I won't make you regret hiring me."

Kirk believed him, and wanted to help . . . and not just so he could enjoy the scenery. Getting a first job could be really hard, especially in a small town like Lanville. The people here tended to keep their jobs for years.

Which made Kirk wonder about Josh's hometown.

"Where are you from, Josh?"

"Dallas." He leaned back in his chair again. "I'll be honest. I come from a well-off family. My father wants me to be happy, but he's disappointed I didn't join his law firm as soon as I passed the bar. I told him I wanted the chance to drive and see parts of the country I've never seen. I've flown a lot, but I've never driven."

"Lanville can't be on your list of places to see."

Josh grinned. "Actually, it is. I have a friend who has relatives here. They've always raved about the town. I decided it would be a good place to start my travels."

"So you don't plan to stay here long?"

Josh shook his head. "I'm thinking two, three months. After

that . . ." He shrugged one shoulder. "I don't know. It depends on how I feel at the end of those three months."

Three months to see this man several days a week and dream about what could never be. Kirk should tell Josh that wouldn't work, that when they hired someone, they expected the person to stick around for a while. Josh had no work experience. He came from a rich family, meaning he'd probably whine the first time he got a callus on his hand.

So it surprised Kirk to hear the words "Okay, I'll give you a try" come out of his mouth.

Josh smiled and stood. "Thanks, Kirk."

He offered his hand over the desk. Kirk accepted it. That flash shot up his arm and through his body again.

I'm an idiot to put myself through this torture.

"Do I need to fill out some paperwork?" Josh asked. "When do you want me to start?"

"Be here at eight tomorrow morning. You can fill out the paperwork then, and I'll give you a tour of the store and grounds."

"Eight tomorrow morning. I'll be here."

Kirk watched Josh walk out of the office before he sat down again. Loneliness settled like a heavy wool blanket around his shoulders. He wasn't like his brother. Kory only cared about having a good time and fucking as many women as possible. He'd told Kirk he doubted if he'd ever get married.

Not Kirk. He wanted to share his life with someone. He wanted to hang his clothes in the same closet, cook meals together, spend an evening in silence while watching a favorite TV show. All those little things that meant commitment. Devotion. Fidelity.

Love.

He'd tried online dating, but the few dates he'd made had ended up disasters. It hadn't taken Kirk long to realize that just because he'd been honest while filling out his profile didn't mean everyone told the truth about themselves. And while he believed the inside of a person mattered more than the outside, he'd learned that people often put up pictures that looked nothing like them in real life.

The mental image of Josh flashed through his mind. Kirk pushed it aside. His new employee hadn't given any indication that he might be interested in a relationship with a man, even a short one. Kirk would be Josh's employer, nothing more.

As much as he loved his hometown and hated the thought of not having his family close, Kirk knew he'd have to leave Lanville to find the man meant for him.

2

Josh slid behind the wheel of his car. For a moment, he simply sat and ran his hands over the steering wheel. Growing up in a grand home with all the material things he could ever want could've given Josh a swelled head and made him conceited and rude. He'd figured out at a young age when a friend's family lost their fortune to never take anything for granted.

After he came into the trust fund from his paternal grandfather on his twenty-sixth birthday in July, he'd tucked it into the bank and indulged in only one luxury—this Mercedes SLS convertible. What a sweet ride.

The Mercedes wasn't the only thing that would be a sweet ride.

When he first met Kirk Wilcox, he thought he'd detected a flash of interest in the man's blue eyes. It had disappeared so quickly, Josh decided he must have imagined it. Too bad. Spending some naked time with the hunky blond would be very nice.

He had no idea if any gay men lived in this town, but he'd bet if they did, they didn't flaunt their sexual preference. Small towns could be unforgiving toward someone they perceived as "different." Finding a lover wouldn't be easy. But many things in Josh's life hadn't been easy—despite his family's money—and he'd learned to go with the flow. If he had to drive to a larger city to meet men, so be it.

Now that he'd acquired a job, he needed to find a place to stay. Thanks to his friend's cousin, Jeremy, he'd contacted Country Woods bed-and-breakfast and booked one of their cabins. He'd thought about staying at The Inn on Crystal Creek, which he could easily afford, but decided to try the out-of-the-way place close to the Rose River.

Once he checked into his cabin, he'd search for some lunch. Jeremy had told him some of the places to eat in Lanville. He remember some hamburger place that Jeremy had raved about. That sounded like a good place to try first.

Kirk slid into the booth across from his brother and opened the menu. He didn't know why he bothered. He came to The Purple Onion so often, he'd almost memorized every word of the menu.

"What are you having?" Kory asked. "As if you need to tell me. You always order the barbecue burger."

"Not always."

"Okay, you order it ninety-five percent of the time."

Kirk couldn't argue with Kory about that. He grinned. "Why mess with a good thing?"

Kory shook his head. "You should be more adventurous. I've tried every burger on the menu."

"I've tried a lot of them. I like the barbecue the best."

Jami walked up to their table carrying two glasses of iced tea. "One sweet . . ." She set a glass in front of Kory. "And one unsweet," she said, setting the other glass in front of Kirk.

Kory smiled at her. "Thanks, Jami."

He looked at his menu, so didn't see the longing pass over Jami's face. Kirk saw it. He didn't understand why his brother constantly chased other women when a sweet young woman like Jami cared so much for him.

"Are y'all ready to order?" Jami asked. "Kirk, your usual?"

Kory burst out laughing. Kirk glared at his brother before looking back at Jami. "Yeah."

"Kory, how about you?"

"I'll have the peppercorn burger today. I haven't had it in a while."

"Got it. They'll be right out."

Kirk watched Jami walk away, then turned to his brother. "You're an idiot."

Kory stopped with his glass of tea raised halfway to his mouth. "Why do you say that?"

"Jami's crazy about you."

Glancing toward the waitress, Kory frowned. "So?"

"So she's a sweetheart and really cute. Why don't you ask her out?"

He shrugged one shoulder. "She's not my type."

"Since when do you have a 'type'? I thought you'd fuck any gal who spread her legs."

His brother's frown turned into a scowl. "I'm not that bad."

"Damn near. You keep going to the Metroplex to date women you'll never see again instead of staying close to home and being with someone who cares about you."

Kory twirled his glass on the tabletop, making the ice cubes tinkle. "If you think Jami is so great, why don't *you* go out with her?"

"She isn't crazy about *me*, she's crazy about *you*."

Kory took a long drink of tea, returned his glass to the table with a loud *thunk*. "I'm not interested in anything permanent. Jami is a permanent kind of gal."

Kirk would've argued more with his stubborn brother, but a prickling along his neck made him glance toward the entrance. Josh stood next to the hostess station.

He could pretend he hadn't seen Josh, or be friendly and invite him to join them. Kory needed to meet Josh anyway, so it would be a good time to do so.

"There's our new employee."

Kory turned his head to look at Josh. "Oh, yeah? Invite him to join us."

The decision made, Kirk raised his hand to wave at Josh. A quick nod of his head proved Josh had seen him. He spoke to Jami a moment, then headed toward their booth.

Kirk's cock thickened the closer Josh got.

"Hey," he said to Kirk. "I didn't expect to see you again until tomorrow morning."

"Small town." He gestured toward Kory. "Josh Stafford, my brother, Kory Wilcox."

Josh offered his hand and Kory accepted it. "Nice to meet you."

"You, too."

Kirk scooted over in the booth. "Join us."

"Thanks."

Josh slid in beside him, leaving about eight inches between their legs. If it were up to Kirk, he'd press his leg against Josh's and find out if it was as muscular as Kirk suspected.

Jami returned to the booth with a glass of Coke and a menu for Josh. He waggled one finger back and forth between Kirk and Kory. "I'll have whatever these guys are having."

"Kirk ordered the barbecue burger and Kory ordered the peppercorn burger."

Josh looked at Kirk. "Barbecue, huh? Is it good?"

This close and with Josh facing the window, Kirk could see

specks of gold in the man's brown eyes. He imagined Josh staring at him with those amazing eyes right before he kissed him.

Kirk swallowed so his voice wouldn't come out husky. "Yeah, it's really good."

Josh swung his gaze back to Jami. "I'll try it."

"You got it," she said, flashing him a flirtatious smile.

Kirk noticed Kory watched Jami walk away, a frown wrinkling his forehead. He wondered if his brother could be jealous of the way she had smiled at Josh.

Maybe Kory cared more about Jami than he wanted to admit.

"So, Josh," Kory said, "what brings you to Lanville?"

"I told Kirk during my interview that I've been in school forever and needed a change. I want to travel, but I also want some job experience. I don't have any."

Kory's eyebrows shot up. "You've never had a job?"

Josh shook his head. "Hard to believe, huh?"

"You rich or somethin'?"

"My family is. But I want to make it on my own."

"You won't earn much working in a lumberyard."

"I don't need much." Josh shifted on the seat, which brought him a couple of inches closer to Kirk. "To be honest, I'd never have to work a day in my life thanks to an inheritance from my grandfather. But I don't want to be the spoiled rich kid. It's nice having the cushion in the bank, yet I want more out of life than partying all the time."

Kirk's admiration for Josh rose several degrees. A lot of people would blow the inheritance without thinking about what they would do for money in the future. Josh had brains as well as good looks.

And he smelled incredible.

Conversation halted when Jami brought their food. Kirk

chuckled to himself when Josh picked up the large slice of purple onion on his plate and stared at it. "Am I supposed to eat this or wear it as a hat?"

"I recommend eating it," Kirk said. "It's sweet and delicious."

Josh looked at him. "I'm all for sweet and delicious."

It might have been his imagination—or wishful thinking—but Kirk thought heat flashed through Josh's eyes before his lids narrowed a bit.

Kirk hadn't detected any interest from Josh when they first met, but perhaps Josh did the same thing as Kirk—hid his true feelings until he knew it would be safe to reveal them.

His heart pounded in his chest at that thought.

"Okay, I'm game." Josh lifted the top bun, placed the slice of onion on the meat. "Luckily I don't plan to kiss anyone today."

"No little honey waiting for you at home?" Kory asked.

"Nope. Haven't had a honey in a long time."

"You should come with Kirk and me to Fort Worth Saturday night. We're gonna hit some clubs."

"I appreciate the invitation, but I promised to have dinner with my parents and sister Saturday."

Kory straightened his shoulders. "You have a sister?"

"Yep."

"Single?"

"Yep."

"Pretty?"

Josh grinned. "You're way too transparent, Kory."

"Damn," Kory said, snapping his fingers. "And I thought I was being subtle."

"You're about as subtle as a freight train." Kirk squirted a generous amount of ketchup by his fries. "Don't give him any information about your sister, Josh."

"Oh, come on, bro." He grinned wickedly at Josh. "I promise to show her a really good time."

"You apparently don't have a sister or you wouldn't suggest what you're suggesting." Josh bit a French fry in half. "Pass."

Kirk grinned to himself. Josh may have spent most of his life in school, but he'd learned some life lessons along the way. He could handle himself fine.

"Born to Be Wild" came from Kory's cell phone. He wiped his hands on a napkin before he unclipped the phone from his belt and checked the display. He smiled. "Maybe I won't go clubbing this weekend after all. Excuse me."

Kory rose from the booth and walked toward the restrooms as he answered the call. He stepped out of range before Kirk could hear anything he said that might indicate who had called him. Kory met women all the time, so he could be speaking to anyone.

"What kind of club do you and Kory go to?" Josh asked.

"Kory likes country music, so we usually go to a place this side of Fort Worth. I call it a bar, he calls it a club. Lots of dancing."

"You like to dance?"

"Nah. I have two left feet. I like to sit at a table and watch people. Kory's the party animal."

"Y'all have to be twins to look so much alike, yet you're very different from him."

"Kory's the one who wants to tease and play and never settle down. I'm quieter. I'm happy to stay home and read a good book. I don't think Kory has opened a book since high school."

Josh washed down his bite of burger with a gulp of Coke. "Who's your favorite author?"

Kirk didn't even have to think about his answer. "E. P. Payne."

"No kidding?" Josh's smile spread from ear to ear. "He's mine, too. Loved *Black Illusion*."

"I still love it. I've read it at least five times."

Kory groaned as he slid back into the booth. "Don't tell me y'all are talking about reading shit."

"Some of us like discussing things other than the best brand of beer to drink, bro."

"Yeah, yeah, whatever." Kory popped a fry into his mouth. "Change of plans. That was Anna Hopkins. I met her at Boot Scootin' a couple of weeks ago when she was in town visiting a friend. She invited me to a party at her place Saturday night. Said there will be between twenty and thirty people there. I asked her if I could bring my brother and she said yes." He grinned and bobbed his eyebrows. "She said brothers are sexy."

Which meant Kory would try to convince Kirk to participate in a ménage. Kirk had gone along with his brother once, and once was enough. He couldn't help but get off with the woman's warm mouth wrapped around his dick, but an orgasm didn't mean enjoyment.

Before Kirk could comment, he remembered what he and Kory had promised to do Saturday after closing the store. "Hell, Kory, we can't go. We promised Dad we'd do that inventory spot check while he and Mom are at the home improvement show."

"Shit," Kory muttered. "I forgot about that."

"Is there something I can do to help with your inventory?" Josh asked.

"Yes," Kory immediately said. "You can take my place."

Kirk scowled at his brother. "Kory, you can't ask Josh to do that. He hasn't even started working for us yet."

"I don't mind, Kirk. That way your brother can still go to the party."

"What about your dinner date with your family?"

Josh shrugged one shoulder. "I'll call my mom and tell her I'll come next weekend. She'll understand if I have to work."

"Great!" Kory beamed. "Then it's settled." He offered his hand over the table. "Thanks, my man."

Josh accepted Kory's handshake. "No problem." He looked at Kirk again. "Unless you have a problem with it."

It wouldn't be easy to be alone in the store with Josh and keep his hands off the other man. But Kirk would do it. Despite the pull he felt toward Josh, Kirk would never do anything to make him uncomfortable.

"No problem at all."

Kirk watched Josh ring up Mrs. Campbell's purchases. He gave her a wide smile, which made the elderly woman blush adorably.

No one would be able to tell Josh had never held a job by watching him now. He'd worked at Wilcox Lumber for four days and caught on almost immediately to whatever Kirk showed him how to do. First-time clerks sometimes had trouble with the cash register, but Josh had breezed right through Kirk's lessons, enough to where Kirk put him at one of the checkout stations on their busiest day of the week.

He'd turned into a much better employee than Kirk anticipated.

Once Mrs. Campbell left Josh's station, he rolled his shoulders a couple of times before he smiled at the next customer waiting in line. Kirk knew Josh had to be sore from working outside in the yard the past two days. Even someone who worked out regularly in a gym would be sore after lifting and hauling lumber and bags of cement since they used muscles rarely utilized. He'd bet Josh would pay just about anything for a massage.

Kirk would happily give him one for free.

A glance at his watch showed Kirk it would be time to close the store in five minutes. He'd already called China Palace to deliver his and Josh's supper about six-fifteen. They'd eat first, then work on the inventory. Kirk figured it shouldn't take more than a couple of hours to finish the spot check, which would leave Josh plenty of time to enjoy the rest of his Saturday night.

Kirk had caught Josh watching him several times over the last four days. Kirk wanted so badly to see interest in Josh's eyes, yet couldn't honestly say he had. Josh treated all the employees and customers to his friendliness and smiles.

Every day working with Josh had been part pleasure and part misery. He wished he could touch the other man, wrap his arms around him, kiss those full lips. He wanted to take what he knew would be a magnificent cock down his throat, taste Josh's cum.

Before his dick responded and let every customer in the store know his thoughts, Kirk moved to the front door. He slid the sign to "Closed" and waited while the last two customers bought their items. Once they left, he locked the deadbolt.

Kirk said good night to the other three employees in the store. By the time they clocked out and left via the back entrance, the delivery guy from the Chinese restaurant arrived at the front door. Kirk took money from the register to pay for the food and tip, then locked the front door once more.

Facing Josh, he held up the two large white sacks. "Hungry?"

"Starving."

After turning off the lights by the entrance, Kirk led the way to the break room. Josh took a Coke for him and Dr Pepper for

Kirk from the refrigerator and set them on the table. "Want silverware?" he asked.

"Yeah." Kirk began removing the small cartons from the bags. "And plates. I ordered a bunch of different dishes since I wasn't sure what you like."

"If it's Chinese, I'll eat it." He selected two forks from the silverware drawer. "How many spoons?"

"Six."

Josh set six large serving spoons on the table, along with two plates. "Anything else?"

"Grab some paper towels, too." Kirk quickly located the egg rolls and bit into one.

"Hey, no fair eating before me."

Kirk offered the container of egg rolls to Josh. "Here."

Josh bit off half a roll in one bite. "Damn, that's good." He took the chair opposite Kirk. "What else did you order?"

"Broccoli and beef, pork chow mein, sweet-and-sour chicken, fried rice, teriyaki wings, shrimp lo mein, and mushroom chicken."

"How many people you planning on feeding?"

"Just you and me. But do you know what's so great about Chinese food?"

"What?"

Kirk grinned. "Leftovers."

Josh returned his grin. "Amen to that." He spooned some of everything onto his plate. "So, boss, how am I doing?"

"You know you're doing great."

"I feel like I am, but I want to be sure. I've enjoyed every-thing I've learned so far." He rolled his shoulders the way Kirk had seen him do after waiting on Mrs. Campbell. "Even if every muscle in my body hurts."

Kirk chuckled. "Told you you'd be sore." He unscrewed the cap from his drink. "You have a natural gift with conversation. The customers enjoy talking to you."

"I enjoy talking to them, too. Especially the older people. The elderly woman I waited on right before closing was sweet."

"That was Mrs. Campbell. She's a widow. Married sixty-four years before her husband passed away two years ago."

"Wow. That's a long time to be together." Josh stabbed a large mushroom. "It's a lot of work to be with one person your entire life."

"Yeah, but worth it if you find the right person."

Josh selected a wing from its container. "Finding that right person ain't easy."

"Nope."

Kirk could feel Josh watching him as he chewed his bite of wing. "I've seen Kalinda flirting with you."

"We're just friends."

"She's pretty. And smart. And obviously has a thing for you."

"We're just friends," Kirk said again.

Wiping his hands on a paper towel, Josh leaned back in his chair. "Why?"

It seemed as if Josh taunted him to tell the truth, to admit women did nothing for him. Kirk didn't know if Josh asked because he might be interested in Kalinda, or if he might be interested in Kirk.

He yearned for the second option.

If Josh wanted the truth, Kirk would give him the truth. He set his fork on his half-empty plate. "Because I'm gay."

"So am I."

Even with Kirk's hope that Josh might be gay, it still surprised him for the man to admit it. "I thought you might be interested in Kalinda and that's why you asked about her."

"No." He laid the paper towel next to his plate. "The only one I'm interested in is you."

Kirk's heart took off at a gallop. His dick swelled in his briefs in anticipation of Josh's lips wrapped around it.

"How about you?" Josh asked. "Are you interested in me?"

"Yeah." His voice came out husky, rough. "I'm very interested."

Josh pushed back his chair and rose. Kirk's gaze snagged on the other man's fly as Josh rounded the table. The large bulge behind the jeans zipper proved Josh's interest ran as high as Kirk's.

Josh tugged on Kirk's chair until he turned it to face him. Leaning over, he placed his hands on the seat on either side of Kirk's thighs so their faces were level. "I hoped, but you didn't give off any signals."

"I've become really good at hiding how I feel."

Josh's gaze traveled from Kirk's eyes, to his lips, and back to his eyes. "I don't want you to hide anything from me."

Kirk only had enough time to inhale before Josh kissed him. He released the air in his lungs on a long moan. Josh's full, soft lips moved over his, turning one way, then the other, in a gentle kiss of hello.

"Nice." Josh cradled Kirk's face, gave him another long kiss. "I want more."

"So do I."

Josh's gaze dropped to Kirk's lap. One side of his mouth quirked. "I can tell." He looked into Kirk's eyes again, all traces of humor gone. "You want some help with that?"

Kirk swallowed, but his voice still came out hoarse. "Yeah."

Josh dropped to his knees between Kirk's wide-spread legs. He took his time unbuckling Kirk's belt, unfastening the buttons of his fly, as if trying to build up Kirk's anticipation of what would soon happen. Kirk didn't need any buildup. His cock felt as if it would blow with the first touch of Josh's tongue.

"Lift up," Josh commanded softly.

Kirk did as instructed. Josh grasped the waistbands of Kirk's jeans and briefs, tugged them past Kirk's hips. His dick sprang up full and hard against his belly.

"Mmm, yeah." Josh ran one fingertip down the heavy vein. "*Very* nice."

Kirk clenched his hands into fists to keep from grabbing Josh's head and forcing his cock into the other man's mouth. It would happen soon. He just had to be patient.

Being patient didn't sit at the top of his to-do list right now. Josh pressed his nose against Kirk's balls and inhaled sharply. "You smell good."

"Jesus, Josh."

Holding tightly to Kirk's cock by the base, Josh ran his tongue up the vein to the tip. "I like to savor."

"Savor later. Suck now."

He chuckled. "This is going to be fun."

Josh's definition of fun must be completely different from Kirk's. He couldn't imagine how slow torture could be fun.

Then Josh opened his mouth and engulfed Kirk's dick until his mouth touched his fist. Kirk jerked and arched his hips without thinking about possibly choking the other man. Josh must have anticipated that might happen and that's why he'd wrapped his hand around the base of Kirk's cock.

Whatever the reason, Kirk closed his eyes to better enjoy the sensation of that wet warmth surrounding his hard flesh.

"I have to warn you," Kirk managed to say between pants, "it's been a while for me. I probably won't last long."

"Good." Josh ran his tongue around the rim, licked the top of the crown. "I want to taste your cum."

"Ah, *fuck!*"

"Later. But for now . . ."

Josh took him again, even deeper this time. Helpless to do anything except enjoy, Kirk tunneled his hands into Josh's hair. He loved the way the wavy strands curled around his fingers. He also loved watching the way his shaft disappeared into Josh's mouth, only to appear again when Josh pulled back to the head. Saliva coated his flesh, making it easier to slide in and out of Josh's mouth.

The tingling started at the base of his spine, the first indication of a building orgasm. Kirk hated to come too soon, hated to remove his cock from Josh's mouth. Yet Josh said he wanted to taste Kirk's cum. That would happen far sooner than he probably expected.

His balls tightened. Gripping Josh's head firmer, he pumped his hips to drive his dick farther down Josh's throat. So close. Just a little longer . . .

A wet finger shoved into his ass sent Kirk over the edge. He cried out as the orgasm barreled up his shaft to explode in Josh's mouth.

Realizing he was pulling Josh's hair, he slowly released his grip. Josh gave Kirk's cock a final lick and suck before he sat back on his heels. "I knew you'd be delicious."

Kirk leaned forward, grabbed Josh's head again, and kissed him. He didn't give him the soft, tender kisses Josh had given. He kissed the other man with passion, with hunger, with all the yearning he felt deep inside.

Heat flashed in Josh's eyes when Kirk stopped the kiss. "Damn, Wilcox, you do know how to kiss."

It pleased Kirk that Josh thought so. "I like kissing."

"So do I. And I like blow jobs." He stood, reached for his belt buckle. "You want to return the favor?"

"Definitely."

Kirk pushed up Josh's T-shirt while Josh unfastened his belt and jeans. Dark hair swirled around Josh's navel, climbed up his torso, made a nest at the base of Josh's cock. Kirk planned to explore every bit of this man's body later. Right now, his mouth watered at the thought of taking Josh's dick as deep in his mouth as Josh had taken his.

Josh pushed down his jeans and briefs to reveal a long cock with a curved tip. Pre-cum leaked from the slit, making Josh's mouth water even more. He swiped his tongue across the head, gathering the salty essence.

Josh cradled the back of Kirk's head. "I won't last long either," he whispered.

Which worked fine for Kirk. He longed to taste even more of Josh's essence, have it fill his mouth, slide down his throat. Kirk cupped Josh's balls in one palm, gently massaged them as he slowly slid his lips down the hard column of flesh. He slipped his other hand over Josh's hips to grip a tight cheek.

"Push a finger inside me."

Kirk released Josh's dick long enough to wet his forefinger. Locating the tight rosette, he pushed his finger inside Josh's ass as he engulfed his cock again.

Josh sucked in a sharp breath between his teeth. "Mmm, yeah. Go deeper."

Not hesitating to obey, Kirk pushed his finger as far inside Josh's ass as he could. He moved it around until he found the sensitive spot that would make Josh go wild. One caress of it and Josh hissed. His cock jerked in Kirk's mouth.

"Fuck, that feels good."

Josh gripped Kirk's head a little tighter, moved his hips a bit faster. Kirk let him take control, let him move however he needed to. Kirk continued rubbing his prostate and balls, giving Josh as much pleasure as possible.

Kirk could tell by Josh's heavy breathing and jerky thrusting that his orgasm would soon hit. He waited a few moments, studying Josh's movements. When he suspected it was the right time, he rubbed Josh's gland harder and took his cock all the way to his balls.

"*Shit!*"

Josh stilled and released a loud groan before his cum shot into Kirk's mouth. Kirk swallowed again and again, wanting every drop.

Knowing Josh's legs would be weak, Kirk slid his arms beneath Josh's ass to help him continue to stand. Once Josh's cock had softened a bit, Kirk let it slip from his mouth. He pressed his forehead to Josh's abdomen, not wanting to let go of him yet.

Josh ran his hands through Kirk's hair. "Hey."

Reluctantly, Kirk lifted his head and looked up at Josh to see him smiling. Kirk returned it. "Hey."

He ran his fingers through Kirk's hair again. "I have an idea."

"I'm open to ideas."

"How about if we do the inventory thing we're supposed to do, then take all this food to my place for a snack after we make love?"

"Where's your place?"

"I rented one of the cabins at Country Woods."

Which had only one bed in one bedroom. Kirk could leave after he and Josh made love, but cuddling and falling asleep together sounded so much nicer. His apartment had two bedrooms. If Josh stayed over and for some reason someone asked about it, Kirk could say he offered his extra bedroom to Josh since he didn't want to drive after drinking.

"Do you want to spend the night together?"

"Of course I do."

"Then come home with me. I have a really nice apartment with a huge TV and lots of movies on DVDs."

"Do you think we'll want to watch a movie?"

"We have to rest sometime."

Josh grinned. "Speak for yourself."

Kirk grinned, too. He liked Josh's sense of humor. "Okay, I have a lot of movies if we feel like watching one. What do you say?"

"I say it sounds perfect."

4

Josh followed Kirk to an apartment complex a few blocks from Wilcox Lumber. He counted six fourplexes. Though not large, he could tell the owners maintained the complex by the neat lawn and trimmed shrubs.

Kirk and Kory seemed very close. Josh wondered why the twins didn't live together.

Josh wondered a lot of things about his new lover . . . things he hoped to discover before the night ended.

Kirk stuck his hand out the window and pointed to an empty parking spot in what must be visitor parking. Josh pulled into it while Kirk drove a few yards farther before pulling into a spot next to one of the units. He got out of his small pickup, holding the sacks from the supper they hadn't completed, and waited until Josh joined him. Silently, he led the way to apartment number eight and unlocked the door.

"Wait a sec while I turn on a light."

Josh stood in the doorway while Kirk moved away from him. A moment later, he heard the click of a switch before lamplight filled the living room.

"Come on in."

Closing the door behind him, Josh looked around the living room. Not white-glove perfect, but not dirty by any means. The room looked lived in with an empty saucer and glass on the coffee table, and an afghan partly on the couch and partly on the floor.

"You can hang your jacket there," Kirk said, nodding toward a coat stand in the corner. "I'll heat up our food."

After Josh hung up his jacket, he walked in the direction Kirk had gone. He found him in a small but modern kitchen. The refrigerator, stove, and dishwasher looked shiny and new. The round table sat beneath a window that Josh thought faced east. He and Kirk could sit there in the morning and enjoy the sun while they ate breakfast.

Kirk had hung his jacket over the back of one of the chairs. Josh watched him take two plates from the cabinet and silverware from a drawer. He'd already removed all the little white cartons from the sack and set them on the L-shaped countertop. Josh let his gaze slowly sweep across Kirk's shoulders, down his back, over his ass. He hadn't had the chance yet to see that ass, much less feel it.

That needed to be corrected right now.

Walking up behind Kirk, Josh wrapped his arms around his lover's waist. "I thought we were going to make love again before we ate."

Kirk dropped the spoon back into the container of pork chow mein when Josh cupped his fly. "I didn't want to assume anything."

"Assume all you want to." He kissed the side of Kirk's neck while he caressed the rapidly hardening cock beneath his palm. "I'm assuming you'll show me to your bedroom soon."

"How about now?"

"Now works for me."

Kirk took Josh's hand, led him out of the kitchen, and down

a short hallway. They passed a couple of darkened doorways before Kirk guided Josh into a room. A nightlight plugged into an outlet gave Josh enough illumination to make out a bed and nightstand before Kirk turned on a lamp. The covers had been thrown over the pillows, but hadn't been straightened.

"I changed the sheets two days ago," Kirk said, "but I'm not much for making the bed."

"I don't care if it's been a month since you changed the sheets. As long as you're on them with me, they're perfect."

Kirk smiled, then cradled Josh's nape and drew him closer for a kiss. Josh slipped one arm around Kirk's waist, the other around his shoulders, and stepped closer until their bodies touched. Kirk's hard cock pressed against his. Josh could hardly wait to feel that connection when clothes didn't get in the way.

"How do you feel about sixty-nine?" Josh asked.

A slow, sexy grin spread across Kirk's lips. "Love it."

"Then let's get naked."

Between more kisses and intimate caresses, Josh managed to undress Kirk while Kirk undressed him. Josh climbed on the bed with Kirk right beside him.

Arms and legs entwined as their lips met again. Bare skin pressed to bare skin. Their dicks bumped with every movement, raising Josh's desire to possess this man in every way possible.

A thrill shot through him when Kirk pushed him to his back, leaned over him, and wrapped one hand around his cock. Josh liked that bit of dominance. While he preferred to top, he had no problem bottoming with the right man.

Kirk's lips covered his. He parted his lips, sucked Kirk's tongue into his mouth. A little shifting on the bed and he wrapped his hand around Kirk's dick, exactly the same way Kirk's did his. He copied Kirk's movements as he pumped and squeezed, let his hand glide down to fondle tight balls.

Much more of the hand job and Josh wouldn't be able to hold back his climax.

Releasing Josh's cock, Kirk slid his hand up Josh's torso until he cradled his jaw. The kiss gentled, becoming more tender than sexy. Josh released Kirk's shaft and pulled him closer, wanting to touch as much of his lover as possible.

Kirk kissed his lips once, twice, before he moved down his neck. Josh closed his eyes to better absorb the feeling of Kirk's hands caressing his body. Kisses and tiny bites fell over Josh's shoulder, his collarbone, his chest. They continued down the center of his torso. Kirk's tongue circled his navel. More kisses and nips scattered across Josh's hip bone and down his thigh.

Warm breath blew over his cock. Josh clenched his fists and his teeth. Despite having a strong orgasm a couple of hours ago, he sat on the edge of another one. "You're making me crazy, do you know that?"

"Good." Kirk blew on Josh's dick again. "Sex is hotter when you're crazy."

If the sex got any hotter, Josh would combust. He opened his mouth to tell Kirk that, but a groan came out instead when Kirk licked the crown.

"Mmm, salty." Kirk licked again, then circled the rim with the tip of his tongue. "Love the way you taste."

Only one of them tasting didn't work for Josh. He'd playfully asked Kirk how he felt about sixty-nine, but part of him had been serious. He wanted to suck Kirk's dick while Kirk sucked his.

Josh shifted on the bed again until he lay diagonally on it, his mouth even with his lover's cock. Pre-cum oozed from the slit to slither down the side of Kirk's shaft. Josh lapped it up with one pass of his tongue.

Delicious.

Josh opened his mouth over Kirk's crown. He took the shaft

all the way into his mouth, pulled back to the head as his lover did the same with Josh's cock. It took a few times for Josh to coordinate with the other man until they moved perfectly together. In, out, sucking, pulling back. Josh pressed one finger into Kirk's ass, searched for that sweet spot that gave so much pleasure. A loud moan came from Kirk when Josh found it.

Rubbing the area of sensation, Josh took Kirk's cock even deeper down his throat. He licked the heavy veins, circled the crown, darted his tongue into the slit. He laved the tight balls until they were nice and wet, then took Kirk's dick down his throat again. Every movement he made, Kirk copied. Josh tried to concentrate solely on the other man's pleasure, yet his lover made that difficult with his talented mouth.

Josh's balls tightened. He sucked harder on Kirk's cock, wanting his lover to come at the same time. He could tell by the way Kirk thrust his hips that he had to be close.

Pleasure charged through Josh's limbs and to the tips of his fingers and toes. It dashed down his spine, into his balls, and erupted from his shaft. His body trembled, his hips bucked, as he spilled his cum into Kirk's mouth.

It took only a few more moments for Kirk's essence to fill Josh's mouth. He swallowed quickly to savor every drop.

Not wanting to release Kirk yet, Josh kept running his tongue along the softening flesh. A drop of cum formed at the slit. Josh licked it off, then gently sucked the head back into his mouth.

Kirk copied Josh's actions, laving the semi-soft cock in his mouth. Josh knew it couldn't get hard again, not after already having two orgasms this evening. He doubted if Kirk's could either. That didn't mean he didn't want to taste Kirk's beautiful dick as long as possible.

It amazed Josh when Kirk's cock began to harden again. It amazed him even more to feel his own shaft responding to the light suction of Kirk's lips. Thankful for the pleasant surprise, he continued sucking and licking the male flesh in his mouth. It grew as his did, until both were as hard as before their climaxes.

Now that coming didn't dictate his every move and thought, Josh took it easy and concentrated more fully on his partner's satisfaction.

Apparently, Kirk felt the same way. His mouth slowed, his licks teased. He added a gentle massage to Josh's balls as his tongue bathed the hard column.

Desire reached fever pitch again. Josh added a pumping action with his fist while he tongued and sucked the head of Kirk's cock. Mere moments passed before he received the reward of a third taste of his lover's cum.

Knowing Kirk had found pleasure again sent Josh over the top once more. Although not as powerful as the first two orgasms he'd experienced this evening, this one still left his limbs weak and his lungs struggling for oxygen. He reluctantly released Kirk's shaft so he could draw in more air.

Kirk let Josh's cock slide out of his mouth. "Jesus, did you get the license plate on that truck that just ran over me?"

Although he could barely breathe, Josh chuckled. "I think it was more like a convoy."

Kirk fell to his back, covered his eyes with one arm. "You're trying to kill me."

Josh turned around on the bed so he could look at Kirk's face. He lay on his side, his bent arm supporting his head. "That was amazing."

"Yeah." Kirk uncovered his eyes, rolled his head toward Josh. "I didn't think it was physically possible for me to come twice so close together."

"I guess anything's possible with the right incentive."

Kirk reached out, drew the back of a knuckle down the center of Josh's chest. "You're definitely the right incentive."

"Know what else I am?"

"What?"

"Starving."

Kirk grinned. "Me, too. And cold. I forgot to turn up the heat."

Now that the physical activity had stopped, Josh noticed the chill in the air. "It is cool in here."

"Let's get dressed. I'll turn up the heat and start warming the food."

" 'K."

Two minutes later, Josh helped Kirk load up their plates to warm in the microwave. "There's beer in the fridge," Kirk said as he spooned sweet-and-sour chicken over his fried rice. "I don't have any Cokes, but I have Dr Pepper and Pepsi."

"Beer sounds good. Want one?"

"Yeah."

Josh got a beer for each of them while Kirk warmed the food. He also gathered forks and paper towels, placed everything on the table by the window. His stomach growled in appreciation when Kirk set the plate in front of him.

"I'm warming the wings now," Kirk said. "There's still some of everything if you want more."

"This will do for a start."

He waited until Kirk joined him at the table before picking up his fork. Years of etiquette drummed into him by his mother and grandmother wouldn't let him start eating before everyone sat at the table.

He took several bites before starting the conversation again. "You and Kory seem really close. I'm surprised you don't live together."

"We did when we first got out of high school, but then we got our own places when I went to college and Kory started working full-time for our dad. He knew we would inherit the business someday and saw no reason to earn some piece of paper to hang on the wall when he already had a successful job.

Dad and Mom saved the money to send both of us to college. Kory told them to take his part and go on an extended vacation. He didn't care anything about a degree. I did."

"What was your major?"

"Business management. I learned a lot about organization. Dad pretty much turned the store over to me and I run it. Kory's happy doing whatever I tell him to do."

Josh studied the man seated across from him. He could see where Kirk would be good at organization and running a business. He had a level head on his shoulders and got along well with people. Several of Wilcox Lumber's customers had said how much they liked Kirk and Kory.

Word of mouth meant a lot in a small town. A business could quickly die because of negative comments.

"I'm amazed at how different you and Kory are. I mean, you favor each other because you're twins, but even then you look different. His hair is longer; you're more muscular."

"Kory does a lot of physical work in the yard, but if he can get someone else to do it, he will. I like jumping in to help. It keeps me in shape."

And in very nice shape. Josh hadn't had much time to admire the ripples of Kirk's stomach, but he'd definitely noticed them. He planned to run his tongue over every inch of them.

"You still sore?" Kirk asked.

"Getting better, but yeah. I've used muscles this week I didn't realize I had."

"Maybe you need a massage."

Josh noted the smoky look in Kirk's eyes. He liked the idea of having his lover's hands all over him. "Maybe I do. Do you know a good massage therapist?"

"I'm sure I can find one for you."

Josh grinned. "Works for me."

Kirk selected a wing, took a bite, and licked the sauce from his bottom lip. Josh's cock stirred with interest, which he didn't think could be possible for at least a day. "You plan to find that therapist tonight?"

"Mmm-hmm." Kirk finished the wing, laid the bone on his empty plate. "I bet he'll show up about the time I get the leftovers put away."

"If I help you with that, maybe he'll show up sooner."

It didn't take but a few minutes for Josh to clear the table while Kirk put away the food. He rinsed the plates and silverware, left them in the sink as per Kirk's instructions. Hand in hand, they walked back to Kirk's bedroom.

5

"Take off your clothes," Kirk ordered.

Josh obeyed him while Kirk threw back the bedspread and blanket. He straightened the top sheet over the fitted one so there were no wrinkles. He wanted Josh to be as comfortable as possible during the massage.

Kirk had pulled a muscle in his arm a couple of months ago and saw Dax Coleman a few times for a massage. Dax gave him a small bottle of massage oil to use at home. Kirk located it in the bottom drawer of his nightstand. Setting it on top of the stand, he began to remove his clothes while Josh laid on the bed on his stomach. He admired Josh's body as he undressed—the line of his back, the rounded buttocks, the long legs lightly dusted with dark hair. Josh didn't have the muscles of a body-builder, but that didn't mean he didn't have an incredibly sexy body.

He glanced at Josh's face to see his lover watching him. Kirk removed his jeans, the last barrier covering his body. Three strong orgasms tonight didn't seem to matter to his cock. It hardened a bit more with every moment that Josh stared at it.

Massage now, sex later, he told himself. Picking up the bottle of oil, Kirk straddled Josh's thighs. "I promise I know what I'm doing."

"I have complete faith in you."

Kirk poured a generous amount of oil in his palm, pressed his other hand over it to warm it. He rubbed his hands together to distribute the oil evenly, then placed them on Josh's shoulders. One press with his thumbs and Kirk could feel the tightness.

"No wonder you're sore. Your shoulders are like rocks."

"You shouldn't have worked me so hard."

"You shouldn't have volunteered to work in the yard two days in a row when you aren't used to all that lifting."

"Lesson learned, boss. One day outside, one day inside. How's that?"

"I'll make sure of it when I make up the work schedule."

He concentrated on Josh's shoulders for several minutes before moving down to his shoulder blades. "I'm not as good at this as Dax, but I picked up a few things from him."

"Dax?"

"Dax Coleman. He and his two brothers own Coleman Construction. You met Rye Wednesday, remember? He came in to order a special doorknob for the back door of his house."

"Tall, broad shoulders, dark hair and mustache, very good looking?"

"That's him."

"Dax is a massage therapist?"

"Yeah, and a damn good one. He's converted a room in his house to give massages, but doesn't consider it a business and doesn't charge anyone."

"That's pretty generous."

"People give him stuff for their massages, even though he doesn't ask for anything." Kirk pressed his heels into Josh's lower back, ran them up the sides of his spine. "He wanted to repaint his laundry room, so I took him enough paint for that when he helped me."

Josh lifted his head, looked at Kirk over his shoulder. "Were you hurt?"

"Pulled a muscle in my arm. No big deal. It was okay in a few days." He pushed in the center of Josh's back. "Lie down."

After Josh did as ordered, Kirk ran his heels up Josh's back again. He could feel the muscles slowly relaxing. He repeated the action several more times before moving to Josh's lower back. "How are you doing?"

"I'm trying to stay awake. That feels incredible."

"Dax told me the best compliment he gets when he gives a massage is for his client to fall asleep. That shows complete trust that he won't hurt them."

"I trust you won't hurt me."

No, Kirk would never intentionally hurt Josh. Even though they'd only known each other a few days, Kirk already cared for the man lying beneath him. Not that caring for Josh would do Kirk any good. Josh had already been clear about his plans to stay in Lanville for a short time before he moved on to the next part of his journey.

Falling in love would *not* be a good idea.

But being in lust worked fine. Having an incredible lover for a short time worked fine. As long as he protected his heart, Kirk could say good-bye to Josh when he decided to leave and not have any regrets.

Kirk scooted farther back so he could massage Josh's buttocks and upper thighs. He added more oil to his palms, spread it over the round cheeks. A therapeutic massage turned into one of exploration when Josh shifted and spread his legs a couple more inches.

Taking the movement as an invitation, Kirk slipped one knee

between Josh's legs. Josh immediately widened his legs even more. Instead of the easy, gentle breathing from the massage, his breathing turned choppy, heavy. Kirk gripped the other man's cheeks, pulled them up and apart to expose the tight rosette. He touched it with one slick thumb, causing Josh to inhale sharply.

"Want me to play a little?" Kirk asked.

"Yeah," Josh said in a strangled voice.

Kirk spread oil around Josh's anus. Josh arched his hips, as if silently asking for more. Kirk caressed a bit, then dipped his thumb past the entrance before caressing again.

"God," Josh muttered. "Don't stop!"

Kirk replaced his thumb with two fingers so he could rub faster. He knew how good it felt to have all those sensitive nerve endings stroked. He fondled Josh's ass while he increased the movement and pressure of his fingers. Josh bucked his hips, but couldn't move much since Kirk held him.

His cock rose to a hard column of aching flesh. Kirk wanted to pound it into Josh's ass, but wouldn't do that until Josh came again. He slid his other knee between Josh's legs and pushed them farther apart. Kirk dipped down to squeeze Josh's tight balls before returning to his anus.

"If you don't stop, I'm gonna come all over your sheets. Let me turn over."

Kirk helped Josh roll to his back, then pushed up his legs until they almost touched Josh's chest so he could continue playing with his hole. He stared into his lover's eyes while he rubbed the sensitive tissue. Josh's eyes rolled back and he released a long, loud moan.

Unable to wait another moment to be inside this man, Kirk reached in the top drawer of his nightstand and grabbed a condom. He donned it and smeared it with the massage oil still on his hands before he drove into Josh's ass.

He kept his thrusts slow and easy, giving Josh time to adjust.

Once Josh lifted his hips and met Kirk's thrusts, Kirk knew his lover could take more. Propping himself on straight arms, Kirk pumped faster, deeper.

"Yeah, that's good," Josh whispered. "So good."

Kirk agreed, but lust tightened his throat and left him unable to speak. He could only feel—the sheen of sweat forming on Josh's skin, the tight grip of his ass, the bite of fingernails when Josh dug them into Kirk's arms. Everything combined to send Kirk's desire higher than it had ever been.

Streams of cum erupted from Josh's dick to splatter on his chest and stomach. Pulses from his lover's climax squeezed Kirk's dick. Heat flashed through his body, stars burst behind his eyelids. Kirk rammed his dick all the way inside Josh's ass when his own climax barreled out the end of his cock. It went on and on, until he'd finally emptied his balls.

Kirk slowly pulled out of Josh and fell to the bed. His legs shook so much, he didn't believe he could stand. "I think you were right," he said between gasps of breath. "It was a convoy, not just one truck."

Josh shifted closer, laid his hand on Kirk's chest. "A convoy of bulldozers."

"I believe that." He turned his head toward Josh. His lover's eyes appeared slumberous and a satisfied smile curved his lips. "You okay?"

"I am beyond okay. You?"

"Yeah. But don't expect any more tonight. I'm wiped."

"Me, too. How about a shower before we go to bed?"

"As soon as my legs work again."

Josh grinned. "Am I gonna have to help you?"

"How can you help me? You should be as wiped as I am."

"I am. But I think we can do it together."

Agreeing with that, Kirk took Josh's hand and used his other to push himself off the mattress. He gingerly scooted to the edge of the bed and placed his feet on the floor. "So far, so good."

Josh stood and offered his other hand to Kirk. He accepted it, groaned when his legs protested moving so quickly. "Hell, I think my legs are dead."

"The hot water will revive them."

Grinning, Josh walked backward out of the bedroom and into the bathroom. Kirk released one of Josh's hands to flip on the light, but held the other one. He didn't want to break the connection yet.

"You like the water hot or lukewarm?" Kirk asked.

"As hot as I can stand it."

Exactly the way Kirk liked his shower. He turned on the water in the tub. "Washcloths and towels in the cabinet," he said over his shoulder while adjusting the water's temperature. Once it reached the degree he wanted, he pulled up the lever to switch on the shower. After disposing of the condom in the trash, he stepped beneath the spray.

"I figured one washcloth was enough." Josh held it out to Kirk, then stepped into the tub next to him.

"You first. Get yourself wet and I'll wash your back."

Kirk moved to the back of the tub after wetting the wash-cloth so Josh had more room beneath the spray. He poured a generous amount of body wash on the cloth, worked up a thick lather. Josh turned his back to Kirk, propped his hands on the wall. Kirk started at the base of Josh's neck, swiped the cloth across his shoulders. He followed the washcloth with his hand, enjoying the feel of the lather on Josh's warm skin.

He made his way down Josh's back to his ass. He dipped the cloth between Josh's buttocks, which earned him a soft moan.

"Sore?"

"A little." Josh smiled at him over his shoulder. "But it's a good sore."

Not wanting to cause Josh any discomfort, Kirk moved the washcloth back up his lover's spine and laid it on Josh's shoulder. "My turn."

Josh took the cloth and quickly swiped it over the rest of his body while Kirk moved beneath the spray to wet his skin. He took the same position Josh had, resting his hands on the wall while Josh washed his back. When he reached Kirk's ass, Kirk widened his stance as much as he could so Josh could easily find his anus.

Josh rubbed the sensitive area while he wrapped his arm around Kirk and cradled his balls. "Your ass is mine tomorrow."

"It's yours tonight if you want it."

"Love to." Josh nipped Kirk's earlobe. "But my dick is dead."

Kirk laughed. "Not dead, just recuperating."

Josh handed the cloth to Kirk, who used it to wash the rest of his body. He rinsed off the lather, moved aside so Josh could do the same.

Once they'd dried, Kirk took Josh's hand again. Instead of leading him back to his bedroom, he led him across the hall to his spare bedroom.

"This is a combination office and catchall room," Kirk explained as he turned on the overhead light. "But the sheets on the bed are clean. I figure it's easier to sleep in here than change the sheets on my bed since *someone* made a mess on them."

Josh stuck his tongue out at Kirk, which made Kirk laugh.

"Get in bed. I'll grab another blanket in case we need it and turn off the light."

After laying the blanket at the foot of the bed, Kirk turned off the light and crawled between the sheets next to Josh. He shared several soft, loving kisses with Josh before urging him to turn over so he could hold him. Cuddled up to Josh with his arm around his lover's chest, Kirk sighed in contentment and closed his eyes.

*　*　*

The smell of bacon cooking had Kirk inhaling deeply to savor the aroma. He blinked to force himself away from sleep and back to reality. He didn't have any bacon in the refrigerator, which meant Josh must have gone to the store.

He had no idea of the time since he'd never put a clock in this room, depending on the clock on his computer or his cell phone for the time. But the grocery store on the main highway through town opened at eight, so it must be at least as late as that in order for Josh to go out and buy food.

Kirk smiled. He liked waking up to someone cooking breakfast.

Throwing off the covers, Kirk padded back to his bedroom. He drew on a pair of sweats and thick socks, not bothering with briefs. He grabbed the covers from the floor and tossed them over the soiled sheets, making a mental note to change them later today.

Following his nose, he found Josh in the kitchen. He wore his clothes, plus shoes, so Kirk had been right about Josh going out. He walked up behind his lover, kissed the side of his neck.

Josh smiled. "Hey, good morning."

"Good morning." Kirk leaned against the cabinet and peered into the skillet. "I know I didn't have bacon, so you must have gone to the store."

"You didn't have much of anything, besides beer. Your three eggs had an expiration date from two weeks ago, so I threw them out and bought fresh ones."

"I'll pay you back for wha—"

A quick kiss cut off Kirk's words. "You won't pay me back for anything. I'm eating, too." He nodded toward the coffeemaker. "Coffee's done. How do you like your eggs?"

"I'm not picky."

" 'K, then I'll scramble them. You're in charge of the toast."

Working side by side, Kirk finished buttering the last piece of toast as Josh spooned scrambled eggs onto two plates next to slices of bacon and orange. Kirk noticed Josh had already placed two juice glasses, silverware, paper towels, and a jar of strawberry preserves on the table.

Very domestic, which Kirk loved.

"There's OJ in the fridge," Josh said, "if you want some."

"Do you?"

"Yeah."

Kirk placed his mug of coffee on the table, then poured a glass of orange juice for both of them. He sat down as Josh placed a plate in front of him.

"Wow. This looks great."

"I like my bacon done, but not too crisp. Hope that's okay."

"It's perfect." Kirk picked up a piece, bit off half of it. "Oh, yeah. Perfect."

This whole scene seemed perfect to Kirk. Spending the night next to Josh, waking up to find the man cooking breakfast, sharing that breakfast with the sun shining warmly through the window. Kirk didn't know how it could be any better.

"Any plans for today?" Josh asked.

"Are you into football?"

"Duh. That's a dumb question."

Kirk grinned. "The Cowboys play the Packers at noon. We can watch the game together."

"Noon's three hours away. We'll have to think of something to pass the time until then."

"We can wash the breakfast dishes. And I need to change the sheets on the bed. That'll take a few minutes."

"True. Then what?"

He loved the humor shining in Josh's eyes. "I believe you said something in the shower last night about my ass being yours today."

"Yes, I did say that."

"Maybe we can mess up the sheets on the spare bed before changing those, too."

Josh grinned. "I like the way you think."

The front door opened and closed. "Yo, bro!" Kory called out. "Where are you?"

Kirk's perfect world collapsed.

6

Josh saw Kirk's eyes widen in terror at the sound of Kory's voice. That reaction verified Josh's suspicions—that he hadn't told his family about being gay.

He didn't have time to reassure Kirk that he would handle everything before Kory walked into the kitchen. "Hey, there you . . ." He stopped, did a double take when he looked at Josh. "Hey, Josh."

"Hey, Kory. Want some coffee? It's fresh."

"What are you doing here?"

"I crashed here after a few too many post-inventory beers."

"Ah." That seemed to satisfy Kory. He walked to the cabinet that held the mugs, took one, and filled it with coffee. "I've done that a few times, too. Lucky Kirk has another bed. If you'd been at my place, you would've had to sack out on the couch."

Josh winked at his lover. Kirk smiled and his shoulders visibly relaxed.

Kory turned the chair around and straddled it. "So, y'all got the inventory thing done?"

"Yeah," Kirk said. "Everything worked great. How was the party?"

"It sucked." Kory snatched a piece of bacon from Kirk's plate. "I mean, I got laid, but the party was a dud. I left a little after two and came home. Mmm, good bacon."

"Josh cooked breakfast."

"Yeah?" He reached over and nudged Josh's arm. "Wanna stay over at my place and cook breakfast?"

Kirk almost choked on his orange juice. Josh fought back a grin while Kory reached over and patted his brother's back. "You okay?"

"Yeah," Kirk croaked. "Just swallowed wrong."

"Careful, bro. I don't want to have to give you mouth-to-mouth." He shuddered.

I'd do it in a second. Josh didn't say the forbidden thought aloud. Instead, he selected another slice of toast from the saucer in the middle of the table. "I can scramble you some eggs if you want them, Kory."

"Nah, I'm good. I grabbed a breakfast burrito from Sonic." He looked at his brother. "Dad called me right before I got here. He asked us over to watch the game. Mom's frying chicken." Kory switched his attention back to Josh. "You're welcome to join us, Josh. My mom makes the best fried chicken you'll ever eat."

Josh couldn't read Kirk's expression, so didn't know if he should say yes or no. "I don't want to intrude on family time."

"You wouldn't be. There's nothing my dad likes better than having a bunch of guys there to watch the Cowboys. And my mom loves to feed us."

"That's true," Kirk said. "Our mom is happiest when she's cooking for a crowd."

Figuring Kirk wouldn't have said that if he didn't want Josh at his parents' house, he nodded. "Then I accept."

A rumble of thunder sounded in the distance. Josh looked

out the window where sunshine had shone through only minutes ago. Now gray clouds filled the sky. "Is it supposed to rain
today?"

Kory shrugged. "I didn't watch the weather last night, but
it's cloudy and feels like rain."

"We need it," Kirk said, forking up his last bite of scrambled
eggs.

Josh heard more thunder, this time louder and closer. He
looked out the window to see a jagged slash of lightning streak
across the sky. Then a loud *boom* shook the apartment enough
to rattle the window next to him.

Both Kory's and Kirk's eyes widened. "Jesus Christ, what
was that?" Kory asked.

Kirk pushed back from the table and ran toward the front
door with Kory and Josh right behind him. All three men
stepped onto the small landing, scanning the area. Josh didn't
see anything out of the ordinary, but he didn't know what he
should be looking for.

"There!" Kory pointed to the east, where black smoke bil-
lowed into the sky.

"That can't be good," Kirk said.

Four beeps came from the pager attached to Kory's belt. He
pressed the button to silence it, then looked at his brother.
"Meet you at the fire hall."

"Right behind you."

Kory ran down the steps and to his pickup. Josh followed
Kirk back into the house and to his bedroom. "What's up?
What did Kory mean about meeting you at the fire hall?"

"Kory and I are on the volunteer fire department. Four
beeps means a structure fire that isn't a house." Kirk pulled off
his sweatpants, tossed them on the unmade bed. "That smoke is
in the direction of the saltwater injection disposal site about
seven miles east of town." He pulled on briefs, walked into his
closet, and came out with a pair of jeans and boots.

"What does that mean?"

"It's owned by Tharwood Energy. Could be lightning struck one of the storage tanks." He sat on the edge of the bed long enough to pull on his boots, then grabbed his cell phone, keys, and wallet from the top of the dresser. "I have to go."

"Go. I'll clean up the kitchen and lock the door when I leave."

Kirk gave him a quick kiss before he jogged past him, stopping only long enough to grab his jacket from the coatrack before he ran out the door.

"Holy shit," Kirk breathed when the fire truck pulled to a stop several yards from the fire. Black smoke shot straight up before being caught by the wind and whipped into a hideous dance. Six of the eight storage tanks burned.

"Let's go, let's go!" Clay Spencer, their fire chief, yelled.

Kirk hurried over to where Dylan Westfield and Quade Easton prepared to fight the fire with the department's new foam truck. Thanks to a generous contribution when one of Lanville's citizens passed away in September, the department had been able to purchase the truck that dispensed firefighting foam. The foam was used to fight specific types of blazes, including oil- and gas-related fires. Several of the firefighters had been instructed on how to use the foam, including Kirk. Made to extinguish flammable liquids, it coated the fuel source, preventing contact with oxygen, which snuffed out the fire.

Lanville's ambulances arrived, along with fire trucks from neighboring towns. Kirk noticed them out of the corner of his eye, but he focused on getting in position on one of the two hoses that would disperse the foam. He gripped it tightly, knowing there would be a kick when the foam started flowing through his hose.

Several other firefighters got into position to help. A shift in the wind blew the black smoke toward the men. Kirk couldn't see for several moments, but trusted his leaders to guide him and the other firefighters.

Rain began to fall as the foam left the hoses. He stood two men back from Quade, who held the nozzle that would adjust the foam's flow. Lightning lit up the sky, thunder rolled. The rain increased until it came down so hard, it bounced off the cement almost to Kirk's knees. Thankful for the protection of his turnout gear, he kept his position on the hose for almost thirty minutes, until the last flame died.

Kirk knew there would be spot checks to be sure all the fire had been extinguished. He waited for instructions from his chief as to the direction he should take. Kory joined him, and Clay sent them in the same direction.

Now that the danger of the fire had passed and the routine cleanup started, Kirk let his mind drift back to last night with Josh. He wanted many more nights exactly like it, falling asleep with his arms wrapped around his lover. Having those nights in Lanville would be impossible if he wanted to keep his secret. He couldn't leave town without telling Kory, and his brother would wonder why Kirk would go out of town without taking Kory since they did so many things together.

He could do what he should've done years ago—be honest with Kory.

Kirk blew out a heavy breath. He didn't look forward to that conversation at all.

Josh paced back and forth in his cabin, unable to do much of anything else with the rain pouring down outside. He kept going to the window and looking out, hoping to see Kirk drive up. Although Kirk hadn't said anything about seeking out Josh once the fire had been extinguished, Josh hoped he would.

Kirk, a volunteer firefighter. Josh already admired the man for his work ethic and the way he got along so well with people. Now he had another reason to admire him. Josh thought fighting fires to be one of the noblest, most courageous occupations a man could have. And Kirk did it out of the goodness of his heart, simply to help people. He didn't get any kind of compensation for putting his life out there to save someone else's life.

Warmth spread throughout Josh's chest at having met such a special man.

He already cared more for Kirk than he had any other man in his life. He hadn't come to Lanville looking for love. He'd come here to work for two to three months before he moved on to the next town in his journey across the U.S. While he liked the small town, he couldn't see living here the rest of his life.

Perhaps Kirk would go with him. They could travel together, see the entire U.S. Josh had plenty of money to support them for the rest of their lives.

As soon as that thought formed, Josh knew it wouldn't work. Kirk had a life here with his family and his friends and the business that would be his and Kory's someday. Josh had no right to try and take him away from everything and everyone Kirk loved.

The slamming of a car door filtered through the rain pounding on the roof. Josh hurried to open the cabin's door. He pulled it wide as Kirk raised his hand to knock.

Kirk smiled. "Hey."

"Hey, yourself. Get in here."

Kirk stepped over the threshold. Raindrops dotted his hair. An invisible trail of the rain-scented liquid soap Kirk used followed him. He must have gone home to shower after putting out the fire, before he came over here.

Needing to know for sure his lover hadn't been injured, he drew Kirk into his arms, held him tightly. "I was worried about you."

Kirk returned his hug. "I'm fine."

"So everything went okay with the fire?"

"Yeah. We put it out and did the cleanup in about an hour." Kirk stepped back, took off his jacket, and draped it over the straight-backed chair at the desk. He wore a blue crewneck sweater almost the same color as his eyes. His gaze swept the room. "This is nice."

"It's comfortable. Nice bed and cable is included in the rental price." He motioned toward the small kitchenette with its combination microwave and convection oven, mini-fridge, and two-burner cooktop. "Not as nice as cooking in your kitchen, but I make do."

Kirk stepped closer to him. "You can cook in my kitchen any time you want to." He cradled Josh's nape. "Or sleep in my bed."

The desire in Kirk's eyes sent blood rushing to Josh's dick. Now that he knew for sure Kirk hadn't been hurt, he could concentrate on getting him naked. Grabbing a fistful of Kirk's sweater, he tugged it away from Kirk's chest. "This has to go."

In a flash, Kirk pulled off the sweater and tossed it in the direction of the desk. Josh took a moment to admire the wide shoulders and strong arms before he kissed the center of Kirk's chest. He kissed his way to a nipple, gave it a long lick before drawing it between his lips to suckle.

"God," Kirk muttered.

Taking that to mean Kirk liked the attention to his nipple, Josh switched to the other one. As he licked and sucked the hard nub, he slid his hand to the fly of Kirk's jeans. A thick bulge pressed against the zipper. Josh unfastened the waistband button, lowered the zipper. His knuckles brushed hard flesh.

Kirk hadn't bothered with underwear.

A low groan came from Kirk's throat. He cradled Josh's face, kissed him passionately. Josh accepted the kisses while he tugged apart the placket of Kirk's jeans. His lover's cock sprang up, full and hard. Wrapping his hand around it, Josh pumped the firm column while they continued to kiss.

Soon only touching Kirk's dick wasn't enough. Josh ended their kiss, guided Kirk to the bed. As soon as Kirk sat down on the edge, Josh leaned over and took his partner's cock in his mouth. Kirk released that sexy groaning sound again and arched his hips.

"*God,* Josh, you do that *so* good."

Doing something he loved took no effort at all. The fact that it pleased Kirk made it even sweeter for Josh. Running his tongue along the heavy veins, he slowly moved back to the crown. A drop of pre-cum already seeped from the slit. Josh lapped it up.

"You taste good." Josh licked his way down to Kirk's balls and nuzzled them. "You smell good, too."

Gripping the back of Josh's shirt, Kirk tugged on it until Josh lifted his head. Fire flashed from Kirk's blue eyes. "You. Naked. Now."

Josh wanted the same thing. Rising to his feet, he quickly pulled off his henley and threw it in the direction of Kirk's sweater. He pushed his jeans and briefs down his legs, pulled them and his socks off at the same time. Leaning over once more, he gripped the waistband of Kirk's jeans. "Lift."

Kirk did. One good yank and Josh sent Kirk's jeans, socks, and boots to land somewhere on the floor.

Kirk uncovered one of the pillows on the bed, stuffed it beneath his stomach. He lowered his head to his folded arms and spread his legs wide apart.

Josh suspected what Kirk wanted, but had to be sure. He stretched out on top of his lover, his dick nestled in the warm cleft between Kirk's buttocks. "You want to be fucked?"

"Yeah."

A nip on Kirk's earlobe made him moan again. "How about my tongue in your ass first?"

"God, yes."

Josh kissed Kirk's nape while caressing his shoulders. He could see the pulse pounding in Kirk's neck, could hear his rapid breathing. Josh continued to drop kisses down the center of his lover's back until he reached his ass. Each cheek received a gentle nip with his teeth. "You have a great ass."

Kirk arched his back and lifted his ass higher. "Stop being so slow."

"I told you I like to savor." He ran his tongue down the crack, stopped at the top of Kirk's anus. "I like the buildup."

Rising to his elbow, Kirk looked at Josh over his shoulder. "I've been anticipating your dick in my ass ever since you mentioned it last night. That's enough buildup."

Josh considered teasing Kirk a bit more, but the lust darkening Kirk's eyes changed his mind. Josh pulled apart Kirk's cheeks, drove his tongue into his partner's ass.

"Fuck!" Kirk yelled.

Kirk could yell all he wanted to. In fact, Josh wanted to hear that sound of Kirk's pleasure. He had purposely picked the most isolated cabin for privacy in case he met someone in Lanville and they came here for sex. Plus the pounding rain created a natural barrier to sound.

Pulling Kirk's cheeks even farther apart, Josh began tongue-fucking his ass. Kirk lifted his hips to meet Josh's tongue every time it dove inside, lowered them when Josh withdrew. It took only a few moments for them to establish the perfect rhythm, one he hoped would bring Kirk to a climax.

On second thought, he wanted to see Kirk come.

Josh rose to his knees. Kirk groaned again, but this time in protest. "Don't stop! Man, that feels good."

"It'll feel even better as soon as I get my dick in your ass."

Josh reached in the nightstand by the bed, removed lube and a condom. He rolled on the protection, then applied plenty of lube to his dick and Kirk's anus. "Do you need me to prepare you with my fingers?"

"No. Just fuck me."

Placing the head of his cock on the puckered hole, he slowly pushed until the crown slipped past the tight muscle and stopped to let Kirk get used to it.

Leaning forward, Josh braced himself with his straight arms and slid his dick in another inch. He pulled back, pushed forward a bit more. Back, forward, back, forward, until his balls rested against Kirk's skin. He remained still for several seconds, letting Kirk adjust some more, before he moved again. He drew back until only the crown remained inside his lover's ass, then glided his cock all the way inside him again.

"My God, that feels good," Kirk said in a raspy voice.

It felt good to Josh, too, but he wanted more. He wanted to look into Kirk's eyes while they fucked.

He pulled all the way out, nipped both cheeks with his teeth. "Turn over."

Kirk did as ordered. He held both his legs behind the knees so they spread wide open. Josh wasted no time in thrusting completely inside the other man again. He watched Kirk's eyes slide closed as a look of pure bliss covered his face.

Josh began a gentle pumping motion. "Jesus, you're tight." He picked up the speed of his thrusts. "Love the feel of my dick in your ass."

"So do I." Kirk opened his eyes, stared into Josh's. "It's perfect."

Josh slid one arm beneath Kirk's leg so Kirk could release it and have one hand free. Kirk touched Josh's shoulders, chest, stomach, hips. Fingertips dug into Josh's butt, urged him closer. Josh answered Kirk's silent request and pumped quicker.

"Yeah, like that." Kirk's eyes almost singed Josh with their heat. "Just like that."

Needing even more contact, Josh wrapped his free hand around Kirk's hard cock and milked it while he drove his shaft more firmly into Kirk's ass. The base of his spine tingled, his balls drew up tight. He wouldn't be able to hold back his climax much longer.

Veins popped out in Kirk's neck and temples. His body quivered, his cock twitched. Warm cum shot from the slit to land on his belly and chest.

Now that his lover had come, Josh thrust his dick all the way into Kirk's ass and let his orgasm envelop him.

7

Kirk lay in the circle of Josh's arms beneath a quilt, content to be close to his lover while he listened to the sound of the rain. The thunder and lightning had stopped, leaving a slow, soaking rain that would help put a dent in the drought.

"Are you asleep?" Josh whispered.

"No. Just enjoying the rain."

Josh slowly caressed Kirk's chest and stomach. "Aren't you supposed to be at your folks' house for lunch?"

"Yeah, at one-thirty. Kory called them on the way to the fire to tell them we'd be late." Kirk glanced at the digital clock radio on the nightstand. "Which gives us about twenty-five minutes to get there."

"Do you still want me to go with you?"

Unsure why Josh would ask that question, Kirk turned over so he could look into his lover's eyes. "Of course I do. Why wouldn't I?"

Josh scooted closer until their flaccid cocks brushed together. "I don't go around shouting 'I'm gay,' but I don't hide it either. If for some reason the subject comes up with your parents, I won't tell them we've been together, but I won't lie about my sexuality."

"You think my parents are gonna say, 'hey, Josh, are you gay'?"

"Not that crass, no, but the subject could come up."

Kirk played with the dark hair on Josh's chest. "Do your parents know you're gay?"

"Yeah. I told them as soon as I figured it out. They were and still are very supportive. They only want my happiness." Josh propped up on one elbow. "You should tell your parents, Kirk. You'd feel better if you didn't carry around such a huge secret."

Kirk rolled to his back, ran his hands over his face. "How do I do that? I can't just blurt out, 'oh, by the way, I'm gay.' "

"A little more finesse would be good, but basically that's what you do. You have to be honest with them, and with the rest of your family and friends. Don't you think they'll wonder why you aren't getting involved with any of the women around here? You're a very good-looking guy and several women who come in the store obviously have the hots for you. Kalinda would attack you if you gave her any hint of interest."

Frustration welled up inside Kirk at the thought that he would have to go through this. "Why is it such a big deal to some people who someone has sex with? Being gay doesn't define who I am. I'd still have blond hair and blue eyes if I was straight."

"That's true. And I know it can be maddening. I've gone through some gay bashing from people I considered friends. One minute I'm a great guy and fun to be around, the next I'm an outcast simply because I prefer men in my bed. Never has made sense to me." Josh laid his hand on Kirk's stomach. "You've been with women, haven't you?"

"Yeah, several times. I've partied with Kory and that always meant women. They never . . . appealed to me."

"The same with me. While my high school buds were ogling

the cheerleaders, I was admiring the football players' asses in those tight uniform pants."

Kirk grinned. "I know what you mean." His grin faded as quickly as it formed. "I don't want to lose anyone I love."

Josh cradled Kirk's cheek in his palm. "If they truly love you back, you won't lose them." He leaned over and gave Kirk a gentle kiss. "Now, we should get dressed and head for your parents' house. I'm hungry for your mom's fried chicken."

Kirk agonized over when and how to tell Kory and his parents about being gay over the next week. He finally decided he'd wait for a natural time to bring up the subject. He wasn't quite sure what would be a "natural time," but putting it off as long as possible seemed good to him.

His plan fell apart when Josh invited him to go to Dallas over the weekend. Josh said they could have dinner with his parents Saturday night, then spend Sunday doing whatever Kirk wanted to do—eat out, go to a movie, go to the Cowboys game since they played at home this week. His father's law firm owned a suite at the stadium and Josh could go to any home game he wanted.

Kirk couldn't tell Kory he might go to a Cowboys game Sunday and not invite him. Kory would be crushed.

The "natural time" popped up a lot sooner than Kirk wanted. He couldn't put off talking to his brother any longer.

Instead of hunting down Kory at work, Kory found him right before lunch. He stuck his head in the office while Kirk sorted bills for payment.

"Hey, bro, want to come over tonight and watch *Thursday Night Football*?"

It would be the perfect opportunity to talk to his brother. "Sure."

Kory smiled. "You pick up a pizza, I'll get the beer."

"Deal."

Once Kory left, Kirk leaned back in his chair and blew out a breath. He and Kory had shared so much since the day they were born. Kirk didn't know what he'd do if Kory pushed him away after Kirk admitted the truth regarding his sexuality.

"Hey."

Kirk looked up to see Josh leaning against the door frame. As always, his heart sped up at the sight of the handsome man. "Hey."

"You wanna get some supper after work?"

"Can't. I'm going over to Kory's."

Josh must have sensed something by Kirk's expression. He looked both ways in the hall before speaking again. "Is this the night?"

Kirk nodded. "It's time. I don't want to hide the truth any longer."

"Good. Call me later and tell me how it went. Or . . ." He looked in the hall again. "Come by and tell me in person."

"It might be late."

"I'm off tomorrow. Late is fine."

"I'll call you and let you know for sure."

Josh nodded, although he seemed confused. "Okay."

He turned toward the store, where Kirk had scheduled him to be at the checkout counter today. Kirk didn't blame Josh for being confused. They hadn't been alone together since Sunday since Kirk kept coming up with things he had to do, which kept him and Josh apart. Josh had been great with his parents and they liked him, too. His dad said he wished everyone he hired worked as hard as Josh. His mother doted on him like a third son. Yet Kirk's stomach had churned with guilt the whole time, making it difficult to eat his mother's delicious cooking. Having Josh in his parents' home without them knowing how much he cared about the other man didn't seem right.

He'd tell his brother first. Then he had to tell his parents.

Unable to concentrate on the bills—and worried he'd pay something wrong—Kirk closed out the accounting program. Maybe doing something physical would help take his mind off what would come later.

A truck holding sacks of cement pulled into the yard as Kirk walked out the back door. Perfect. Unloading the truck meant he could put his body on autopilot and not have to think.

"Hey, Kirk," Gus said as Kirk joined him and Don. "Whatcha doin' out here?"

"Thought you guys might need some help unloading the cement."

"Shouldn't you be doing payroll today?" Don asked with a grin.

Kirk returned his employee's grin. "Already done. You'll get your check tomorrow, just like every Friday."

"Good." Don rubbed his gloved hands together. "I have plans with a cute little sweetie this weekend."

Gus rolled his eyes at Kirk. "He's almost as bad as Kory. I'll get the forklift."

Movement at the back door of the store drew Kirk's attention. Josh stepped outside, shrugging into his jacket. "Hey, Don, phone call for you. I'll take your place out here."

"Thanks, Josh."

Josh stopped next to Kirk in front of the bin where the cement would be stored, stuffed his hands in his pockets. "You okay?"

"Yeah, sure." Kirk blew out a breath. "No."

"Look, don't do anything you aren't ready to do just because I suggested it. I'll be out of here in a couple of months. I don't have to live around your family and friends. You do."

The reminder that Josh had no intention of staying in Lanville cut into Kirk's heart, but he refused to let his pain and disappointment show. He'd known from the moment he interviewed Josh that the other man wouldn't be around for long.

Kirk shouldn't have let his heart rule over his brain. "It was a good suggestion. It's time. I should've been honest with my family a long time ago."

"Come by my cabin later, no matter what time it is. I want to be with you."

Kirk wanted that, too. He nodded. "I'll be there."

"Oh, man, did you see that?" Kory asked in a frustrated voice. "How could he have dropped that pass? It was perfect!"

Kirk thought the same thing as he bit into a slice of cold pizza. He and his brother had devoured most of the pizza as soon as Kirk opened the box, but the remaining two pieces had been sitting there for a while. Kirk didn't care. He loved pizza, whether hot or cold.

Besides, eating gave him the excuse not to talk.

With halftime only a couple of minutes away, Kirk decided he'd stalled long enough. "Hey, can I talk to you at halftime?"

"Sure." He grinned. "Is it the kind of talk that needs a fresh beer?"

"Could be."

Kory's grin faded. "Hey, bro, what's up? You okay?"

"I need to tell you something and I'm not sure how to do it."

Picking up the remote control, Kory muted the TV's sound. "You can tell me anything, Kirk, you know that."

"It can wait until halftime."

"Fuck the game. You're more important."

Kirk tossed the rest of his slice back into the cardboard box on the coffee table. Leaning forward, he clasped his hands between his spread knees and stared at the floor. "You ever wonder why I don't date as much as you do?"

"Not . . . really. Why?"

"It's because there's no one in Lanville who interests me."

"Me, either. That's why we hit the clubs in the Metroplex. Lots of great-looking babes there."

"That's the problem, Kory. I don't want any great-looking babes." Kirk lifted his head, looked directly into his brother's eyes. "I prefer the company of men."

Several moments passed before Kory's eyes widened so much, Kirk would've laughed if the situation hadn't been so serious. "You're gay?" he squeaked.

Kirk nodded.

"But you've had sex with women lots of times. I know because I was there some of those times."

"Let's be honest, Kory. If someone is sucking your dick, you're gonna get off."

"Yeah, that's true." He ran one hand through his hair. "Wow. I never suspected anything like that."

Here came the hard part . . . the question Kirk dreaded asking. "Does it make a difference with us?"

Kory frowned. "Difference?"

"Yeah. Between you and me. Are we okay?"

Kory's frown turned into a scowl. "What the *hell* kind of question is that? Of course we're okay. We're brothers. Just because you're gay doesn't mean I stop loving you."

Kirk's shoulders sagged in relief. "God, I was so scared to tell you, scared you'd push me out of your life."

"Jesus, Kirk, I would never do that. I'll always have your back, no matter what. Why should I care who you have as sex partners?"

"Desiring men makes me different. That matters to a lot of people."

"Then they're idiots because it's none of their business."

Kirk glanced at the floor again before looking back at his brother. "Do you think Mom and Dad will feel the same way you do?"

"You haven't told them yet?"

Kirk shook his head. "I wanted to tell you first."

Kory scooted closer to Kirk and placed his hand on Kirk's shoulder. "I think Mom and Dad love you and will be there for you, no matter what."

Emotion clogged Kirk's throat, making it impossible for him to speak without bursting into tears. He laid his hand on top of Kory's, gave it a quick squeeze.

Kory picked up the pizza box. "Okay, now that true confessions time is over, I'll get us another beer and we can watch the rest of the game."

And just like that, what Kirk feared would happen when he confessed to his brother vanished into the air like a wisp of fog.

He hoped he experienced something similar with his parents.

"Kory."

His brother stopped halfway between the couch and kitchen. "Yeah?"

"Hold off on that beer for me. I need to go see Mom and Dad."

"You sure you want to do that now?"

"Yeah. I think it's best if I get it done."

Kory came back to the living room. "You want me to go with you?"

Warmth spread through Kirk's chest at his twin's offer. "No, but thanks."

Kirk stood, picked up his jacket from the back of the couch. At the front door, he faced Kory, who had followed him. "Thanks for being such a great brother."

Kory smiled, then tugged Kory into a back-slapping hug. "Backatcha."

Kirk stepped into the cold night, hopeful his parents would be as understanding as his brother.

* * *

Josh glanced at the digital clock when he heard the soft knock on his cabin's door. 10:05. Not as late as he expected Kirk to arrive.

He opened the door to see Kirk standing beneath the small overhang, his hands in his jacket pockets. He couldn't tell by Kirk's expression what happened tonight. Silently, he opened the door wider so his lover could enter.

"What happened?" he asked as Kirk removed his jacket and draped it over the desk's chair.

"Nothing." Kirk turned to face Josh. "I was expecting to be thrown out of the family and maybe even ordered to leave town. Kory was great, my parents were great. Kory had no idea I'm gay, but my parents said they suspected it since I'd never been involved with a girl or dated anyone more than once." Chuckling, Kirk pushed his hair off his forehead. "I thought my dad would be furious. He was even more understanding than my mom. He said as long as I'm happy, that's all he wants."

Thrilled coming out had worked so well for Kirk, Josh drew him into a hug. "I'm glad."

"You might not be for long." Kirk pulled back, a worried expression on his face. "I told my folks that you invited me to Dallas for the weekend. Dad mentioned that we've been spending a lot of time together and asked if you're gay, too. I said yes."

"I don't have a problem with that, Kirk. I told you I don't flaunt my sexuality, but I don't hide it either."

Relief flashed in Kirk's eyes. "I was worried you'd be angry."

"No." He cradled Kirk's face in his hands. "I could never be angry with you. I care about you way too much for that."

8

With Kirk's lips so close, Josh couldn't resist tasting them. They softened, parted, at first contact. Kirk laid his hands on Josh's waist and tilted his head to allow Josh to deepen the kiss.

Lips caressed.

Tongues tangled.

Breaths mingled.

With their lips still pressed together, Josh guided them toward the bed. Even though Kirk said everything had gone fine with his family, Josh knew his lover had been stressed and nervous. He wanted to do everything he could for Kirk to relax him and show him that he cared.

Josh pulled Kirk's sweatshirt over his head. Kirk reached for the hem of Josh's T-shirt, but Josh held his hands before he could remove it.

"No. Let me take care of you first."

Kneeling at Kirk's feet, Josh untied his shoes and slipped them from his feet. He unfastened Kirk's belt, unsnapped and unzipped his jeans . . . not an easy feat since Kirk's hard cock filled the fly. Josh tugged on Kirk's jeans and briefs until his dick popped free. A drop of pre-cum already dotted the slit. Josh swiped it off with his tongue.

Kirk moaned.

Josh loved that sound and planned to do everything he could so Kirk would make it over and over again. He tugged down Kirk's jeans and briefs to his knees for more room to fondle Kirk's balls. They tightened in his palm, drew up closer to Kirk's body.

Josh's mouth watered with the desire to taste Kirk's cum again.

Standing, Josh took Kirk's shoulders and gently pressed until his lover sat on the edge of the bed. Kirk's jeans, briefs, and socks landed on the floor on top of his sweatshirt. He pushed again, this time on Kirk's chest until his partner lay crosswise on the bed, his legs hanging over the side.

Josh took a few moments to simply look at his lover. He admired the shaggy blond hair, scorching blue eyes, shapely lips, broad shoulders, wide chest that tapered to a trim waist. Kirk had no hair on his chest, just a line that ran down from his navel to flow into his pubic hair. Soft, dark blond hair scattered over his arms and legs and formed a nest for his cock.

"I want to look at you, too," Kirk said in a husky voice.

"Soon. Let me enjoy the view for a bit."

"You can touch me and still enjoy the view."

Kirk's cock jerked, making Josh grin. "Eager, are you?"

"Always."

Josh ran his hands up the outside of Kirk's thighs. "Do you have any idea what an incredible body you have?"

"Yours is incredible, too."

Josh shook his head. "I'm on the lean side while you're more muscular."

"Just because you're lean doesn't mean you don't have an amazing body. Which I'm still waiting to see."

Josh grinned. He liked teasing Kirk. It made the passion so

much sweeter. "You can wait a little while longer. I want to play first."

Before Kirk could utter another protest, Josh leaned over and licked the full length of Kirk's dick. His lover's hips jerked, and so did his cock. Josh licked again, traced the thick vein with the tip of his tongue. He laved Kirk's balls for several moments before he drew them, one at a time, into his mouth and sucked gently.

"You're killing me."

Kirk's voice sounded raspy, as if he couldn't get enough air into his lungs to talk. Knowing his breathlessness came from pleasure and not pain encouraged Josh to continue his playful torment. He nuzzled beneath Kirk's balls, licked that sensitive area between them and Kirk's ass. His partner propped his feet wide apart on the bed, let his knees fall open to expose the rosette. Pulling apart the puckered hole with his thumbs, Josh licked around the edge of Kirk's asshole.

"Oh, *fuck!*"

Not yet, but Josh had every intention of fucking this man before the night ended. Or maybe Kirk would fuck him. Either way worked for him, which had never occurred in his life. He'd bottomed a few times and enjoyed it, yet preferred to top. With Kirk, as long as they made love, Josh didn't care what position he took.

This relationship with Kirk differed from relationships with other men. He'd liked other men, enjoyed sex with them. Everything with Kirk seemed so much bigger, so much more special.

He cared so much more about this man than any man in his life.

Josh pumped his tongue in and out of Kirk's ass for a few more strokes before he moved back to his balls. Once he'd licked every spot on them, he ran his tongue up the length of

Kirk's dick again. When he reached the crown, he gripped Kirk's cock by the base so it stood straight up from his body. Josh circled the rim, darted into the slit, took the entire head into his mouth. He watched Kirk's face while he worshipped the hard flesh in his hand and mouth. His lover's parted lips and closed eyes proved his pleasure mounted with each stroke of Josh's tongue.

Knowing Kirk had to be close to coming, it surprised Josh when Kirk tunneled his hands into Josh's hair and lifted his mouth away.

"With me," Kirk whispered. "Come with me."

While Josh loved that Kirk wanted him to also experience pleasure, Josh greedily yearned for another taste of his lover's cum. "In round two. Right now, I want to take care of you."

Josh took Kirk's cock's head in his mouth again, using his tongue and a gentle suction at the places he knew to be the most sensitive. Kirk kept his hands in Josh's hair, but no longer pulled him away. He pumped his hips in time to Josh's sucking, slowing when Josh slowed, speeding up when Josh sucked harder and faster.

Kirk's breathing became choppy. His chest rose and fell with his heavy breathing. Knowing he had to be right on the edge of a climax, Josh decided to help him fall off that edge. He shoved a finger into Kirk's ass. His lover's hips rose off the bed as Kirk cried out. Warm semen filled Josh's mouth, trickled down his throat.

Josh placed his hands on either side of Kirk's waist and stared at his face. Kirk still breathed heavily through his mouth with his eyes closed. Josh smiled. He liked completely wearing out his partner so he could barely move.

"You okay?" Josh asked.

"No." He peered at Josh from one eye. "You keep hitting me with trucks."

Josh chuckled. "Want me to stop?"

"Hell, no." He opened his other eye. "But I do want you naked."

Deciding he'd teased long enough, he straightened to do as Kirk requested. Holding his lover's gaze, he pulled off his T-shirt and let it fall to the floor. Jeans and briefs came next, then socks. Once he stood naked before Kirk, Josh palmed his cock and slowly—so slowly—ran his hand up and down his hard flesh.

Kirk sat on the side of the bed, his gaze riveted to Josh's hand. "Keep doing that." His voice broke on the last word and he cleared his throat. "I want to watch you come."

Not something Josh expected Kirk to say, but he had no problem jerking off if that's what Kirk desired.

Reaching into the nightstand drawer, Josh pulled out a bottle of lube. He poured a generous amount in his hand, applied it to his cock. Now his hand slid easier over his shaft. He paid extra attention to the crown and the sensitive spot beneath the rim. Kirk lifted his gaze every few moments to Josh's eyes, but then returned it to the scene a foot away from him.

"It won't take long for me to come if I keep doing this."

"Good. Don't stop."

Josh noticed Kirk's clenched fists, as if he didn't know whether or not to touch Josh. Feeling his lover's hands would only add to Josh's pleasure. "Touch me, Kirk."

Kirk placed his hands on the outside of Josh's thighs. He ran them up Josh's sides as far as he could reach, repeated the journey back to his thighs. He made one more trip, then reached for the bottle of lube on the nightstand.

Anticipation of what Kirk planned to do had Josh's heart pounding. He increased the speed of his hand as his lover coated two fingers with the clear gel. "Spread your legs," Kirk ordered.

Josh did. Kirk touched his asshole with slick fingers. Josh's movement on his dick faltered.

"Don't stop." Kirk pushed the tips of his fingers past the ring of muscle. "Keep touching yourself."

Josh groaned when Kirk's fingers slid all the way into his ass. Bending his knees, he widened his stance to give Kirk more room. Kirk pulled his fingers all the way out, pushed them back in. Josh altered the rhythm of his stroking to match Kirk's. As Kirk moved his fingers faster, Josh moved his hand faster.

"I'm gonna come."

Kirk didn't stop.

"I'll shoot all over your chest."

Kirk pushed in his fingers and massaged Josh's prostate. That did it. Josh couldn't have stopped his orgasm if a tornado whipped through the cabin. His balls tightened, drew up close to his body. Cum barreled up his dick to explode out the slit, splattering on Kirk's chest and stomach.

Josh grabbed Kirk's shoulder with his free hand and locked his knees to keep from falling. "God, that was hot."

"I'll say." Kirk dragged his finger through the cum on his chest, lifted it to his mouth. "Mmm, tastes good."

"So do you." Josh leaned over and gave Kirk a long, passionate kiss. "I'll get a washcloth for you."

It took a moment for his legs to work right, then Josh walked into the bathroom. He cleaned himself first, wet a fresh washcloth to take to Kirk. He found his lover lying on his back on the bed, Kirk's skin still dotted with Josh's cum. Despite the earth-shattering orgasm he'd experienced, Josh's cock stirred at the sexy sight.

He sat on the edge of the bed, gently bathed Kirk's chest and stomach. "Do you have any idea how sexy you look lying there with my cum all over you?" He lowered the washcloth toward Kirk's abdomen and bumped his hardening cock. He grinned. "I guess you do."

"Watching you jerk off was one of the hottest things I've ever seen."

Josh tossed the washcloth to the floor, laid his hand over Kirk's dick. He didn't caress it, didn't pump it, he simply touched it. "Everything with you is hot."

Unable to resist the lure of Kirk's lips, Josh bent over and kissed the other man. Kirk wrapped his arms around Josh, pulled him closer. Josh rolled them so they lay on their sides, facing each other. His cock began to respond to the feel of Kirk's skin against his.

He groaned when Kirk gripped both their dicks in his hands. Josh continued kissing his lover, running his hand up and down Kirk's back, while Kirk worked their cocks together. It felt good, but he would need more stimulation to come again.

Apparently, Kirk felt the same way. He pulled back, looked into Josh's eyes. "On your knees."

Curious about what Kirk planned to do, Josh didn't hesitate to rise to his knees on the bed. Kirk also rose and faced Josh. He moved closer until their hard cocks touched. Once more gripping them, Kirk rubbed them together as he kissed Josh again.

Having Kirk working their dicks left both of Josh's hands free to explore his lover's body. He kissed the spot beneath Kirk's ear that he knew gave Kirk so much pleasure. He tugged on his partner's earlobe with his teeth, kissed his way along Kirk's jaw back to his mouth.

He would never tire of kissing this man.

Emotion swelled in his chest, an emotion he'd never experienced with another man. Since Josh had never been in love, he didn't know how it felt. This breathless, heart-pounding, want-to-be-with-Kirk-all-the-time feeling had to be love. He couldn't imagine calling something so strong anything else.

The pre-cum leaking from his and Kirk's slits made their dicks easily slide together. Josh drove his tongue into Kirk's mouth, moaned when Kirk sucked on it. Sweat covered his skin, and Kirk's. Desire built, peaked, resulting in his second orgasm grabbing his balls only seconds before Kirk jerked from his own release.

Josh's legs gave out on him. He wilted to the bed, his arms still wrapped around Kirk so his lover went with him. They once again lay on their sides, facing each other. Josh didn't even have the strength to open his eyes for several moments. When he did, he saw Kirk staring at him with tenderness and caring.

Josh touched Kirk's lips, smiled when Kirk kissed his fingertips. "If you have any more tricks up your sleeve, they'll have to wait until another day. I'm wiped."

"If you think I can do anything else tonight, you're way overestimating my abilities."

"I don't think I'm overestimating anything. Your abilities are awesome." He gave Kirk a soft kiss. "We still on for this weekend in Dallas?"

"If you think I'm gonna turn down seeing a Cowboys game live, you're nuts."

Josh chuckled. "You hungry? I have a couple of slices of leftover pizza I can pop in the microwave." He glanced down at their cum-splattered stomachs. "Maybe we should shower first."

"Definitely shower first."

"I'll warn you, the shower stall is made for one person. It'll be a tight fit for both of us."

Kirk gave him a lazy grin. "I love tight fits."

9

Two Months Later

Kirk blinked open his eyes shortly after six to see Josh lying next to him. Smiling, he reached out and ran his thumb down Josh's cheek. Love not only filled his heart, but overflowed to occupy every part of his body.

His smile faded. He hadn't told Josh of his feelings. Nor had Josh said anything about loving Kirk, although Kirk knew Josh cared. They'd spent the past two months together as much as possible without discussing where their relationship could be going.

Even though Josh said he didn't hide his sexual preference, he hadn't done anything to push his beliefs on Kirk. There were no public displays of affection at work, or even around town. Josh never took Kirk's hand while they walked, never tried to sneak a kiss. Kirk appreciated that, but he couldn't help feeling a little guilty about not being truthful with his friends. His family knew about his relationship with Josh, and while others might suspect he and Josh spent more time together than mere friends would, no one had said anything. There had been no snickers, no finger pointing, nothing that Kirk noticed from customers or people he passed on the sidewalks.

He considered that a good thing, since Josh would probably leave Lanville soon. Josh had told Kirk he'd be here two to three months when he accepted the job at Wilcox Lumber. Two months had already passed. Kirk suspected Josh would leave any day.

He would take Kirk's heart with him, but Kirk would never stand in the way of Josh's plans or happiness.

Josh opened his eyes. He gave Kirk a sleepy smile. "Hey."

"Hey back."

"Wha' timezit?"

"Early. Go back to sleep."

" 'K."

Josh closed his eyes, but opened them again seconds later. "Why aren't you asleep?"

Kirk shrugged one shoulder. "Don't know. I woke up a few minutes ago."

"Maybe cuddling will help you fall asleep again." Josh scooted closer until his hard cock bumped Kirk's. "Or there are other options."

While Kirk always enjoyed making love with Josh, he would rather talk this morning than have sex. "How about if I start breakfast for us? I'm in the mood for pancakes."

A surprised look crossed Josh's face. He apparently didn't expect his offer of sex to be rejected. "Uh, sure. If that's what you want to do."

Kirk rose from the bed, crossed to the chest of drawers for socks and briefs. By the time he'd donned those, Josh sat up in bed with the covers to his waist, his arms resting on his raised knees. "Is something wrong?" he asked.

"Nope, I'm just hungry." Kirk fastened his jeans, reached into another drawer for a T-shirt.

"You're scaring me, Wilcox."

"I don't mean to." Kirk sat on the side of the bed, reached for Josh's hand. "Everything is fine."

"I hear a 'but' after that sentence."

Kirk blew out a breath. He didn't know how to bring up what he wanted to discuss with Josh. "Let's talk over breakfast, okay?"

He saw Josh's throat work as he swallowed. "Okay."

Kirk started the coffee first, then gathered the ingredients to make pancakes. He'd poured Bisquick into a bowl when Josh joined him. "Can I help?"

"Yeah. I bought a canned ham yesterday. You can slice it."

Before Kirk had the chance to add milk to the bowl, Josh held his arm. "I won't be able to eat anything without knowing what's wrong."

Kirk doubted if he'd be able to eat either. He wiped his hands on a dishtowel. "Let's get some coffee and sit down."

After pouring mugs for both of them, Kirk joined Josh at the table. He didn't like the anxiety in his lover's eyes and hoped he could quickly erase it. "I've, uh, been thinking about when you interviewed for your job. You said you didn't plan to be here but two or three months. You've been here for two. Are you planning to leave soon?"

Josh set down his mug without taking a sip of the hot brew. "You may not believe this, but I'd planned to talk to you about that today."

Kirk managed to give him a small smile. "Great minds."

"Yeah." Josh stared down into his mug, as if searching for the right words to say. "I've been getting . . . itchy to hit the road." He lifted his gaze back to Kirk. "I like Lanville, I really do, but it was never my intention to stay here for very long."

"I know that. You were honest about your plans from the start."

Kirk silently toasted himself that he could make his voice sound so steady and calm while his heart slowly crumbled.

"I never expected to meet someone as special as you in this small town." Josh pushed aside his untouched coffee, reached across the table, and laid his hand on top of Kirk's. "Come with me."

Not what Kirk expected Josh to say. "What?"

"We can see the U.S. together. I have plenty of money, more than I could ever spend by myself. We'll go first class all the way. If we get tired of driving, we'll get on a plane and fly. Europe, Asia, Australia . . . wherever you want to go."

Kirk had no doubt his brother would jump at the chance to be "kept." Kirk wouldn't. Maybe he'd consider it if Josh said, "I love you." Those words hadn't yet come from Josh's mouth.

He slowly drew his hand from beneath the other man's. "I have a life here, Josh."

"I know you do, but we could have a lot of fun together."

Fun. Not a relationship, not together forever, just fun. Josh didn't want a lifelong partner, he wanted a travel and fuck buddy.

No matter how much he wanted Josh to stay, Kirk would never beg him to remain in Lanville if staying would make Josh unhappy. He loved Josh enough to put his lover's happiness before his own.

"I'm sure we *could* have a lot of fun, but I can't go with you, Josh. My dad depends on me to run the company, which will be mine and Kory's someday. My life is here."

The crushed look on Josh's face almost made Kirk change his mind. He pushed aside any sympathy for his lover's hurt feelings. Kirk knew staying in Lanville was the right thing to do. He didn't want the kind of life Josh wanted. He wanted forever. He wouldn't get that with Josh.

"When do you want to leave?" Kirk asked.

"I was thinking around the first of March. That'll give you time to hire someone to replace me."

Less than three weeks from now, the man he loved would drive off in his fancy Mercedes convertible and Kirk would never see him again. "I appreciate the advance notice."

Josh sat back in his chair, his eyebrows drawn together in a confused frown. "So is this it? Are we saying good-bye?"

"I guess we are," Kirk said softly.

Pain flashed through Josh's eyes and Kirk felt a moment of hope that Josh would change his mind. That hope died with Josh's next words.

"Then there's no reason for me to stay any longer. I'll head for my cabin."

Kirk followed Josh to the door, where Josh took his jacket from the coatrack and slipped it on. Kirk clenched his hands into fists to keep from pulling Josh into his arms and begging him to stay, despite swearing he would never do that.

Josh reached for the doorknob, but stopped before he turned it. He faced Kirk again, cradled Kirk's nape, and gave him a gentle kiss. "Thanks for everything," he whispered.

"You, too," Kirk managed in a choked voice.

Kirk closed the door behind Josh, then wandered back to the kitchen. Pancakes held no appeal now. He put the milk in the refrigerator. He started to pour the Bisquick back into the box, but couldn't since his hands shook. His knees gave out and he dropped to the floor. Sobs tore from his throat. Lowering his head, he let the tears fall.

Josh checked around the cabin once more to be sure he hadn't forgotten anything. Living in such a small space for the last two-and-a-half months had been an adventure after living in his parents' huge house in Dallas. But he'd proven to himself that he could get and hold a job on his own without his father's help. That meant a lot to him.

Something else meant a lot to him, or he should say *someone* else—Kirk. He'd so hoped Kirk would agree to go with him, but he wasn't surprised Kirk wanted to stay. The two of them would have had a blast together driving across the U.S. from east coast to west coast and all the places in between.

Josh wanted to share that experience with the man he cared about so much.

Releasing a heavy breath, Josh sat on the edge of the bed. He hadn't wanted to admit to his strong feelings for Kirk, afraid they would interfere with the independence he'd sought for so long. But he couldn't deny he'd fallen in love with the handsome blond. That didn't matter, since Kirk hadn't returned his feelings. If he'd loved Josh, he never would've let Josh leave his apartment so easily two weeks ago. He would've said the words Josh longed to hear.

You didn't say the words to him either. You can't blame him for something you didn't do.

Josh ignored the voice inside his head. It didn't matter now. Josh would leave here, go by Wilcox Lumber for his last paycheck, and be on his way.

Alone.

After stopping at the Country Woods's office to turn in his key and settle his bill, Josh drove to Wilcox Lumber. Part of him wanted to see Kirk, and part of him didn't want the pain of seeing him. He supposed he had no choice, since Kirk would be the one to give him his paycheck.

Josh pulled up to the back of the store and parked in the employees' lot for the last time. He waved at Gus and Don as he got out of his car. He'd said his good-byes to everyone Saturday, his last day to work. Since the workweek stopped on Wednesday and checks were generated on Friday, he had three days' pay due him. He'd told Kirk not to worry about paying him for the three days, but Kirk insisted he'd have the check ready today.

He walked into the back door and headed straight for the office. Kirk sat behind the desk, papers spread before him. Josh's heart clenched at the sight of him. "Hey."

Kirk looked up. Josh thought he saw a flash of longing in Kirk's eyes, but it quickly disappeared. "Hey."

"Just came by for my last paycheck."

"You headed out of town?"

Josh nodded.

"Where are you going?"

"East. I'll hit Highway 67 in Glen Rose and stop in Dallas to see my folks and sister once more before I take the interstate into Louisiana."

Kirk's gaze passed over Josh's face, shoulders, and down to his fly before he pulled open a drawer in his desk and removed a white legal-sized envelope. Rounding the desk, he handed the envelope to Josh. "Have a safe trip."

"Thanks."

There didn't seem to be anything else to say, yet Josh couldn't make himself leave the office. He stared into Kirk's gorgeous blue eyes and wanted so badly to ask Kirk if he cared about Josh as much as Josh cared about him.

Instead, he slapped the envelope against his palm and backed toward the door. "Well, thanks again for everything."

Kirk nodded.

Josh turned and hurried out the back door and to his car. He had to blink back tears before he could see to start the car and back out of the parking spot.

"You know you're an idiot, don't you?" Kory asked from the office's doorway.

Battling tears, it took Kirk a moment to find his voice to speak to his brother. "What are you babbling about?"

"Y'all love each other. How could you let him go?"

"He never said he loves me."

"Did you tell him how you feel?"

Kirk didn't answer, but his silence spoke for him for Kory frowned. "I knew it. You waited for him to say it first. When he didn't, you let him go instead of fighting for him like you should have."

"He didn't want to stay here, Kory. I was a fuck buddy, nothing more."

"I don't believe that. I saw the way he looked at you, Kirk. He loves you as much as you love him. You need to go after him before he gets too far down the road and tell him how you feel."

A tiny sprig of hope bloomed in Kirk's heart. "Do you really think so?"

"Hell, yes, I really think so. Do you know where he's heading?"

"Yeah, to Glen Rose and then up 67 to Dallas."

Kory pointed toward the parking lot. "Then get your ass out of that chair and into your truck and find Josh before it's too late."

Kirk debated no more than five seconds before he decided Kory had a great idea. He jumped up from the chair, grabbed his jacket from the hook on the wall. After hugging his brother and whispering "Thanks" in Kory's ear, Kirk ran out the back door.

He had his hand on the handle of his pickup when a squeal of brakes drew his attention. Kirk turned his head to see Josh's car slam to a stop less than two feet away.

Kirk's heart took off at a gallop.

Josh opened the driver's side door, stood between it and the car while he stared at Kirk with longing in his eyes. Kirk took a step closer, then another. "I was on my way to find you."

"I got a couple of miles outside of Lanville when I realized I couldn't leave you."

Kirk didn't know who moved first, but in the next instant he held Josh in his arms. Josh gripped him tightly, their bodies pressed together from chests to groins. "Someone will see us," he whispered in Kirk's ear.

"I don't care." He rested his forehead against Josh's. "I love you."

"God, I love you, too."

Kirk kissed him, pouring all his love into the kiss. A wolf whistle from the yard made him pull away and glance over his shoulder.

"Get a room," Gus said with a grin.

Josh chuckled. "Think he suspects you're gay?"

"I'd say that's a good bet. Guess I didn't hide my feelings for you so well after all."

"Except from me." He clasped Kirk's hands. "I was so stupid not to tell you how I feel. I was wrapped up in finally having my independence and didn't see the very special thing I had right in front of me."

"I didn't want to hold you back from doing what you wanted to do."

"What I want to do is be with you."

Kirk smiled. All the sorrow and pain floated away with Josh's words. "I want the same thing."

"So, I guess we have a lot to talk about, huh?"

"I guess so."

Josh squeezed Kirk's hands. "I was thinking I could get my job back here and you and I could take extended trips two or three times a year. Would that work?"

"I'll make it work."

Josh's smile lit up his face brighter than the sun. "Great! I'll go back to Country Woods and see if I can rent my cabin again."

Kirk shook his head. "No, you won't. You're moving in with me."

Josh's smile faded. "Are you sure? If I live with you, it won't be long before the whole town knows about our relationship."

"I don't care. I'm tired of hiding who I am. I love you and I'm not ashamed of that."

Josh's smile returned, tender and full of love. "I'm not ashamed of loving you either."

This time Kirk squeezed Josh's hands. "Then move that piece of junk you drive into your parking spot and get back to work."

"Yes, sir," Josh said with a grin.

GREAT BOOKS, GREAT SAVINGS!

When You Visit Our Website:
www.kensingtonbooks.com
You Can Save Money Off The Retail Price
Of Any Book You Purchase!

- **All Your Favorite Kensington Authors**
- **New Releases & Timeless Classics**
- **Overnight Shipping Available**
- **eBooks Available For Many Titles**
- **All Major Credit Cards Accepted**

Visit Us Today To Start Saving!
www.kensingtonbooks.com

All Orders Are Subject To Availability.
Shipping and Handling Charges Apply.
Offers and Prices Subject To Change Without Notice.